ELVIS AND TIGER

Myles Goodwyn

Dedicated to the memory of friend
and Canadian golf great,

George Knudson

Disclaimer

This is a work of fiction. Names, characters, businesses, places, events and incidents are either the products of the author's imagination or used in a fictitious manner. Certain characters may be composites, or entirely fictitious. This book is designed for entertainment to readers.

Edited by Patricia MacDonald
Cover design by Brandi Doane McCann
Book formatting by Steve Walters at Carolyn Flower International

Title: Elvis and Tiger
Format: Paperback
ISBN: 978-1-7752088-1-5
Publisher: : Northern Goody Two Tunes Inc.

ISBN/ISMN Published Heritage Branch

Library and Archives Canada / Government of Canada
bac.isbn.lac@canada.ca / Tel: 819-994-6872 or 1-866-578-7777

PROLOGUE

Antigua, August 2001

Elvis stood on the fourteenth tee. The hole was a 157-yard par three. The sky was clear and the air sweet with the mixed scent of exotic flowers. It was an ideal morning for a round of golf—sunny but not too hot yet. That was the way Elvis liked it and the reason he teed off in the morning, so he could be finished before the sun was in the middle of the sky and the temperature well into the nineties. Elvis really enjoyed golf, although it surprised most of his entourage that he even played at all. Back in the States he had shown no interest. But that was the past. A different Elvis.

Bob Royce, his swing coach, occasional caddie and good friend, wiped a six iron clean and handed it to him. Bob had the look of a middle-aged athlete no longer in his prime but not so out of shape as to be considered fat. There was still lots of muscle there and he still had a full head of curly hair, the color of desert sand. "Slight wind left to right, Aaron."

"Yeah, I can feel it. I'll play to the left a bit and we'll see what happens. I don't want it to stay left though and have it come up short in the damn front bunker."

"Just hit it firm and it'll be just fine. I'll watch it. You stay down."

After arriving on the island and becoming healthy

enough to consider what he wanted to do with all the free time he suddenly had on his hands, Elvis decided to try saltwater fishing. Fishing was a natural choice. When he was young growing up in Tennessee, he loved to fish in the rivers and streams in the Tupelo and Memphis areas, for a variety of freshwater fish such as bass, walleye, crappie, perch, grass and jack pike, and of course the good-eating but homely catfish. All were in abundance back then.

For Elvis there was nothing like fishing with surface lures for bass, lures such as poppers, jitterbugs and even frogs. He could be *"walking the dog"* with that poor frog by quickly twitching the rod during the slow retrieve. *"Popping"* was a similar technique that he used a lot, and it was accomplished by jigging the bait along the surface of the water. This attracted the fish, and if all went well, it would result in a fish grabbing and swallowing the bait. And when a largemouth bass hit that bait and started to fight, well, it sure got young Elvis's heart racing.

Trout was another favorite catch. Eating fresh-caught trout, pan-fried on an open fire, was one of the fondest memories Elvis had from those early fishing days when life was innocent and pure of heart. As the song says, *summertime and the livin' is easy; fish are jumpin' and the cotton is high.*

Elvis could still remember the state record for a trout caught back in the day, when fishing was more important than music and girls: a whopping 102 pounds and about 50 inches long.

"A trout that size you don't eat it, no sir, boy. You

get it stuffed and mounted," his daddy had said emphatically to young Elvis.

Although saltwater fishing was quite different from the fishing he was used to back in the United States, he grew to really enjoy it, and he became an avid fisherman all over again.

Golf on the other hand was something he had never tried until he got to Antigua, but try it he did, and he quickly became hooked. Passionately.

Elvis played golf right-handed, same as he played the guitar, when he bothered to play at all these days. His grip was strong, with the left hand turned over so the V in that hand pointed to the middle of his right shoulder. He wasn't as flexible as he once was as a young man, but a far cry better than he had been twenty or more years before. A lifetime ago. His workout routine over the subsequent years was good for him, and he enjoyed the fact that he looked and felt great. The way things had been going back in Memphis all those years ago, he wouldn't have been able to swing the club hardly at all. *Praise the Lord*, thought Elvis, and he smiled despite himself.

It was 2001, and Elvis was sixty-six years old.

"Aaron, don't think too hard about it, just let it flow. Your body knows what to do. Just don't get in your own way."

Bob was one of the pros teaching at the golf course where Elvis was a member. He had met Elvis at the course and they hit it off. Literally.

Teamed with Elvis's best friend and confidant,

Tommy Jefferson, the threesome went on to win the semi-annual eighteen-hole staff tournament together, and their friendship grew quickly on and off the course.

Elvis heard Bob's advice but didn't reply. His focus was all on the ball, and his mind tuned out everything else. He waggled the club, turned his chin slightly to the right as his golf hero Jack Nicklaus had done, gave the club another waggle and then slowly drew back the MacGregor six iron, as far up and back as his body would comfortably allow. A moment's pause at the top and then he started the swing down to meet the Titleist with a smooth and powerful forward motion, making solid contact and completing the follow-through in balance. Elvis held his gaze down until the ball was well on its way, and only then did he look up to see that the result was quite good indeed. *Well hit*, he thought as he tracked the ball's flight to the left center of the green. The pin was back center. A gentle wind coming in off the bay coaxed the ball to move slowly left to right. When the ball hit the small green it checked up slightly and then started to roll toward the flag stick. The speed was perfect. The ball looked determined to make Elvis's day . . . Elvis was now beginning to think, *Could it be, finally, a hole in one?* His first.

He heard Bob saying, "Go in! Go in!" They say the odds of a hole in one by an amateur are about 12,750 to 1.

"Go in, ball," Elvis said, almost a whisper.

Well, that darn ball was listening, because it rolled straight up to the hole, leaned against the flag stick for a second, and then dropped in and straight to the bottom of the cup.

A hole in one!

Elvis felt like singing for the first time in long while.

INTRODUCTION

My uncle says that was the happiest he had ever seen Aaron Smith. The most excited. As a nongolfer, I confess that I do not really understand the euphoria. Getting the golf ball in the hole, on a short hole, on your first try, was very nice indeed, but let's be honest, it wasn't exactly a miracle, now was it? As a matter of fact, I have heard it said that it is just good luck—a fluke—and it could happen to anyone. Nevertheless, he was "*over the moon*," my uncle told me in confidence.

Uncle Normand told me all sorts of things about Aaron Smith behind closed doors and in confidence.

My name is Craig Tenn Kincaid, and I am twenty-two years old. My parents would occasionally visit my uncle at the villa when he worked there for Aaron Smith. My parents, Fergus Blaine Kincaid and Sarah Lace Fisher—my mom is Uncle Normand's "baby" sister—started taking me with them when I was quite young, and I enjoyed the visits very much. As a family, we went to the villa to see Uncle Normand when he wasn't working because the villa was also his home. A few of the staff members lived there. My uncle, as majordomo of the estate, was required to live on the premises full time, and his living in this beautiful mansion and being second in command to only the Boss himself suited my uncle just fine, thank you very much.

I was always welcomed at Villa Selena. Aaron Smith liked me and was kind to me, and it is easy to like a kind person, is it not? Even for a child; perhaps especially for a child.

There was a festive mood at Villa Selena upon Aaron's triumphal return that day, like a hunter back from the hunt, boasting enthusiastically about the kill.

He told everyone he was thankful Bob had been there as a witness. He was his friend, his golf instructor and now his witness. Bob was beaming with pride at the great value Aaron placed on his being there. Thank goodness there was a *witness* . . . sounds like pretty serious stuff, this elusive hole in one.

Knowing now what I've been told by my uncle regarding those times at Villa Selena and the man who owned it—the American with the smooth southern drawl, clear blue eyes and great smile, the man who was my uncle's boss and friend—I realize that I missed a special moment for this great man that day and that there were and are, no doubt, millions of other people around the world who would have loved to have been there that afternoon.

My uncle Normand was there, and he told me all about it.

Yes, things were loud and festive, said my uncle, as the house staff were delighted for their boss and congratulated him warmly and were happy to do so. Aaron Smith was well liked by all who knew him. Actually, to say they knew him is not very accurate. In fact, few really knew him at all. Where did he come from and what was his story and what were the circumstances that enabled him to achieve his great wealth and eventually, mysteriously, end up "retiring" here in Antigua?

Life at the villa over the years was good for everyone. My uncle was happy, his staff were loyal—a domestic quality not always easy to find here on the island—and his boss became a good friend. It sounds idyllic, does it not? Everything appeared perfect, and in a way, I suppose it was. The good life. Yes, it was!

Now, I wonder if anything is really as it appears on the surface. In life, I mean. I thought I knew everything there was to know about the life and the people at the villa. Turns out I knew *shit*.

Regardless, my uncle Normand knew everything about the goings on at the villa, and he finally started sharing it all with me on the afternoon of March 7, 2012.

It was a sad day.

"Aaron died last night, Craig." My uncle sat on a bench I had made from some driftwood and salt-stained crates, looking thoughtfully out across English Harbour.

It was a clear, warm afternoon with a gentle southeasterly breeze, and I was working on a small, older wooden pleasure boat that had been purposely beached, requiring a repair to the transom where some rot had started its cancerous assault on the dark mahogany. I work primarily on larger boats that are moored either at a fisherman's wharf in one of the bays or harbors along the coastal shores of the island or, in the case of the various-sized pleasure boats, at one of the yacht clubs in the area. But this 16-footer with a 60-horsepower Merc outboard lay like a willing patient waiting for me to make her better, right on the beach with her stern lifted a few feet in the air, supported by a few logs that had washed ashore long before.

"Oh, my God, what happened?" I had heard nothing of Aaron Smith being sick. "Was he in an accident?" I asked, confused and shocked by the truth of it. *Aaron Smith was dead.*

Uncle told me he died peacefully at the villa in his sleep.

"Peacefully? Why, he wasn't that old was he?"

"He was seventy-seven," my uncle answered. "No, not that old in actual years I suppose, but he did a lot of hard living before he came here, Craig, and the consequences of that cannot be denied. The doctors say something just stopped working while he slept. There will be an autopsy, of course." He sounded tired.

I said, "But he was in great shape for seventy-seven. He was active—I mean, he was swimming and still playing golf several times a week." I stood up. "He never drank alcohol that I know of, and he never smoked, either. Seems all wrong." Pacing now, I was having a hard time accepting that he was really gone.

Still looking across the bay, his gaze steady, my uncle said to me, "Craig, a person is like a car: If you have 300,000 miles on that car, but then you hardly drive it at all, it's still the same car. You might even put it in a garage and never drive again, but it will still have 300,000 miles on it. That's a lotta miles. Can't change that." He looked to me. "Know what I mean?"

I knew what he meant but it was still wrong.

My dear uncle was never quite the same after Aaron Smith passed on. He had to move out of the villa. He was unemployed, not that that mattered to him monetarily; he was financially secure. But with no interest in working for anyone other than Aaron at Villa Selena, he seemed lost. He was, until that day, a happy, fun-loving, active man of sixty-two, but within a short time after Aaron's death, he looked and acted much older. Mentally and even physically, he was a different man. He lost his boss. His *friend*. It was tough for him.

It was a few months later that my uncle came to visit me at my cottage on Old Parthem Road. I had not seen him in a while, and I was happy that he dropped by.

"So how have you been, Uncle? Still on vacation?" I asked lightly with a slight smile. We were now sitting in my kitchen having a cup of tea. He was looking troubled . . . resigned, even, as if weighed down by something of importance that he needed to share.

My uncle is a tall man, and even at sixty-two years of age, his lean frame was still well toned. His hair was thin now and still mostly black but with some gray at the temples, combed straight back. He turned his chair to one side and sat at the table sideways with his long legs stretched out before him. His ankles were crossed, one gray runner lapped over the other. I sat barefoot, in red beach shorts and a white T-shirt, with my arms resting on the table, alert as to why my uncle had dropped by, *out of the blue*. It was unlike him not to call first. He was old fashioned that way. I waited for him to say something.

"Craig, I have decided to tell you a story, one I have never shared with another living soul. It is a secret like no other. But I need you to promise me that you also will never tell anyone else, ever. Before I start I want you to know this is very important to me, and you are the only person I trust enough to discuss what I feel I must say. The only one. It is a secret I have kept to myself for fifteen years, and it's about Aaron, may he rest in peace."

I often went to my uncle when I needed good advice. He is very smart and has an uncommon degree of common sense that I could rely on when needed, but it was clear that he really needed me right now. Why, I had no idea, but I was about to find out.

You should know that my uncle and I have always been close, and although he had girlfriends over the years, he was never married. He had no children, and I was like the son he never had. We were friends, and we loved and respected each other, as they say, *unconditionally*, like families should.

Over the years Uncle Normand and I have fished countless hours together, traveled to the out islands by boat, and explored the beaches and local culinary treasures that could only be found in places such as Turtle Cay and Coral Lagoon. We shared some real

good times, he and I, over the years. Uncle encouraged me to finish my education when all I wanted
to do was drop out and start my career as a carpen-
ter specializing in custom boat work. I was turned on
to wooden boats by a friend of Dad's who lived near
English Harbour, Peter Reid. I spent many weekends
hanging around and helping out on boat projects
Peter was working on. He was glad to have an extra
hand, and I became good at doing the work. I had
the imagination and the desire to do the best I could
. . . it was like a calling to me. And so I knew what I
wanted to do toward the end of my high school days,
and I declared that I was dropping out of school at
the end of third term that year. But I took my uncle's
advice, and my parents', of course, and remained in
school and got my diploma.

The following year, at nineteen years of age, I went
to university and majored in English for a year, but
that following summer I got restless to get on with
my life and dedicated all my time to my first love,
working on boats, classic wooden boats in particular.
Using my hands to build, repair and create. So I did
not return the second year, and I have not regretted
it. My dear uncle understood this and even helped
me get my first real job at the yacht club where Aaron
Smith kept his boat at the time.

But before I impart to you what my uncle told me,
and the purpose of this narrative, let me state for the
record that I am not a professional writer. I'm an arti-
san, a builder not a storyteller. Neither is my uncle a
writer, and that is one of the reasons I will relate this
story to you and not him. And the fact that he trusts

me more than anyone.

He confided to me the truth about Aaron Smith and the details of what transpired over the years he had been employed at the villa. I had many questions, and he was patient and he added more and more details. It was as if the more he had to say the better it was for him. I could see in his body language that there was relief in the telling. It poured out of him. He was hemorrhaging years of bottled-up emotions, finally able to talk about a topic that had been taboo for decades. I was stunned time and time again. It would have been impossible to believe most of what I heard that night if not for the fact that it was my Uncle Normand telling it.

He left me alone with my thoughts as the sun was coming up. For days I carried on as usual, dealing with the regular schedules and commitments in my life, but my thoughts were focused on what I now knew about Aaron Smith. It was amazing. I laughed out loud at times, shaking my head, feeling a mixture of amusement and awe, like someone who learned the secret of a magic trick that fooled him every time . . . until it was explained. I also felt an odd sense of letdown for the same reason. Wasn't it a hell of a lot more fun when I didn't know how they did it? *But now I knew.*

Several weeks after my uncle sat with me in my kitchen and unleashed this spew of facts that left me numb and overwhelmed, I realized I wanted people to know the truth. Everybody needed to know the truth. Deserved it. I was convinced of this and set off to convince my uncle. I knew it would not be easy.

So there I was, at twilight, heading for his home in Falmouth Point. It had recently stopped raining and the roads were wet and shiny, but I was driving my silver Jeep a little too fast regardless. I intended to convince my uncle that I could write this story of Aaron Smith and the events surrounding his coming to the Island of Antigua. I had thought it through time and time again over the past weeks. I knew I could do it, and I believed it should be done as soon as possible. When I got to his house he answered the door himself and let me in. I was talking a mile a minute as I stepped through the entrance and into the living room, dripping water and leaving footprints as I did.

"Uncle, we gotta do this."

"Do what?"

"Tell Aaron's story. Elvis. Tiger Woods. The whole thing, especially the Elvis part."

"Don't be ridiculous, Craig."

"I'm serious."

"Have you been telling people?"

"No, I haven't."

"Good. Now, what's with you talking like this? Stop it before someone hears you. For God's sake, enough!" My uncle was clearly upset with me.

"OK, Uncle, let's sit and talk . . . please."

For hours we talked.

Yelled.

Whispered.

That's right, we whispered. *God forbid someone should hear us.* Finally I had said all I had to say for one night and got up to leave.

"Uncle, please, seriously, think about what I said. I love you. Good night."

I left him at the door, finally speechless.

I didn't hear from him the next day, so I called him. He didn't wanna talk about it. OK, I said.

This went on for several weeks. I would not relent on this. I could think of nothing else. I started writing. Making notes. Doing research.

And I kept after my uncle, asking to meet and talk about it some more, and he kept saying no. Then one evening he called me at the cottage. He told me to come see him. He wanted to talk.

I grabbed the keys to the Jeep and flew out the door into the humid darkness, my heart pounding in anticipation that my uncle was ready to give me the green light to start writing this story.

Let me say at this point that I believed I could tell the story Uncle Normand had told me. I was not expecting to write a Pulitzer Prize–winning piece of nonfiction, I assure you, but I knew what I was told and I felt I could put pen to paper and simply repeat it with a bit of wiggle room for a few embellishments and some anecdotes . . . yes, I could do it. See it through. Get it done.

Some of you might think, why not simply convince my uncle to arrange a press release and be done with it? He could tell them this unbelievable story, I suppose, but would they laugh at him? Think he was crazy or delusional? Probably . . . but we will never know because my uncle would never, ever, do that sort of thing!

No, that would never do. I wouldn't want him to, either. I wouldn't want to see him take the risk of being humiliated and embarrassed publicly. No, sir.

There was another way, I figured. A "tell it like it is" kinda way, on our own terms. His and mine.

He wanted to talk. We talked.

Well, it turns out I had asked my uncle if I could try authoring this story in the form of a novel so often that he was finally worn down by my persistence and gave me the go-ahead to give it a try.

When Aaron Smith decided to confide in my uncle, he did so with great passion and detail. My uncle said that events, perspectives and even conversations were notable when it came to Aaron Smith, and my uncle kept a kind of diary because there was so much, too much to ever remember without keeping some kind of record. All these records he now offered to me. Uncle Normand wanted me to tell the story as he knew it. *All of it.* He had decided it would be an injustice to the great man's memory if he did not share his experience with Elvis.

I love to read. Two of my favorite authors growing up were Wilbur Smith and Clive Cussler. I discovered these great authors when I was about eight years old. I believe my dad had all their books, and one day I found an old Cussler Dirk Pitt novel, a story from the National Underwater and Marine Agency—the NUMA series. Wow! Dirk could do it all. I loved the fact that all the adventures dealt with intrigue and espionage, and ships on the high seas and all kinds of treasures in the depths of those seas. When reading these wonderful books, I was Dirk Pitt and I was taking care of business!

Around that time I also discovered my dad's Courtney series written by Wilbur Smith, and again I was hooked.

Smith writes of incredible adventures in the territories of Africa, and they are spellbinding. Epic. I devoured these divine books as well, and when I finished a series, I would start again. I tried writing short stories around that time too; that and my love of reading are what led me to choose English as my major in college after graduating high school. But it wasn't meant to be. After a while the truth became obvious, that my calling, my first love, was as a craftsperson specializing in custom wooden boat work.

Nevertheless, I like words, and to be honest with you, some say I have a certain way with them. And as naive or even as brazen as that may sound, putting them on paper, certainly in this case, seemed doable to me.

Although this story is a serious one, it is not without some humor, so, and with my uncle's blessing, I will attempt to inject some from time to time.

I like to share a good yarn, although I'll admit I've been accused of being a bit long in the tooth at times. But embellishment is what can make a good story great, don't you think? And besides, I'm good with details if I do say so myself. But no worries; I will not bore you with too many details, nor will I use too many words, fancy or otherwise, to tell this story. There is no good reason for exaggeration or frippery when telling a story that is, simply put, extraordinary. And the telling of it seems as right as rain.

There is an expression in golf that I heard once and liked: "Keep it simple, stupid." Another tip I like in particular, referring to the mental aspect of the game, is don't get in your own way. No, friends, I promise. I will not let my ego get in the way of such an important story.

As I reminded myself early on, I do not need to *write* a story here—the story has been written. I do not need to devise a beginning, a middle and an end and all the rest of it—it's all been done for me. No great imagination is required in this task. Besides, truth is often stranger than fiction. This is truth. It's history; I only need to write it down. Anybody could do it. It just turns out that I'll be the one because I heard about it firsthand, from the only person I know who knows the truth.

And as I said to my uncle Normand many times over the last few weeks, the world deserves to know, finally. It is *that* important, I insisted.

He relented. God bless him.

He made me promise to tell the truth, the whole truth and nothing but the truth. When he said that, those very words, it made me laugh, of course, which was his intention. Sincere guy with a good sense of humor, my uncle Normand. He also made me promise not to rush it, to wait until the timing was right.

So I've taken my time, trying my best to do the story justice, and waiting for the right moment. This year is the fortieth anniversary of Elvis Aaron Presley's "death." As far as the rest of the world knows, he's been dead almost as long as he was alive. But I know better. And it's the perfect time to reveal what really happened that day back in 1977.

Here, then, is the story. A story that has been, until now, perhaps one of the greatest never told.

The story of Elvis and Tiger.

CHAPTER ONE

R ed West first met Elvis back when they both attended Humes High School in Memphis, Tennessee. One afternoon, Red saved Elvis from a group of ruffians who had him trapped in a school bathroom, about to cut his Tony Curtis–style haircut into the crew-cut style that was popular back in the day. But it was not only his ducktail haircut that incited the hostility but also his Beale Street pimp-style clothes and his whole cooler-than-cool persona, which he had adopted from watching movies like *Curtis's City Across the River* and its visual portrayal of the working class in the neighborhoods of New York City during the early '50s.

Red West took pity on Elvis that afternoon, and so he intervened and put a stop to the harassment by threatening to bust a few heads. West was a tough cookie, and this was to be the first of many, many times he would save Elvis's hide over the next quarter of a century.

That was in 1951. By the time Red and his cousin Sonny West and friend Dave Hebler got their walking papers, Elvis Presley had gone from being a poor, shy, pimply teenager to a truly worldwide phenomenon.

Through his records, his movies and his celebrated live performances, he became a living legend, worshipped and adored by millions of fans and, of course, extremely wealthy. He'd also become a drug addict.

Elvis made his professional recording debut in the summer of 1954 at Sun Records in Memphis, Tennessee. It's been well documented that studio boss and owner-producer Sam Phillips was looking to find a white singer with the sound and feel of a "Negro" performer. When he heard Elvis during a demo recording session in his studio one night, he was convinced he had found his man. Phillips recorded an old blues song that evening called "That's All Right," and that recording marked the beginning of a career unparalleled by any other popular singer, ever.

With the response the song generated locally when played by radio stations in the Memphis area, Phillips knew he had a winner in Elvis Presley. And not only was Elvis's voice unique, but live, his sex appeal was undeniable. A combination of the music's rhythm and his nervousness during performances resulted in him shaking his legs as he sang, causing the women to start screaming. *They never stopped screaming!*

The King! Elvis the Pelvis!

His fortune and good looks enabled the King to have most anything or anyone he desired. The world was his oyster, and man did he indulge . . . that is, until it all finally caught up with him. The drugs his doctors prescribed for him—codeine, morphine, Valium, Quaaludes, and many more—brought on a delusional and paranoid Elvis who became self-destructive and vindictive toward others, including his friends at the time. Friends who would have done anything for him. Would have taken a bullet for him. These were guys he insisted be taught to intimidate, to fight and to carry firearms, in order to protect His Majesty— Elvis Aaron Presley.

These were guys who, in the beginning, respected him.

It was said that he fired Red and Sonny West and the others in July of 1976, for being too "physical" in their roles as protectors of the King of Rock and Roll. The main reason given for the dismissals was the number of mounting lawsuits by people claiming to have been beaten by his bodyguards, aka the Memphis Mafia.

It is very likely that his mental state at this time caused any number of phobias, including believing that Red West's success as an actor overshadowed his own acting ability. Because of his connection to Elvis, West did some television acting jobs during the '70s.

After all their years of devotion to Elvis, this unfair and hypocritical act of firing the boys caused Red, Sonny and Hebler to retaliate by recounting their memoirs in a book called *Elvis: What Happened?*

The book was scheduled to come out in August of 1977.

Presley was paranoid when he heard the news of its release. His drug addiction was known by all close to Elvis, and the last thing he wanted was for his fans to know the truth. He had in fact been hospitalized on several occasions for detox treatments and almost died a few times of overdose. There was no question there would be consequences resulting from the publication, and Elvis was beside himself. Unable to stop the book's release and terrified of being humiliated by its truth, he was inconsolable. Even the Colonel, his now longtime personal manger, was unable to make the problem go away.

Elvis was able to finagle a copy of the book a few months before its official release, and upon reading the sections that described his drug use, he knew he had to do something desperate to stop the bleeding.

Elvis decided he would throw himself into the upcoming summer tour. He would put together his best show ever. But then self-doubt crept in, and the more he thought about it, the more he wanted out. Now! Out of everything. He'd simply had enough. Elvis was certainly not thinking clearly, but he wasn't a stupid man. He knew the drugs were killing him and that he was very fortunate to still be alive. There was no getting around the fact that he was addicted to prescription drugs.

They say the first step to recovery is admitting you are helpless over your substance (or substances) of choice and that your life has become unmanageable. Without that first step, there is little chance of recovery. There is also the belief that perhaps a person who can't stop the abuse hasn't suffered enough.

Elvis decided that he and those close to him had had enough suffering.

Long live the King!

CHAPTER TWO

As much as Elvis wanted to escape from the self-imposed hell he was living in, he couldn't just turn off a switch and have it all end.

The machine that fueled Elvis's personal decline into overindulgence and dipsomania couldn't be shut down, its doors closed and sealed and shut forever. Or even for a minute. His image was the second most recognizable in the civilized world, right behind Mickey Mouse. There was no escaping that monumental degree of popularity.

Even if he was somehow able to get off the pills and get healthy physically and mentally, the stress of being the biggest and most beloved entertainer in the history of popular music, with absolutely no chance at a normal existence, would keep him using and abusing substances—and he knew it. It would be impossible.

His world was one where his every move, every word and every action were scrutinized relentlessly. How does one handle that kind of incredulous pressure? He couldn't say, honestly. He could only carry on and hope, and even pray, that he could survive . . . *somehow*. Amen.

So Elvis started doing what he'd always done over the years when preparing for a new tour: He started attempting to get in shape. He was fat, weighing in at about 270 pounds. It wasn't going to be easy, but then again it never was. He worked out in his gym by stretching and light lifting. He wasn't ready to run, but he was on the treadmill and walking. And of course he indulged in his on-again, off-again passion for karate.

There were vocal exercises every day. Preparation for rehearsals at the end of the month required song selection, key changes and arrangements, and there were wardrobe issues, choreography . . . the whole shebang. Two weeks into the dieting and daily workouts, he was in trouble.

Lordy, he was so freaked out and distracted about the *Elvis: What Happened?* book, set to be released in a matter of weeks, that it became impossible for him to concentrate properly.

It was gnawing at him, causing him to sleep poorly despite the pills he took to ensure slumber. Pills to wake up and pills to sleep and pills to wake up again.

Enough!

He decided he had to get away from Graceland for a while, and so he called a meeting. He told his staff he was going to a small island in the Caribbean to chill out. A place to relax and rejuvenate. To break the ruinous routine of pill popping. What he really wanted was a destination where he could escape all the hoopla surrounding this book. A book that was written, in his opinion, solely to destroy his image and undermine his career! But he'd show them all a new Elvis. A new slimmed-down, tanned and in-control

Elvis. He just needed to get away from Memphis for a while.

He wanted to leave as soon as possible, so he started orchestrating the trip by shouting orders to the staff. It was typical of Elvis to do things impulsively. Whether it was buying a dozen cars or an airplane, if he wanted it, he wanted it right NOW! It was also typical for him to shout out orders and then go off and hide in his room. Not this time!

He was inspired . . .

But there was one problem. He was being watched like a Tennessee Cooper's hawk. Graceland was under constant observation, even more so than normal because of the damn publicity and building notoriety around the much anticipated release of *Elvis: What Happened?*

Leaving Graceland and Memphis, even for a few weeks, would be very difficult to keep a secret, as remarkably, public interest in his whereabouts and his every move still remained as high as ever.

He decided then and there to do what he had done a number of times before. *Get a fake Elvis!*

He wanted to use the same impersonator he had used as a decoy in previous situations like this. Those times when he wanted to get away undetected by determined fans and the obnoxious paparazzi that were always waiting and watching. This man had proved himself reliable, and he kept his mouth shut. His loyalty to the King was unwavering. Besides, he was a good old boy from Tennessee, or at least that's what Elvis had been told when Red originally suggested using the guy.

Elvis couldn't remember the impersonator's real name, though, as his mind was somewhat befuddled from all the drug abuse. He wasn't even sure if he ever knew it. Neither Tag nor Tommy knew how to reach him, either; they said Red always took care of it. So Elvis had a problem. He needed the help of the West cousins to find him; it had always been their job to contact the guy, hire him and get him to Graceland whenever they needed him. But there was no fucking way he was gonna call those bastards now.

But there wouldn't be a problem finding an Elvis impersonator, would there? *They're practically falling out of the sky*, he thought, and he started to laugh. This brought on a coughing fit and it worried him, as he immediately thought of his throat and his vocal chords. At that time singing was still his one true passion.

"Tommy, Tag . . . get in here," he managed in that slurred drawl that was so recognizable. Tommy came in right away, with Tag right behind him.

"What's up, Boss?"

"I need you guys to find a new me!"

CHAPTER THREE

Tom Jefferson met Elvis when his catering business worked one of the King's shows a few years previous. Tom stood at five-ten and weighed in at about 175. He was of average build and moved gracefully. He wore his hair in a neat Afro and was proud of his African-American heritage. Tom had an easy, open way, and Elvis always felt at ease around him. Most called him Tommy.

Tag Koury worked security at the estate and loved his job. Tag was big—football defenseman big—and always dressed in black. His hair was black, and he had a neat but thick moustache . . . Fu Manchu style. He was *daunting* and Elvis liked that.

They got lucky fast.

The Elvis they hired was a good find under the circumstances. He had the general body shape and overall size required to be an Elvis decoy, but most important, he was not about to run home and tell his friends all about being *fake Elvis* and living in a mansion. He was from another state, with no family ties, he confided in Tommy. He was basically a homeless drifter with an insatiable thirst, which was apparent from the look and smell of him when he approached Tommy in line for some soup and spare change.

"And how are you doing, sir?" asked Tommy.

Dressed in blue jeans and a black sweatshirt, Tommy was busy doling out vegetable soup and salted crackers at a help shelter where he was an occasional volunteer.

"I'm tired . . . and hungry," the man replied, not taking his red-veined eyes off the Styrofoam bowl Tommy held in his hand. A lazy steam wafted off the hot soup.

Tommy passed the hot meal to the man. "Well, here you go. This will fix you right up."

"You spare some change? I'm broke and ain't been working lately, my friend." His breath omitted the smell of cheap sherry wine, causing Tommy to turn his head to one side.

"Sorry, can't help you there."

"OK," replied the man passively as he turned and headed off with his ration of soup and saltines. The shelter was situated in the basement of a Methodist church on Griffith Avenue in the old section of Memphis. The church opened its doors to folks in need of an evening meal. The fellow went to sit with some other sad cases at a table across from where Tommy was working the line.

Tommy forgot all about him until the guy started singing. Not well, mind you, but Tommy could tell the tune was one of Elvis's, although the words came out uncertain and somewhat slurred. It got his attention for a moment or two, though. He smiled and shook his head as he prepared the next bowl.

A week later Elvis was needing a *fake* Elvis, ASAP.

"*I need you guys to find a new me*," remembered Tommy from earlier that very afternoon.

It was Monday, early evening, and Tommy was volunteering at the church. Once again, the same vagrant was in line needing a free meal. Tommy remembered him from the week before, but this time he really checked him out. Elvis's words had been on his mind all day—*ASAP!*—and he almost hadn't bothered to show up that night. Now he remembered that this guy had been singing an Elvis tune the weekend before.

Tonight he looked more closely at the man and saw a vague resemblance to the size and shape of his boss. *Funny*, he thought as he watched the guy getting closer to him in line, *how a man who's without means and the money to buy all the food he wanted could be overweight . . . possessing a body shape like that of his boss*. Genetics, he figured.

"And how are doing tonight, Elvis?"

The guy looked at Tommy as if he didn't understand. And of course, how could he?

"What?" he mumbled. The smell of cheap booze was still there.

"You a fan of Elvis, sir?" asked Tommy, a slight smile on his lips.

"You mean Elvis Presley? Damn right I am. Who ain't?" he spat out, causing the smell of his breath to attack Tommy's olfactory senses.

"I thought you might be after hearing you singing one of his songs last week," said Tommy amicably while watching the guy closely as he handed him a plate consisting of a ham sandwich on white and an orange.

"You got any vodka to go with that orange, my friend?" he cracked, reaching for the plate of free food. "I'm awful thirsty." His hand was shaking slightly as he took hold of the offering.

Tommy pointed. "We got all the coffee you can drink right over there."

"Guess it'll have to do for now," mumbled the guy as he wandered off, his feet shuffling in tired sneakers that were tied up with soiled gray string frayed at the ends.

As the vagrant ate his simple meal, Tommy watched him, thinking that maybe, just maybe, this poor fellow could be fake Elvis, if only for a few days. The guy had the shape and height, and his long-ish brown hair could be shaped to resemble Elvis's famous "do." There was nothing that could be done about his teeth, which were the color of old razor blades.

Excusing himself to one of the other volunteers, Tommy walked over to the man and sat next to him, but not too close.

"I was thinking I might be able to help you with that vodka you were wanting." Well, that was all it took to get his full and complete attention.

It didn't take Tommy long to get the guy, who said his name was Bud, into his late-model Chevy and head off for that drink.

"Where you live, Bud?" Tommy knew what the answer would be, but he wanted to be sure.

"Live? I live wherever it is I find myself." Bud chuckled to himself. Tommy wasn't sure if it was at his own remark or the fact that he knew he'd soon be having a "real" drink with his newfound friend. Tommy never mentioned his name.

"You got family?" questioned Tommy.

"Nope. Where we going?"

"Not far. Thirsty?"

*****

When Tommy arrived at Graceland estate with Bud, he drove his peculiar guest around to the back of the mansion and parked. He then led him into the office where Tag was on the phone.

Tag looked up, saw Tommy with his shabby-looking companion and said, "Hey, got to go, later," and hung up.

"What's happening, Tommy?" Tag asked as he stood up from his chair.

The office was in a rectangular-shaped outbuilding behind the main house. Its walls were sheets of cheap fake-wood veneer nailed onto gypsum. The floors were covered in an offending abstract mixed shade of yellow and green, and the two office desks were gray, metal and basic, the kind you could buy cheap at Salvation Army outlets. Overhead the entire ceiling was fluorescent lighting. Framed images of the King, of different shapes and sizes, hung at random or lay scattered about the room, leaning against walls or a desk, as if no one could be bothered hanging them all.

"Hi, Tag. Would you mind getting Bud here a drink? Something medicinal—the man is in need of a pick-me-up. Should be whiskey in the desk."

Until recent times, the office had been used by Elvis's father, Vernon. Vernon wasn't well enough these days to do much in his office, but it was still his office and there was still some Kentucky bourbon at hand, and the boys all knew where it was kept.

"Sure thing, T." Tag reached to his right, opened the lower drawer and removed a nearly full bottle of Dickel No. 8 whiskey. He stood and carried the bottle over to a cupboard that held some basic dishes and mixed cutlery and retrieved a cheap, cloudy looking glass tumbler. He proceeded to pour three fingers of the golden nectar and then took it over to Bud, who was standing next to Tommy trying his damnedest not to appear too in need.

"Here you go, Bud. Name's Tag. Nice to meet you." He handed the drink to Bud, no ice, no apologies. If Bud was taken back by Tag's size and his *man in black* persona, it didn't show.

Tag gave Tommy a look.

"Tag, my new friend here needs some work and a place to stay for a while. We have an opening as of today and, well, I think Bud here looks like he could fit the bill. He might be just what E's looking for."

Tommy could see that Tag understood immediately where this was going.

"You might be right about that. Do you think we can move on this? E is anxious to find some temporary help ASAP." Tag was playing along.

Using Elvis's name was not always wise under certain circumstances for obvious reasons, and this was one of those times. A few of the staff referred to their boss as *E*, including Tag and Tommy. Elvis had suggested that the boys call him that, and so they did.

Meanwhile, Bud was holding his precious drink in two hands, and now only one of the three fingers remained. Physically, Bud's demeanor had improved noticeably. He stood a little taller, he wasn't shaking—not as much, at least—and there was a bit of a softening to his countenance . . . all in all, the picker-upper was working its magic.

"This is good, fellers. Tastes like more." Bud gulped his last finger and looked at them hopefully.

"Sure does, Bud. Let's top that up and then we'll have ourselves a chat, OK?" said Tag.

"Sure, let's do that," Bud answered greedily.

So Tommy and Tag sat Bud down and explained the job description.

"Bud," Tommy began, "we have an opening, a job, that would require you to live here at this address for a while, and that's about it. It'll be for a couple of weeks. Interested?"

Bud was sitting on a metal chair that Tag had pulled up to one of the desks, while Tommy sat in

Vernon's desk chair. Tag remained standing, occasionally sitting on the side of the desk so Bud could see him better when it was important that Bud understand what was being said, and at times eye contact helped.

"You will be starting right now. You will remain inside the house unless accompanied outside, and you will do only what you are told, which is nothing much really. Someone here will dress you and feed you and you'll have your own room with a private bath. Understand so far?"

Bud chuckled. "You're gonna dress me?"

At least he's listening, thought Tommy. It was time to spell it out, make things clear to Bud before he was too drunk to understand anything being said to him.

"I'd love another." Bud held up his empty glass.

"Look, here's the thing, Bud, you're going to pretend you're Elvis Presley while you're staying here with us. That means we'll try to make you look, from a distance, mind you, like Elvis. We'll style your hair and dress you like Elvis dresses, casual like when he's home here at Graceland. Understand?"

Bud started laughing while holding up his glass for another "topper."

"Yeah, Elvis and me look like twins, we do." He was laughing hard. "Another drink, please?" he gasped.

Tag stood over Bud and said slowly and deliberately.

"Thing is, Bud, people see what they expect to see,

and what they expect to see here at Graceland is Elvis Presley. We've done this many times before with other fake Elvises. You wanna drink, you accept this job and you can have all the drinks you want, understand. But right now you gotta hear what we're saying to you and you must understand how it will be. And you must agree to keep it all our little secret if you accept. OK?" Tag's voice was all business.

A twinkle was in Bud's eye when he looked from Tag to Tommy. He actually understood.

With all the seriousness he could muster, under the circumstances, he nodded his mangy head, raised his glass and stated enthusiastically to both men before him: "I accept your kind offer, sirs, and I look forward to my engagement here. Now where's my bathroom? I need to piss like a racehorse."

*****

Before they brought Bud into the main house at Graceland to meet their boss, they took him to a guest house on the property and had him take a long hot shower. Then they shaved off his short, ratty-looking beard but left three-inch sideburns. They greased his now clean dark brown hair and combed it back like E wore his those days. Then they had him try on some basic everyday wear that belonged to Elvis: black leather slip-on shoes with dark blue slacks and a yellow-flowered, high-collared, long-sleeve shirt. The transformation was surprisingly good. Very good. It was time for the fake Elvis to meet the real Elvis.

This could work, thought Tommy, as he and Tag led Bud to meet their boss in the mansion. The staff just needed to keep him reasonably lubricated with the poison of his choice and put up with him up for a few weeks. Which meant keeping a close eye on him so he didn't do something too stupid, and that was about it. Even if he did say something to somebody one day about being fake Elvis and staying at Graceland, nobody but nobody would believe him for a second.

When they brought in fake Elvis to meet the real Elvis, fake E. was all dressed up and ready to deliver a "Hi, I'm Elvis Presley. Thank you, thank you very much," in an attempt to impress by impersonating that famous, unmistakable slurred Southern accent of his hero.

But fake Elvis, upon seeing the real deal up close and personal, could only manage *"Shit, it's really Elvis!"* before passing out.

*****

"Where the fuck did you find him, Tommy?" demanded the King.

"At a shelter where I do charity work a few nights a month." The charity work was a personal payback for his good fortune in working for the King. Good karma, thought Tommy.

He smiled at his boss and added, "It seemed fortuitous, Elvis. He was doing you, Boss, singing "Now and Then There's a Fool Such as I." Although Tommy was barely able to stop from laughing at the thought, his boss didn't seem amused.

"Sorry, Boss, we'll keep looking," he offered.

"No, no, he'll do. Just read him the riot act and have Ron keep a close eye on him while we're away. I don't want him outside wandering around. Tell Ron that; he'll know what to do."

And so fake Elvis was to stay on the estate, where he would almost certainly be spotted from time to time going about his "business" and otherwise helping himself to the newly stocked bar. Elvis instructed his staff to inform people that "Elvis is in training for an upcoming tour" and therefore unavailable for any reason. That was it.

Cheers, fake Elvis!

CHAPTER FOUR

Elvis said good night to the boys after arranging a morning departure schedule. All matters concerning his trip were in place and he could now relax. Elvis went to bed early that evening and slept soundly for a change, partly because of the downers he took before bedtime but also because he was relieved that he was going to be out of there in the morning.

Fake Elvis was out of there much earlier.

Tag made the gruesome discovery. It was 7:30 a.m., and he had just started his preparations for their impending getaway. He noticed a light coming from the upstairs hallway and, upon inspection, saw that the door was open to the guest bedroom where fake Elvis was supposed to be sleeping. Tag peeked into the room after a polite tap on the door and called out a "hello" that received no answer. Poking his head in further to have a look-see, he saw that the light was coming from the bathroom. He called out "Bud" and again received no reply, so he went to the bathroom door and slowly pushed it open. That's when he saw a body looking like his boss, lying on the bathroom floor in an unlikely position. He realized it was fake E and slowly closed the door as he withdrew a two-way radio from his pocket and pressed the talk/send button.

"Tommy, I need you upstairs. Now!"

Tag and Tommy each carried on their person a two-way portable radio that was with them 24/7. When one unit was being used, another was being charged. It had to be this way in a house this size, and when dealing with Elvis's mood swings and demands, instant communication was essential.

When he turned to get to a phone to call for help, the real Elvis was standing at the bathroom door.

Tag let out a gasp and then exhaled deeply as he quickly realized the image of fake Elvis, who had succumbed to the pearly gates, lying in such an undignified position on the bathroom floor, had him spooked.

His boss placed a hand on his shoulder and just stared at the form on the floor. He made no move toward the body and made no comment. Tag assumed the Boss was in shock. "Boss, you OK?" His boss just nodded and backed out the door.

Elvis stood there, his dyed black hair disheveled, wearing only black custom-made suede slippers and a white terry cloth bathrobe with *Las Vegas* embroidered on the front left, looking oddly inspired.

Elvis, Tag, Tommy and Ron, his driver, were the only people in the mansion besides the now-deceased fake Elvis. Elvis wanted no one staying in the mansion overnight, other than Tommy, Tag and Ron. He wanted other staff out of the main house at the end of each day and to take weekends off as well. It had always been that way. When Red West and the rest of his Memphis Mafia friends had been around, it had been a crazy atmosphere. Like the time Elvis shot a television set in anger. For years it was party central and all kinds of shenanigans were going down, and privacy was paramount. Young, beautiful women were a constant at Graceland, as his boys had no problem finding an endless supply of willing beauties who wanted to meet Elvis and were more than willing to do whatever was needed in order to do so. Although it was impossible to keep such things completely out of the gossip circles of Memphis and beyond, some effort was made. It was different these days. These days it was more the paranoia that made Elvis insist on privacy at the end of the day. It was all about secrecy and his ability to cope . . . and do his thing. His thing, of course, was all the drugs he ingested at this difficult time in his life.

The bottom line was that nobody else knew there was a dead man in Elvis's bathroom. The rest of the staff wouldn't be back for at least an hour, and they wouldn't venture up to the second floor unless Elvis called for them. When opportunity knocks . . .

"Boss, you sure you're all right?" repeated Tag.

"Yeah, I'm all right." Elvis moved to a chair and sat down.

At that moment Tommy arrived with Ron at the top of the stairs, both looking confused but alert.

"What is it?" Tommy asked. Both he and Ron looked at Tag for an answer, not about to question their boss, who was sitting in the hallway on a gold velvet Louis XV chair, his head back, eyes closed. Tag pointed to the bathroom where fake Elvis, aka

Bud, lay dead on the floor, but before Tag could say anything, Elvis said, "OK, guys, something unpleasant has happened here tonight, but things are under control."

He was now playing with his pinkie ring, a large gold ring featuring the letter E encrusted with small diamonds. They had no idea what Elvis had in mind with regard to explaining this understated "unpleasant" event to the authorities when they arrived.

"What do you want us to do, Boss?" Tag managed. Although unsure of what was going to happen next, Tag looked as if he could take care of whatever it was Elvis needed him to do. Anything.

Their boss was quiet again. They thought maybe he'd fallen back to sleep. It wouldn't have surprised them all that much. The meds made Elvis nod off in the middle of a sentence sometimes.

Finally Elvis looked up and said, "Listen up, fellas."

He got up from the chair slowly, walked over to the bathroom, looked in and stood there, obviously staring at dead Bud. After a long pause he turned back to the guys and started to speak softly.

"This is unfortunate, boys, but I have an idea how we might be able to turn this situation into a positive." Calmly Elvis began to explain that although this was tragic, something called divine intervention might be at play.

"The dead guy in the bathroom has no one that we can call and inform of his untimely demise, you understand, fellas? He was a transient and a loner. He carried no identification, and he possessed nothing other than a couple of dollars and a few ragged pieces of clothing stuffed into a filthy old athletic bag." Tag looked at Elvis, amazed that he would even know all this. He swallowed but said nothing, but Elvis noticed.

"Tommy told me all about the guy earlier," he directed at Tag.

"Yes, I did," confirmed Tommy. Tag nodded but still looked stupefied.

Elvis then said the police would come, ask some questions and fill out "appears to have died of natural causes" on the form, and then send the body to the morgue for a routine autopsy. Then with no one to claim the body, he would be cremated and the whole thing forgotten.

"It's sad but true, boys. That's just the way it works," he said firmly.

Neither Tag nor Tommy had looked at the dead guy since Elvis started talking. They were spellbound and hung on to every word he was saying. As their boss continued explaining, his voice became more animated.

"On the other hand . . . " He paused for effect, looking from each man in the hallway to the next, and then continued speaking. "The dead man in the bathroom could find fame that has eluded him in his lifetime. Yes, this could be divine intervention. Praise the Lord!"

Religion and spiritualism had been a big deal with Elvis during the mid-1960s and well into the '70s. He read, studied and became obsessed with spiritual writings such as *The Tibetan Book of the Dead, Through the Eyes of the Masters* and his personal favorite, *The Voice of Silence.* For several years he had been preaching to his guys and anyone else who would listen to him as he began to think of himself as a preacher, a sort of spiritual leader on a mission to spread the gospel according to his own bizarre beliefs and interpretations. His drug use fueled the delusions. Elvis became a kind of "evangelist" on an absurd, narcissistic self-imposed mission. The boys had to listen as Elvis spoke to them as if from a pulpit, from a higher place, spewing words of wisdom from his own personal orbit on his expressway to salvation. Ad nauseam.

"Our fake Elvis could literally become the real Elvis in his passing. He will be mourned by millions and buried here at Graceland and have a shrine commemorating his memory praising all his accomplishments here on earth." Preacher Elvis was on a roll. "The Lord works in mysterious ways."

"Say what?" asked Tommy. The Boss's words and the suggestion of what he was saying were sinking in. "Pretend you're dead? That you died in the crapper? Shouldn't we be calling the Colonel, Boss?"

"Quickly, everyone, here's what we're going to do," said Elvis, ignoring Tommy. They edged closer to the King so as not to miss a word. They had little choice.

Elvis truly believed he was a special emissary of God, put on earth not to sing and entertain but as a spiritual leader chosen by God himself, to go forth and teach an enlightened awareness. He believed God was within him, and therefore, he himself was divine.

When fake Elvis died on the crapper that night in Memphis, the real Elvis saw it as divine intervention and God's way of showing him a way out. He decided right then and there to take it. Hallelujah!

And so because the life of a man ended that day in Memphis, Tennessee, a unique opportunity was born. As a southern friend of Elvis's once explained to him, "Life's all about adding and subtracting."

Thank you, Father. Thank you, Brother. Thank you. Sister. "Thank you all, thank you very much."

Amen!

CHAPTER FIVE

The magnitude of what Elvis was considering was huge. The consequences of being caught in this charade unthinkable. But he was determined that the risk was worth it. As far as he was concerned, his life was at stake either way.

On one hand, he was slowly killing himself, and everyone close to him knew that. Ironically, the entourage that helped keep him isolated from all persons outside the organization, those privileged with the responsibility to protect him and keep him out of harm's way, were part and parcel of the problem. By giving the King whatever he wanted, whenever he wanted it, they enabled him.

Then there were the doctors who, with their endless supply of prescription drugs to feed his addictions, were also slowly killing him. The indifference by certain members of the DEA certainly didn't help matters, either, although at this point, they were getting hip to what was really going on and were near the end of their tether as far as turning a blind eye to Elvis's hypocritical anti-drug posturing.

The list of accomplices was long and the blame deep—at least vicariously—and Elvis realized this could very well work in his favor.

Tommy, Tag and Ron were instructed to leave the

dead guy the way he had been found and not to touch anything in that bathroom. So far, no one had actually entered the bathroom or touched Bud's body. Elvis told them to go to the kitchen and make some coffee while he had a quick shower and got dressed. Quietly they made their way to the kitchen and waited for their boss.

As the details of his plan began to take shape in his mind, Elvis became fixated. *Concentrate!* Even the drugs would have to take a back seat to his quest for freedom . . . salvation.

Not to say he would stop using, but he would need to be more heedful with his medication. He needed to be awake and alert so he could make plans and follow through.

He took some uppers. He wanted the pain in his body, caused by a host of reasons, to abate and so he also popped a couple of painkillers, but fewer than normal. He was proud of himself for taking less . . . it was a start. *I'll be all right*, he thought. One step at a time.

Elvis took a hot shower; he wanted to feel cleansed and revitalized. He needed to concentrate. In fact, he needed to concentrate like never before in his life.

Elvis knew what he wanted to do as soon as he'd seen the dead guy lying on the floor in the bathroom down the hall. But he needed a plan. He had an objective and motivation, but right now, right this minute, he needed strategy, and the luxury of time was not in his favor. The challenges were immediate. The first challenge was to deal with the body, and the second . . . to get the hell out of Memphis undetected.

Elvis decided to take a military approach to this daunting task, starting right then. It was war and he was a general, and he would lead his army to victory and to a safe place. In order to have this covert maneuver be successful, he needed allies.

General Presley needed a small task force, a tight-knit team to stand by him, steadfast and with complete unconditional servitude . . . not impossible to find if you're the King.

A year before there would have been no question as to who would man his army. Old habits are hard to break, and for a moment or two Red, Sonny and Dave were right at the top of his wish list of recruits. He even considered calling them, but deep down he knew he could not trust them anymore. No, he needed loyalty above all else.

Elvis knew his army would have to consist of as few as possible. There were only three people he could trust to follow him regardless of the consequences. Fortunately, they were with him that night.

Tommy Jefferson was thirty-two years old at the time. And smart. Unlike so many of E's former guys, he was not from the south but from Pittsburgh. He owned the catering company that was working an Elvis Presley concert in December 1975. Tommy was introduced to Presley at the sound check on the afternoon of the big show: the New Year's Eve concert in Pittsburgh.

After knocking himself out pleasing Elvis all day and evening long, Tommy even drove him to the hotel after the show accompanied by two security guys in the back seat. Elvis wanted Tommy to join him upstairs in his suite. Why? Maybe no reason other than he liked his company; Tommy was a cool guy. It was comforting to have a local at his beck and call, day and night, and Tommy seemed OK with that. Or maybe because Tommy Jefferson was black. Elvis had been known to do remarkable and unexplainable things for people of color over the years.

The story of his giving a Cadillac to an older black woman in a car dealership in Memphis was famous. When he asked her if she liked the Cadillac model she was looking at, she responded, "Why, yes sir, it's beautiful." He bought it for her. On the spot!

One opportunity quickly led to another for Tommy. He was soon invited to Graceland, where he was put in charge of overseeing the household staff. The longer Tommy was part of the team at Graceland, the stronger was his desire to please the Boss. He was a perceptive and efficient team player, excellent at multi-tasking, and it didn't take long before he was indispensable. Hiring Tommy was one of the best moves Elvis had made in a long time.

Big Tag Koury, head of security, friend and confidant, had been with him for years and Elvis flat-out trusted him. Like his boss, Tag had been born in Tupelo, Tennessee. He had moved to Memphis when he was only five years old. As he got older he got much bigger, and his large size, dramatic black hair—combed back in a ducktail—and black-on-black clothing style caught everyone's attention, including Elvis.

The fact that they lived a few doors down the street from each other made their meeting inevitable, and with Tag's impressive look and Elvis's unconventional sense of fashion, the pair became the odd couple in their neighborhood, and that cemented their friendship. As Elvis became successful, Tag tagged along for the ride and provided security when Elvis needed protection from the fans and paparazzi.

The third and last member of his team was Ron Fielding, Elvis's friend, bodyguard and personal driver. Ron had been born and raised in Memphis, and at fifty-two, he was the oldest of Elvis's "boys." His short, thick hair had mostly turned white when he had been in his early thirties. He had a great sense of humor, and he made Elvis laugh all the time. For all their silliness and clowning around, the man was serious about his work and therefore reliable . . . Ron was a guy to be trusted and vital to the success of Elvis's plan to escape from Graceland.

Like Tag he also had been with Elvis a long time. This would be his team for now.

After Elvis went over his strategy with the men, explaining his covert plan to "cease to exist," he dismissed them. He then closed the door to the bedroom suite and went directly to his hidden drug stash. The collection was impressive and deadly. There was Amytal, Quaaludes, Dexedrine, Adderall, Percodan and Dilaudid . . . and lots of each. And there were pills Elvis didn't even remember the names of anymore. He had a strange feeling as he gazed upon the little army of killers, ready and waiting to do what they did best.

Fuck him up. There was more than enough to kill him, so that was one less thing to worry about.

His next immediate objective was to enlist two more recruits.

CHAPTER SIX

D r. Derrick Muir was a pathologist Elvis had gotten to know when his mother, Gladys, passed away. The doctors had wanted to perform an autopsy to determine the exact cause of her death, but Elvis had forbidden it. The autopsy would have been performed by Muir had it been approved by the family, but when Elvis refused the procedure, it was Muir who sided with Elvis's wishes, and that had been enough for a kind of friendship to form between them. The doctor had been invited to Graceland several times since then, a major coup for any resident of Memphis at that time. He was also a major Elvis Presley fan.

Dr. Nick Brass was Elvis's longtime doctor. They got to know each other because of Elvis's many drug-related emergency trips to the hospital, ironic because the excessive drug use could be traced to the variety of drug prescriptions made out by Brass himself.

The two of them sat waiting nervously in the den, Tommy promising that Elvis would be with them momentarily.

The den was a large, curious room and the King's favorite in his castle. There was a huge sofa and two matching dark wood chairs with carved arms and legs, otherwise covered in some kind of fake fur.

The floors were hardwood and scattered with various-sized area rugs. Gaudy and tacky seemed to be the running theme in the sixty-foot-long den. Both men were seated in one of those oversized furry chairs facing a long wall of cut fieldstone from which water flowed to imitate a stream, or perhaps it was supposed to look like some kind of waterfall.

A stuffed armadillo, positioned on a large wooden table staring off into space, caught Deke's eye. "Jeez, will you look at that." He nodded at Nick. "*Creepy.*"

Both Derrick (Deke) and Nick had gotten a call from Elvis himself approximately forty minutes earlier . . . it was now 8:50 a.m. Getting a personal call from Elvis just never happened anymore. Elvis did not pick up the phone to ask for anything. He paid people to do that. When the King told them to get themselves over to Graceland pronto, they did. They were both afraid of Elvis, and for different reasons.

Dr. Nick had been worried for quite a while about Elvis's demands for more and more prescription drugs. He never said no to Elvis, in spite of the health problems and emergency treatments that resulted from the pills he prescribed. Elvis was getting crazier all the time, and that was the potential problem. After an order was placed with Dr. Nick, one of Elvis's gophers would pick up the prescription and bring it to his boss. The prescriptions were forwarded to a pharmacy—different pharmacies around town, never just the same one. On occasion the drugs would be procured by the doctor personally, and a runner from Graceland would exchange cash for the drugs at a prearranged meeting place.

Elvis was his number one patient, and although he was paid very handsomely indeed, being summoned to Graceland made Nick very nervous. The firing of Red West and the others only added to his anxiety. He too knew of the impending release of *Elvis: What Happened?*, and that was keeping him up at nights. He used to be able to deal with those guys when he had to, but with Elvis, well, you never knew what might happen. Elvis wasn't firing on all cylinders these days and the doctor, better than anyone, knew why. As he sat waiting anxiously in the den, he found himself wondering where Elvis kept all his guns.

Deke was more in awe of the King than afraid of him. But afraid he was nonetheless, afraid lest he fall out of favor with Memphis's richest and most famous resident. Derrick Muir felt his life was a banal and uninspired existence. There was the hospital smell that wouldn't go away. His hands were pink from scrubbing. His kids said pathology was gross. Anytime he was permitted into Elvis's world, his sense of excitement went off the radar.

So when the Big Boss-man charged into the room followed by Tag, he nearly jumped out of his chair. Nick also rose to his feet, albeit in a more dignified manner.

"Hi, fellers, thanks for coming over so fast. I appreciate it sincerely." His southern slur was somehow comforting. "Please sit. Welcome to Graceland."

"No problem, big guy." This from Nick, who regretted his choice of words immediately and quickly followed with "So, what's up, Elvis?" He settled back into the oversized chair, looking apprehensively at his patient.

"Deke, you OK?" asked Elvis. Deke was still standing with his mouth hanging open. He slowly sat back down, never taking his eyes off his hero.

Elvis glanced over his shoulder. "Tag, pour the boys a couple of fingers of that fine Kentucky bourbon we got in the bar over there." He looked back at his captive audience. "I think they might need it."

Neither of the fine doctors dared refuse such an early morning libation. When Elvis offered you a drink, you took it. Nor did they look at their watches, although both were wondering how late they'd be for work that morning. Still, they smiled a tight-lipped thank you to their host.

"Gentlemen, I've asked you to come here this morning to help me with a delicate matter. Someone died here at Graceland last night, and I need your help with the situation. Now, your first impression when you hear what I need from you guys might be a bit unsettling, I grant you that, but I believe you'll understand and see things my way when you hear why I'm gonna do what I need to do. Or I should say, *what I feel we must do*, gentlemen, in dealing with this unfortunate situation."

The Boss had the stage and his magic was never more apparent. As his audience went from stupefied to shocked to compliant, he continued to work the room like the truly inspired, virtuoso performer that was Elvis Presley. The King. Number one.

"OK, then, let's get started, shall we?" Nick stood with a bit of difficulty as he was now buzzed from the bourbon.

Though a keener to visit with the King of Rock and Roll and get a buddy thing going, a stunned Deke now looked as if he was going to cry.

Tag got the nod from his boss indicating it was show time, and so he said to the doctors, "Follow me, gentlemen." Tag led them out of the room, passing the mounted head of a long-eared deer and the whole stuffed carcass of a witless warthog in the process.

"Upstairs we go . . . watch your step . . . that's it . . . now turn right . . . very good . . . and here we are," directed Tag. Tommy and Ron were standing outside the bathroom that contained Bud's remains. They were waiting patiently for orders from Elvis.

Tag gestured to the door of the bathroom and said to the doctors, "In there." They slowly looked at each other, wide eyed, and then turned in tandem to peer inside the opened door. Pointing at the twisted form on the bathroom floor, Tag said, "And there's Elvis." He couldn't help himself.

The cry from Nick was extraordinary. It was almost inaudible, but somehow it filled the room.

Deke made a sound that sounded like "Eek!"

CHAPTER SEVEN

No one said a thing. The boys looked to Elvis, waiting to hear what was going to happen next. Lost for what to do exactly, under the bizarre circumstances, Nick and Deke stood silently by, looking as if they were hoping for a miracle to deliver them from this evil. Or direction from Elvis, whichever came first.

"Ron, you get the van ready, then come back and help Tag. He'll tell you what to do."

"OK, Boss. I'll be right back." And Ron was gone.

"Tommy, we got a lot to do before the shit hits the fan when Ron makes the call, so you stay here."

What happened from this point on was crucial to the success of the plan. Everything was moving very quickly, too quickly for comfort, really, but circumstances dictated the pace of play, not he.

Elvis paced as he considered; the next bit was obviously the most daring, switching identities. Having the fake Elvis, become the real Elvis. Smoke and mirrors time.

"Listen up. For this to work I need you all to hear me, and hear me good. Understand?" Elvis had popped a couple of Dexedrine just a few minutes before, and the juices were flowing. "All right then, here's the plan."

"Tag, I need you to arrange a few things for me. Start by calling Joe Bradley, and have him get a plane ready to roll. I wanna be long gone in a few hours." He held out a piece of paper with handwritten notes. "And take care of these few things pronto, all right?"

Tag nodded. "I'm on it, Boss." He snatched the list from Elvis and headed for the den.

"OK, then. Tommy I need you to do exactly as I say, and you need to be quick about it. Fake Elvis is ready for some basic makeup, so I want you to do it."

Tommy looked at E and said, "Boss, I won't be any good at that. I've never done makeup before." His voice was uncharacteristically tense.

"You'll do fine. I'll show you where everything is and you'll do just fine. Remember, we're not entering him in a damn beauty pageant, for Christ sake! Besides people don't look their best after a fatal heart attack, do they, Tommy?" He patted Tommy on the shoulder. "You can do it."

Elvis continued. "Just comb his hair up like mine. You'll add some hair spray to help keep it more or less in place, and add some makeup around the eyes. That's about it. His head is all purple and extremely bloated, and that's good. Leave it that way . . . it will look unnatural, I know, but it would anyway, even if it was really me. I wouldn't look like myself anyway, right?"

Elvis shuddered slightly.

"Follow me, Tommy. I got what you need, and you'll get on with it, son."

"Sure, Boss."

"And when that's finished with, pack a couple of suitcases for me. Basic stuff. I'll get everything else I need when I get to where I'm going. Tell Tag to bring the van 'round back, load it up and be ready to go. Hopefully, I'll be leaving Graceland for good."

He turned to Nick and Deke. "Follow me, please." They did.

CHAPTER EIGHT

Elvis needed to devise a plan with the doctors next. It had to be finely tuned and followed to a tee . . . and quickly!

They gathered in the den and closed the door. Elvis spoke slowly.

"OK, everything will be just fine if we think things through carefully, decide exactly what you need to say to the authorities and follow our plan precisely. Keep it simple, and keep it focused. It will work. Trust me," finished the Boss. This from a delusional drug addict!

Nick and Deke nodded and took deep breaths. They had to be thinking, *God help us!*

When they had finalized their plan and rehearsed what to say when the time came to deal with the authorities, it all sounded plausible—at least it seemed to at that point. Only then did Nick and Deke leave Graceland, both still visibly shaken.

Before the doctors left, they injected a lethal cocktail of prescription drugs into fake Elvis. The autopsy would show that the drugs had been administered after death; but that's where Dr. Deke would fudge things. Under the circumstances, and considering that Dr. Derrick Muir, chief pathologist, had done the procedure himself, there would be few or no questions asked, and no thoughts of foul play. Dr. Nick would handle the medical examination of the body on arrival at the hospital and file the reports and conclusions. He would be the doctor who would confirm findings consistent with Deke's report when the autopsy was done. Case closed. Hopefully.

Elvis Aaron Presley considered all that was at stake. His thoughts returned again and again to his father. Vernon Presley was old and emaciated and lived in a guest house behind the mansion. He had a personal staff of nurses, housekeepers and cooks looking after him. He had already suffered one heart attack, and no doubt the medics, when they realized the emergency call was coming from the most famous address in Memphis, would assume it was Vernon, Elvis's father, who was having a crisis, not the King himself.

Elvis had decided not to let his dad in on the truth, knowing he couldn't be trusted to remain silent. It would be just a matter of time before Vernon, old and quite nearly senile, would be overwhelmed and confused by the pressure of it all and would spill the whole can of beans. Purposely or inadvertently, it didn't matter . . . he must never know. It would be better that way.

Vernon would grieve the loss of his son as he had grieved the passing of his wife, Gladys. Perhaps more so. There was no other way. It was cruel, yes, but necessary. And truth be told, his father was in poor physical and mental health, living mostly in a state of oblivion in any case. Reality was no longer his constant companion.

When Vernon was told of his son's death, his honest reaction would unknowingly add credence to the farce.

Elvis was steadfast; still, this decision did not rest lightly on his conscience. *God forgive me*, thought Elvis.

He wept silently.

His melancholia was interrupted by a shuffling sound at the door of the den. It was Tommy.

Elvis got shakily to his feet and cleared his throat before he trusted himself to speak. His mouth was dry, his throat tight.

"Hey, Tommy. You near ready, son?" he managed.

"I'm good to go, Boss. Ron and Tag are at the van. Need anything?" He pretended to be absorbed with something on his hand. He was understandably uncertain.

"No, we're good. Let's get the hell out of here. We'll talk on the drive."

CHAPTER NINE

"Joe's ready when you are, Boss," Tag told Elvis when he got to the waiting van. "The plane's fueled and stocked. He believes he's taking a record executive friend of yours to the Bahamas. I'll make sure he's discreet and unobtrusive. He's been told to drop his passenger off, refuel and return immediately. No problems. The flight plan is a go; the paperwork is filed and all we need to do is show up. Otherwise, Ron's got all the personal items you wanted to take with you loaded in the van. Right, Ron?"

Ron nodded at Elvis. They then headed downstairs, through the kitchen and out the back door, where they walked quickly to a large navy blue Chevy van.

Elvis, dressed in a gray jumpsuit with a hood and black runners, nodded his approval. "Ron, you good?" Ron was.

"Ron, when you get back, give it a couple of hours and then you can make the call, all right?" Ron was in charge of holding down the fort until the jet was well under way. Elvis was positive his driver was as loyal as they came. He needn't worry about his keeping all this under his hat. Ever.

"You got it, Boss. Tag filled me in. I'll call for help and then I'll call Dr. Nick. Then I'll get your father's caretakers to bring him here. I'll tell Lilly and Lucy we have a serious issue and to go gentle with him."

Elvis knew Nick would need to give his daddy a shot when he was told his son was dead. He wouldn't be seeing the body, though. Nick would see to that, and Vernon was so disorientated these days anyway that it would make no difference.

Elvis spoke again. "Ron, be sure Nick gets here fast! You hear me? My daddy's gonna need his help dealing with all this. And make sure Deke is at emergency waiting. I don't want anyone else examining the body but him."

"Yes, sir."

"What you're doing for me, guys, I'll never forget. Not just for today, but for your loyalty that goes forward from here. No one must ever know the truth." There was a slightly ominous tone to the Boss's voice.

"I'll see that you're all compensated for this, boys. I swear on my mama's grave. Ron, you seem ready for the shitstorm about to descend on my home, so let's do it. I just hate to leave you here alone with this. I wish there was an easier way, but there isn't, believe me."

With that, he approached his small army and gave them each a quick, strong hug. They'd never had physical contact with Elvis Presley before, aside from roughhousing. The moment was special and greatly appreciated. It was almost a religious moment for each of them.

To Ron: "OK, then, get us to the airport."

Elvis ducked into the van. "Tag, Tommy, let's move!"

CHAPTER TEN

The jet taxiing out toward runway number one was a white and blue custom Lockheed JetStar: the *Hound Dog II*.

Almost half an hour had passed since Elvis, along with Tag and Tommy, had left Graceland. Ron parked the van at the steps of the JetStar, which had just emerged from the hangar where all the private planes were kept.

A few minutes earlier, the security guards had opened the gates for them upon their arrival. When they saw Elvis's van approach, they motioned for it to stop. They spoke briefly with Ron while Tag sat shotgun. Elvis and Tommy sat quietly in the back, out of sight. Security had been alerted to a VIP flight, and it was a routine they had dealt with many times before. They quickly confirmed the information they had been given in advance and then waved them through to the private area where Elvis kept his two jets, the other being the *Lisa Marie*.

Captain Joe Bradley was in the cockpit and at the controls of *Hound Dog II* when the guys arrived. Tag boarded the jet first and immediately went to the cockpit to say hello to Joe.

Joe Bradley had been on the Boss's flight team ever since Elvis had bought his first jet, a Convair

880, which he'd named *Lisa Marie* after his daughter. Joe was nicknamed "Balls" Bradley; he was a stone-cold risk taker with a reputation of getting himself, and his men, safely in and out. He had flown a North American P-51 Mustang in World War II and then a Lockheed RF-80 Shooting Star in the Korean War. When the war was over, he went private and flew corporate jets for Air Time Management Inc., a Houston, Texas–based company. He flew Elvis and the Colonel a few times, when the King became the number one entertainer in the United States and was chartering private planes to zip from one date to the next. When he heard Elvis had bought his own jet and the Colonel was discreetly looking for a pilot, Bradley contacted the Colonel in Memphis. One thing led to the next, and he had been the King's pilot ever since. He often joked that being a military pilot was safer than piloting the King of Rock and Roll. The mobs of fans, mostly female, were legendary. Joe was in his mid-sixties and enjoying every minute of it.

"Hey, Joe. Tommy and I really appreciate this. Elvis says we take this record company big shot to Nassau today, and you know E, when he says do it now, it's now. And here we all are." He shrugged his shoulders in an apologetic way.

"No problem, Tag. Nice day for a flight, and it beats sitting home when I can be flying."

"Same for me," echoed Tim Cowan, Joe's copilot. "No problemo."

"OK. Tommy and the exec are outside. I'll get them on the plane now. By the way, Tommy and I will be spending a few days in Nassau and doing a bit of gambling, so you guys will be on your own heading back. Thanks again, fellas."

Tag left the cockpit and motioned to Tommy out by the van. Elvis waited in the Chevy with Ron until Tommy came back for the last of the bags, then he said a final goodbye to his faithful driver, left the van and followed Tommy to the jet.

Joe and Tim, as expected, barely gave their human cargo a glance as the men boarded the aircraft.

When Elvis and Tommy were seated and strapped in, Tag pressed the button for the intercom that was mounted next to his seat.

"We're ready. Take her up, Joe."

"Yes, sir," said the captain. "Roger that."

CHAPTER ELEVEN

A couple of hours later at Graceland, Ron paced back and forth in the upstairs hallway. Fake Elvis was still sprawled on the bathroom floor wearing a pair of blue cotton boxer shorts under a white silk bathrobe. *Elvis* was monogrammed in gold on the front. He was barefoot. The gold pinkie ring that Tommy had given him to wear the evening before looked tiny on his swollen, discolored finger.

Ron looked at his watch. It was almost time for the call. Understandably, his mind was racing nervously over what he needed to do. Had to do. He was no actor, and the pressure of remembering his lines in this fiasco, although few, was daunting nonetheless.

Take a deep breath, he told himself. *You can do this, Ron. Just call it in.* The next part was easy: call Dr. Nick and say the coast was clear and to come on over . . . the hardest parts of this crazy plan were on Nick's and Derrick's shoulders. All he'd have to do when the authorities showed up was look stunned—which he was, anyway—and answer a few questions. "Elvis was sleeping late. I saw his light on so I went in to ask him if he needed anything. . . blah blah blah." *I can do this. I can do this for Elvis.*

He thought of Elvis, drink in hand, sitting back in his seat on *Hound Dog II*, flying off to begin a whole new life on an island in the Caribbean somewhere. Joe Bradley had been instructed to fly the jet to New Providence Island, in the Bahamas, and from there Elvis would disappear from the public eye forever. Yes, by the time the news of Elvis's death was to be made public, the Lockheed JetStar would have touched down in Nassau, and the real Elvis would be ensconced in a suite at the Princess Hotel on Paradise Island. Elvis would have Tag or Tommy monitoring all updates directly, and Elvis would be able to watch the coverage from Memphis on television while he made further arrangements to disappear off the radar.

It was time to deal with matters at hand; the ball of fate was in motion, and the Boss was counting on him. *I have to do this*, Ron thought. *It begins here and now, and Elvis needs me to be strong and to be focused. Focus!*

He picked up the phone and dialed the emergency number. It was 2:33 p.m.

CHAPTER TWELVE

When the news of Elvis's death was officially released at the Baptist Memorial Hospital in Memphis, Tennessee, on the afternoon of August 16, 1977, the world was in shock. Within an hour of the announcement, a thousand mourners were at Graceland and many thousands more on the way.

As television, radio and newspapers were relating the story worldwide, the global reaction was nothing less than remarkable. Millions of people were distraught and disbelieving. How could this happen to their hero? There was little knowledge by the adoring fans that Elvis had been a very sick man. The people who knew the truth of Elvis's lifestyle were not that surprised by news of his death. Elvis Presley was a drug addict. Period.

But many fans would never let themselves believe the King was a victim of complications due to habitual drug abuse. It was just too unthinkable for many fans to accept. Many even refused to believe he was dead.

Regardless, the information kept coming from informed sources, which included released statements from both Drs. Muir and Brass. It was Brass who rushed to Graceland when he got the call from Ron informing him that the medics were on the way. The good doctor was less than two minutes behind them, and when he arrived he took charge and pretended to try to revive fake Elvis; in fact, he even went to the hospital in the ambulance so as to be sure it was Dr. Muir—Deke—who received the body. And of course, Deke was waiting for their arrival. There were no insurmountable problems.

The body that arrived at the Baptist Memorial Hospital was hard to look at. The head was grotesquely bloated and discolored, making the features impossible to recognize properly. His body shape was twisted and contorted in an unnatural way . . . and rigor mortis had started to set in some time ago.

The two medics who were first to see the dead Elvis said the man lying on the bathroom floor was so disfigured that neither of them recognized the most famous man in Memphis.

The surrealistic atmosphere caused by the arrival of a dead Elvis also led to no one realizing it wasn't the real Elvis. And it never even occurred to other medics on call that the corpse was not that of the real King. Nick helped keep it that way by orchestrating all events until the body was in the hands of Deke, at which time he took over.

It's hard to believe today that such a lack of scrutiny and false identity could occur; but it was the King. It was all unbelievable. It was Memphis and it was 1977. And most important . . . it was all manipulated by the chief medical doctors present upon "Elvis's" pathetic corpse's arrival at the hospital. Doc Nick and pathologist Doc Derrick. They took charge of manipulating all the medical examination processes from beginning to end, and then, on behalf of the hospital, they released an official announcement to the press. Simply put, it worked.

Brass told reporters after the autopsy that "Elvis's heart was found to be enlarged, his arteries somewhat clogged by drug abuse, so diseased that it looked like spoiled pate de foie gras." What an image.

Muir, in a press conference, revealed that the death appeared to have been caused by cardiac arrhythmia. He stated that there was severe cardiovascular disease present, and basically it was a natural death. He also said, "The precise cause of death may never be discovered." Like Elvis's mother.

Way to play ball, Deke.

And the media continued relentlessly . . .

"Drug use was heavily implicated in the death of Elvis Aaron Presley."

"No one ruled out the possibility of anaphylactic shock brought on by codeine pills . . . to which he was known to have a mild allergy."

Lab reports filed two months later suggested that polypharmacy might have been the primary cause of death: "Fourteen drugs in Elvis's system at the time of death, ten in significant quantity," one reported.

His death caused a unique breed of media circus fueled by controversy that would continue for decades to come.

CHAPTER THIRTEEN

J ust after the JetStar touched down in Nassau—a mere 20 minutes after Baptist Memorial Hospital announced that Elvis had left the building for good—Elvis called Colonel Parker. There was no way around it—his notorious manager had to be informed of what was really going down. Parker would soon be getting deluged by requests to comment on the passing of his famous client, if he hadn't already. Actually there was no reason not to tell him. There was only a great ally to be gained.

Parker was notorious for any number of things, not the least his insatiable quest for the almighty dollar. If he smelled money, he was on it. A man from a circus background, he was primed for an opportunity like this.

Tag went to the cockpit and instructed Joe and Tim to give them twenty minutes while the record exec made some phone calls and then they'd be on their way. Joe had paperwork to fill out anyway and didn't mind the wait.

Elvis called Tom Parker at a private number used only by the two men for confidential conversations. Ron had already spoken to Parker as per Elvis's directive, so Parker knew his only client was still alive . . . somewhere . . . so before the first ring on his private phone line was completed, Parker picked up and shouted, "What the fuck is going on? Are you all right?"

"I'm just fabulous for a dead guy. Thanks for asking, sir. And you?" jested Elvis.

"Me? Me?!" Parker's voice boomed over the line.

Still shouting, Parker continued, "Frank Sinatra just called me with his condolences! Sammy Davis! Hope! Streisand! They're all calling with questions and condolences, and it's only just started. My other lines are ringing off the hook! I got Lamar and Lacker going out of their minds as we speak. They have no idea your fat ass is parked in a suite somewhere while the rest of the world is beside itself because of your supposed untimely demise!"

The Colonel's voice was like that of an old-time carny barker, demanding and much louder than necessary, which many people found abrasive when having to do business with him. The phone was his megaphone at this moment, and he was venting. Mostly it was blatant old-school posturing, and Colonel Tom Parker was actually enjoying himself immensely. No one could, or ever would, speak to the King like this except the Colonel. Their relationship had become a professional relationship only, based on tolerance by both parties. This call was all business for both.

Elvis couldn't help but notice the thrill that the Colonel, the ultimate Barnum and Bailey throwback, the supreme grifter, was getting from all the extraordinary attention suddenly directed at him. His flimflam juices were flowing, a con artist caught up in the con.

Elvis bristled. "My fat ass is still on my jet, sir, and what I'm doing is what I have to do. I'm through with singing and the live performing, and I'm through doing those ridiculous movies we've been cranking out of Hollywood. It's all over. I'm finished with the nonstop attention. I can't take it anymore, and I know it won't stop unless I'm dead, and we both know even that won't end it, but at least I can have a normal life before this craziness kills me."

Elvis knew the only thing the Colonel really cared about was money and that his manager was only half listening to him. The Colonel's uncommon silence confirmed that the wheels were already turning as Parker pondered how to keep the business alive and the money flowing even though the reason for it all was dead.

Knowing the Colonel, his first reaction would be to take action and get to Graceland, to meet with Vernon, Elvis's dad, in particular. There was business to take care of! New contracts would need to be written up and signed. Old contracts had to be attended to immediately. Opportunists would be coming out of the woodwork en masse, even in this dark hour of incredulousness and profound grief.

Elvis continued. "As for the percentage split regarding present and past contracts, they remain the same. But from now on, for all future deals, the split is 80-20. That's 80 percent for you, 20 percent for me, sir, as long as I remain 'deceased.' Understand? That's the way I want it. Now this is an opportunity for you to rake in some serious dough-ray-me; and if that offends your sense of decency, sir, just say so and our business together is, as they say, history."

"Son, you know I have always been here for you. What do you have in mind?" The Colonel's greed knew no limit.

*****

After his conversation with Elvis, Colonel Parker dialed a private number at the mansion and Ron answered.

Parker informed Ron that he had just spoken with Elvis and that he was on his way to Graceland and that if Vernon was there to keep him away from everyone until he arrived.

"Do you understand me?"

"Yes, sir, Colonel," answered Ron, relieved that he'd have another ally at the mansion to help him deal with all the hoopla that was happening.

"Good, I'll be there shortly," shouted Parker before hanging up.

Graceland is a colonial-style, brown limestone structure complete with a facade of six towering white columns, known as Temple of the Winds columns. The first thing you encounter when arriving at the estate are the entrance gates. These ornate iron gates feature a guitar and a series of musical notes. Once through the gates you ascend stone steps flanked on either side by two white lion statues, and the steps lead to the large oak front door. These doors were closed as usual, but the activity behind them was anything but.

Several persons from the Memphis police force were still milling about while Ron stood in the entrance foyer, exhausted and wanting it all to end. Two policemen stood guard at the front gates, and others around the perimeter of the property kept the curious from venturing onto the estate. Ron had called the emergency number just over two hours earlier, and the body had quickly been taken to the hospital by ambulance, accompanied by Dr. Muir, as planned.

Not long after Parker ended his brief dialogue with Ron, he showed up at Graceland. His Memphis office was only fifteen minutes from Graceland by car. He passed the front gates and went on to the private back entrance, used exclusively by staff and family and close friends of Elvis. He had no problem being admitted onto the premises—everybody knew who he was. He was almost as famous as Elvis. Besides, most people were intimidated by the Colonel. None of the security guards even considered trying to stop him or ask why he was there.

Ron was told Parker had arrived and was already on the move. "Where the hell is Vernon?" he asked as soon as he spotted Ron making his way toward him.

Hearing the Colonel's question as they approached each other, Ron replied, "Follow me, please," and kept walking. He led Parker to a room in the left wing of the building, away from all the commotion in the lower main section of the house. Normally Vernon would be in his own building on the estate, but he had been brought to a room in the big house where there was more space and the medics could keep a closer eye on him.

Vernon Presley was sixty-one years old in 1977. His wife, Gladys, had died in 1958. He had been having health issues for the past several years, primarily related to a heart condition. Although the Colonel was Elvis's manager in the real sense, Elvis was paying his father a fee of $60,000 a year for management services. But Vernon's business acumen was not fit for much more than paying some bills and pretending he worked for his son and was therefore worthy of compensation for his employment. By this time, Vernon's health was vulnerable, and he was doing next to nothing because of his medical condition. He was on various medications, and like Elvis's mother, his body was succumbing to years of a bad diet and other poor lifestyle choices.

Vernon was too medicated and too disoriented to be considered responsible for any kind of business decisions for his famous son, and so when Parker needed to explain to Vernon the urgency of the situation at hand, he knew he needed to keep things simple. He had to get Vernon to sign a one-page agreement he had hastily prepared that would allow the Colonel to run with whatever it was he needed to do to maintain control of Elvis's future royalty earnings and to help him legally keep the other wolves at bay. Of course, eventually, the Presley estate would control all that the Colonel was prepared to fight for that day, but he and Elvis had an understanding and a scheme he was determined to make happen.

Ron led Parker to a room that normally was used as a casual sitting room. It was situated off the kitchen, and it was mostly used by staff as a place to relax. The room was average living room size with a series of three large windows along one side offering a view of a garden. The white, full-length curtains were drawn. The walls were painted pale blue and the floors covered with white tiles specked with silver. Several overstuffed chairs and a large sofa, covered in a matching organic pattern of pastel blues, yellows and white, were scattered about the room. This is where Ron and the Colonel found Vernon. He was lying on the large sofa with his head resting on a pillow and a lightweight comforter covering all but his head. He looked to be sleeping. A nearly empty glass of water sat on a white table alongside.

Two ladies seated opposite Vernon looked over as they walked into the room. One, a registered nurse named Lucy, had been hired to tend to Vernon, and the other was Lilly. Both were live-in staff members from Vernon's house, which was adjacent to the main house. They stood when Ron and Parker entered.

"Excuse us, ladies," said Ron, "but we need to be alone with Mr. Presley for a while. If you'll just wait in the kitchen, we'll let you know when we're through here. By the way, how's he doing?"

Lucy answered, "He's been medicated to help him rest. The news of his son's passing had him understandably upset and, well . . . confused, really. He refused to believe it at first. I think they may move him to the Baptist where they can look after him better." She glanced at the other woman. "Come, Lilly." The two of them left Ron and the Colonel alone with Vernon.

The Colonel had been staring at Vernon the whole time. He placed his briefcase on the table and looked over at Ron.

"Wake him."

Ron walked to the sofa and knelt down before Vernon. He placed a hand on the man's shoulder, gently nudging him.

"Vernon, sir, it's Ron Fielding. Can you hear me?" His voice was soft and filled with honest concern for the older man. Vernon liked Ron and was always respectful toward him, even asking Ron to call him Vernon and not Mr. Presley not long after he began working at Graceland. He also treated Tag and Tommy with the same respect, perhaps because these guys looked after his son and they were loyal.

Vernon opened his eyes slowly and said, "Ron . . . where's my son?"

Unlike Ron, Tom Parker had no time for pleasantries. He was in that room no longer than ten minutes, and when he left he had a signed copy of the document, witnessed by Ron Fielding. Colonel Parker had given himself the power he needed to protect his ass and the fortune available to him now . . . and in the future.

There were three signatures required on the agreement: his, Vernon's and Elvis's. He only needed Elvis's now, and he would have that when Elvis signed and returned the paperwork. Elvis would supply an address where the document could be sent in the next day or so. The hastily typed agreement was dated eighteen months earlier, as the Colonel and Elvis had agreed by phone that afternoon. It all should hold up in court if need be, and Parker knew the day would come when the document would be under attack in a court of law, but for now that was all he could do.

So at Graceland that day, Colonel Parker had Vernon Presley sign all the paperwork that needed signing. Vernon, emotionally and physically spent, must have had trouble writing his own name let alone understanding what he was agreeing to. But sign he did, and with that mission completed, the Colonel was off and running, leaving Ron Fielding and the nurses to comfort a devastated father as best they could. He had more urgent business to attend to; the Colonel knew a horde of hustlers would be having a field day trying to exploit Elvis's name and image, now that they believed him dead.

The thought made the cagey old rogue's blood boil, and that was the reason that within half an hour of ending his conversation with Elvis, he was at Graceland with a hastily prepared agreement in hand, the ink barely dry on the page. Parker accomplished a lot in a short period of time, securing merchandise deals in particular, as that was the future. The annual income going to the estate each and every year was staggering.

There were no flies on Parker that day as he made off like a bandit. Elvis, already very rich, would also increase his fortune. All Parker needed now was for Elvis to set up an account wherever he was going and all his present and future earnings would be funneled there discreetly—all tax free, of course.

And so everything worked out as planned . . . the body of fake Elvis would be buried in Memphis on August 18, 1977. There would be millions of mourners, all the world over. The King was believed dead, and the code of silence promised by that small handful of people Elvis confided in was uncompromisingly maintained, a remarkable sign of a tenacious loyalty to their friend and hero. Elvis!

Elvis's perpetuated secret life was safe. The truth was buried with fake Elvis: unassailable . . . *until now*!

CHAPTER FOURTEEN

The reservation for one suite and a deluxe room at the Paradise Island Regency Hotel was under the name of Thomas Jefferson. No one was to know that Elvis Presley was ever in the building. Tommy was understandably uneasy and apprehensive; there was so much that could go wrong. What if the whole affair blew up in their faces? In his face! How would he be treated for his part in it? How much jail time? He would be disgraced and his life ruined.

Tommy put down his personal American Express card for payment, and after that business was concluded, he and Tag took a trolley outside where Elvis, wearing large sunglasses and a plain black cap, sat waiting in the back of the airport limo. The boys loaded up the trolley and then all three made their way through the lobby, got in the elevator and rode to the top floor. They proceeded to suite 1010. The boys' room was across the hall.

"Here you go, Boss, this is your suite. Let me get the door for you." Tag had the keys, and he opened the door for Elvis and then stepped back, holding the door with one hand. Elvis walked into the room, and Tommy followed with two suitcases in hand. Tag carried in a large leather garment bag. They looked around the suite and were impressed.

"Your home away from home, Boss . . . very nice," said Tommy with a comforting smile.

The suite consisted of a large combination living room and a dining and kitchen area, plus a master bedroom with en suite. The floors were covered in a rich-quality beige carpet, and the walls were painted pearl. The many pictures on the walls featured Bahamian themes, giving the room a distinct feeling of island life and healthy living . . . Caribbean style. The chic furniture was lightweight and covered in earthy shades of brown and gold. Vibrant colors filled the room compliments of the flower-patterned cushions, the pink coral-style lamps with rose decorative shades, and the blue and gold painted vases filled with fresh-cut flowers that filled the suite with a wonderful, natural, sensuous fragrance.

One wall was made up entirely of floor-to-ceiling windows overlooking the beach and the Atlantic ocean. A large balcony ran the length of the main room. The kitchen was modern and well equipped, and a large, well-stocked bar was positioned so that carefree vacationers could mix their drinks while enjoying the spectacular views from the top floor of the highest building on Paradise Island.

The spacious, richly appointed master bedroom was at the opposite end of the suite, hidden behind a French door. The suite was completed by a convenient three-piece powder room off the entrance hallway.

"Not bad, boys. A shame we'll be here only a night or two. I could use some R and R in a place like this." Elvis was standing at the window staring out across the beautiful ocean waters. "Oh, well."

Elvis knew his companions were also emotionally exhausted and needed some private time themselves. He turned and said, "You guys go get settled in. We'll order some room service in about an hour, so come on back when you're ready."

"Sure, Boss. We're across the hall in room 1009. Dial a seven first and then the room number if you wanna call us before we get back. OK?"

"Yeah, yeah, go on. I'll be fine."

Elvis knew his stay in the Bahamas had to be as short as possible. He didn't feel safe there; a person as famous and as recognizable as himself would never be able to go unnoticed in such a place for very long. No, it was crucial to do what needed to be done ASAP and move on to wherever his personal Shangri-la was going to be.

Finally alone, he turned on the large console television in the living room and played with the channel select until he found a U.S. channel that was covering the latest updates on the confirmed death of Elvis Aaron Presley. He went to the sofa, sat down and focused his attention on the satellite feed. There was footage of reporters outside the complex at Graceland. There was an interview with the Memphis Chief of Police, who had no comment other than stating that Elvis was dead. There were interviews with fans now collecting outside Graceland. The rumors and speculations were starting, and the world was listening.

All the conjecture relating to the reasons for his

"untimely passing" was extremely annoying, and the references to his alleged drug abuse were hard to listen to. The comments about his being overweight made Elvis shift uncomfortably . . . and sweat.

Elvis was torn regarding his decision not to let Lisa Marie know that her daddy was still alive. How could a child be expected to understand something as outrageous as faking a death . . . her father's. Maybe someday, when she was older . . . but not now. His father also would never know the truth. What was that expression he had heard a few times? Tough love. Yes, sir, this was tough. Or was it an absurd example of a self-serving, cruel deception, with no regard for family and friends? Or the millions of fans, incredulous and in mourning?

Forgive me, Lord, on my road to salvation.

He turned the television off and sat on a sandalwood-toned lounge chair. As he gazed out at the stunning panoramic view of the Atlantic Ocean, he tried to shut out the images of the television coverage and the reaction to his contrived death.

Enough was enough . . . Elvis got up and removed from his hand luggage a couple of downers, swallowed them quickly and then went to the bar and poured himself a shot of Jack Daniels. Had he been back in Memphis and pissed off at watching something that bothered him so much, he would have taken a 57 Magnum and shot the fucking TV. But that Elvis was dead, and there'd be no more shooting television sets.

The Quaalude and the Aventyl were helping him

relax. He realized the irony of being upset at being called a drug addict, and the need he could not ignore, to pop a couple of pills. *Lord help me.* There was no way he was going to stop taking drugs cold turkey. Not here . . . not now. He knew he would need medical supervision when the time came to get straight, but that could wait, for now was not the time. Being straight was the new Elvis. The future.

There was a knock at the door. Elvis looked at his custom gold watch and realized an hour had passed. It had felt like only a few minutes. He walked slowly to the door and looked through the peephole. His boys were standing in the hallway. He opened the door.

"Come on in, boys, and let's get some food happening. Tommy, call down and have them bring me a steak, well done, and some fries; you guys get what you want."

"I already ordered, Boss," Tommy said. "It should be here in a few minutes. I figured you'd be in the mood for a good steak."

"And some chocolate ice cream," Tag added.

Elvis smiled for the first time in hours.

"You done good, boys."

*****

The first thing Elvis did after dinner was go over a list of things that needed to be done during their brief stay in Nassau, and the first order of business was getting a new passport in the name of Aaron J. Smith.

He and the Colonel had a hurried discussion about this when they had spoken earlier. The Colonel said he would take care of the details and for Elvis to reach him the next day. Elvis explained to Parker that he wanted to use his middle name, Aaron, and his mother's maiden name, Smith. The J. was in acknowledgment of his twin brother, Jesse, who died at childbirth, a tragic circumstance that haunted Elvis all of his days. The passport would state: AARON J. SMITH. Hair: auburn. Eyes: blue. It would claim that he was a U.S. citizen, born in Dallas, Texas, in 1940. He had decided to shave five years off his real age, making himself thirty-seven years old. Getting a false ID was not that difficult for a man like Colonel Parker, especially back in the day. All you needed was the contact and the money. Cash, thank you. Not a problem. The passport would be prepared right there on the island. Nassau was a tax haven and a refuge of sorts, and bogus passports were a sometime necessity for the very rich (and the criminally inclined).

He'd have a fake passport within twenty-four hours; it would need a picture of Aaron J. Smith, and that would be taken the next morning.

Elvis sat on a stool at the bar. "Tommy, I want you to cut my hair and do that coloring thing we talked about."

The shopping list Elvis had given Tag in Memphis before they left had included a bottle of hair dye, an apply-and-wait rinse that Tag found easily at a drugstore. Tommy got what he needed for the job from Tag and brought it with him to Elvis's suite.

"And Tommy, I want to go over this banking thing with you." Tommy had spoken with Parker about this less than an hour before and had made careful notes so he would remember all the details for E.

Tommy was preparing to cut his boss's hair; the electric shaver, cream and other supplies he needed were all from Graceland. "Sure, Boss."

Elvis asked him, "What's this cat's name, the guy from the Bahamian Royal Bank?"

Tommy was placing a towel over Elvis's shoulders when he replied. "Rod Miller. He's the main guy who handles offshore accounts coming from the U.S. He can come to you if you wish, or we can meet him at his office. The Colonel says it will all be arranged in the morning, but I'll call him first to be sure. But there should be no problems. You just need to decide when and where you want this matter handled, Boss."

"We'll do it here. I don't wanna step outside until it's time to ride *Hound Dog* outta here. By the way, Joe's back in Memphis?"

"Yes, sir. We'll call when you need him."

"All right."

All right, mama, any way you choose.

When Tommy finished cutting Elvis's hair, he passed a handheld mirror to his boss.

Elvis's hair was now short—not a brush cut, but short—and parted on the left side. Tommy would color the hair the same shade of reddish brown that Elvis had before he started dyeing it black many years earlier.

Elvis noticed that the short haircut made his puffy face puffier. He couldn't snap his fingers and change that tonight, but a look in the mirror would give him added inspiration to lose the extra weight.

"What an ugly son of a bitch! What have you done?" shouted Elvis. Tommy's legs felt rubbery. It had been hard cutting the King's hair. His famous locks, which would fetch a small fortune if put up for auction, were lying neglected on the hotel room floor, waiting to be picked up and tossed in the trash. What had he done, indeed?

Then he heard a giggle that turned to a chuckle, and to Tommy's tremendous relief, the King began laughing his ass off.

"Well, if that don't beat all. That is one lame-ass haircut! Just what I wanted! Well done, Tommy . . . Look here, that's not Elvis Presley, that's *Aaron Smith*." Elvis continued laughing.

Tommy hadn't heard Elvis's laugh in a long time. *It was musical.*

Chapter Fifteen

Elvis had gone to bed early and gotten up around 9:30 a.m. The old Elvis would have stayed up most of the night and slept well into the afternoon. But a new life called for a new lifestyle. Now he was sipping some coffee from a terra-cotta mug with the slogan I'M ON ISLAND TIME printed on the side in orange and yellow lettering.

Rod Miller, the banker assigned by the Colonel to meet with Elvis at the hotel to have some papers signed, arrived at 10:30. He was led in by Tommy and introduced to Aaron Smith.

Today, Aaron Smith looked nothing like the King of Rock and Roll. Like an actor in a play, Elvis felt as if in costume, ready to become a character in a theatre production. His acting skills could only help in this meeting with Miller, although there wasn't much he had to say or do—signing the name Aaron Smith on some documents was about it. Tommy would serve as witness if need be.

A pair of plain, black-framed nonprescription glasses completed the new look he wanted. At that time, colored contact lenses weren't available or he may have been tempted to wear a pair of those as well, to mask his famous blue eyes.

Elvis was wearing a pair of expensive Bulgarian

blue-cotton slacks and a Caribbean-style canary-yellow floral shirt that Tag picked up for him, along with tan suede topsiders and white ankle socks.

Only Tommy and Elvis met with Rod Miller for the signing of all the documents pertaining to opening an offshore account. He showed no sign of recognizing the famous singer, and all went smoothly.

It was all standard procedure, aside from Aaron Smith being transient at this time. Miller was informed that a permanent address would follow shortly, and that the only immediate action would be the transfer of funds into the new account directly from a U.S. account.

"I don't anticipate any problems, sir," Miller assured his bank's new client. "Your request is not an unusual one for us."

Tommy served as witness to the signing of the legal documents by Miller and Aaron Smith, and soon all the business at hand was finished. And that was that. The banker was escorted to the door.

Turning to address Aaron Smith, Miller said, "A shame about Elvis's death yesterday. Man, did he fuck up or what?"

Elvis almost punched Miller in the face. Instead he made no comment, but he closed the door quickly and firmly, throwing the security lock shut in one swift motion.

****

Tag showed up with a guy with a camera just before noon, and he took Aaron Smith's picture and left. No questions asked. That kind of "passport" service is illegal in most places; it was expensive but worth every dollar. Tag was told the passport would be ready to be picked up by the end of the day. Simple.

It was now 4:32 p.m. in Nassau and Elvis was tired again. He needed rest. He still had to focus on finding a new permanent address, which would take a whole lot more time and energy; he also needed the help of the guys. So before taking a well-deserved siesta, he told Tag and Tommy more of his plan.

"Guys, I don't really need to tell you a lot has happened in the last thirty-six hours, and I'm not just talking about my untimely demise." He smiled and then waited while they chuckled. Elvis knew it would help Tommy and Tag to relax a bit. He could see they were exhausted too.

Tommy and Tag had no idea how the King was feeling about things. Not only the events that had transpired since fake Elvis dropped dead in Graceland yesterday morning and they hauled ass out of Memphis but also how he was dealing with his drug issues. Was he using? Was he high? Did he realize what he'd done, and did he know where he was going? Where *they* were going?

A lot of questions, and they couldn't help but feel anxious knowing they were sitting in a hotel, in hiding, with a made-up guy named Aaron J. Smith—a drug addict masquerading as a rich American just passing through, in town just long enough to set up an offshore bank account and then move on; it was all so fucking unbelievable!

"We need to keep moving, fellers. I need a place to hang my hat. I'm talking about a new home. I'm not going back to Memphis . . . ever." He let this sink in.

"I've been thinking I wanna buy a place in the Caribbean, and I want it far from the U.S. and all the 'Elvis' bullshit. I want a new life. Aaron Smith wants a life."

Elvis moved to the window and fell silent.

"Where do you wanna go, Boss?" asked Tommy, looking at Tag with apprehension in his brown eyes.

"I wanna look at properties in Antigua." He turned to the guys and repeated. "I wanna go to Antigua."

Let's face it, Elvis had been there, done that.

Business and pleasure travel had taken him to numerous sunny destination spots over the years, most notably Hawaii. It was while filming in Hawaii that Elvis fell in love with the whole tropical vibe. The endlessly perfect weather that soothed and enticed one's senses to the point of passion was clearly etched in Elvis's memory, and the brilliant sapphire-blue ocean waters and sandy white beaches all added up to an exhilarating beauty he could not resist. He eventually despised making the dumb beach films, but he never tired of Hawaii, which thankfully made it all tolerable at least. He wanted to live in a place that had palm trees, clean beaches and crystal-clear waters. A permanent vacation.

"Antigua . . . where is that, Elvis?"

"In the Caribbean, Tommy, east of Jamaica; east of Puerto Rico too. I'm interested in the St. John's area. That's the capital city, man. I was there several years ago with Ginger. We spent a few weeks. It's a beautiful, laid-back place that's off the beaten track. We loved it. I believe it has everything I'll ever want. It's worth a visit."

Now the boys gotta be thinking about themselves living on some freaking island, in the middle of the ocean, in the middle of freaking nowhere. Right?

"Uh . . . Boss, you wanna have Joe fly us there? I mean . . . I assume it has a real airport, right?"

"Oh, yeah, it's got a real airport, Tommy. It's the fucking capital of the island of Antigua. And Antigua's a member of the British Commonwealth, if I remember right. What, do ya think Ginger and me swam there?"

"I was thinking boat . . ."

"Tommy, we fly in. Tag, call Joe. I want him here tomorrow night. Tommy, you handle the front desk. We'll be checking out tomorrow after dark."

Elvis went to the bedroom after the guys left and popped several pills. He returned to the bar and poured himself a drink before taking a seat on the balcony, slowly relaxing as he listened to the waves breaking on the shore below him. The sky was clear and radiant. The humidity was like a warm, lush blanket that wrapped around him, like a dear old friend. The intoxicating smell of the salt water soothed . . . he felt at peace. Pure magic. He could get used to this.

*****

Colonel Parker was still Elvis's manager in the real sense of the word. That is, Parker orchestrated and manipulated Elvis's personal affairs. And so Elvis Presley, now Aaron Smith, relied on the Colonel more than ever. Of course, the Colonel needed Elvis's cooperation in order to continue raking in the greenbacks and to cash in on his only client's death through new merchandizing rights and renegotiations of other rights now vulnerable because of Elvis's death. And now the Colonel had his hands full maintaining some of the affiliate businesses he had formed that were directly related to controlling the interests of the Presley estate. Those in conflict with the Colonel's vision had their lawyers cueing up to do battle.

Elvis had called Parker many times over the last two days with questions. And there were multiple requests. Some reasonable, some not so much. Do this, do that. Call this guy, call that person. Transfer all of these funds to this new company that had just been formed in the name of Aaron Smith & Associates. Make it happen. Now!

Parker, who always had power of attorney to sign for Elvis, now had the same privilege for Aaron J. Smith.

He in fact had arranged an agreement in writing, signed by Elvis and witnessed, stating that if Elvis was incapacitated in any way, or if Elvis died suddenly during the terms of his management contract, he, Colonel Tom Parker, would continue to manage the estate's affairs indefinitely. That would soon be contested—by Priscilla, for one—and that added to the high priority of the situation. Besides covering his ass, he needed all of Aaron Smith's affairs in place in case Elvis had a change of heart and miraculously rose from the dead and fought him on this. There was no room for interpretation later on.

Parker's law team of Platt & Ross was competent and could handle the responsibility of making shit stick to the wall, even without knowing the whole truth. And that's often how they preferred it when it came to dealing with the notorious snake-oil salesman, Colonel Parker. The Colonel let them know part of the truth only when it suited him to do so, and their lucrative account with the Parker/Presley organization depended on their ability to accept and obey, even if they suspected that some dealings were unethical.

To his credit, the Colonel dealt with Elvis's demands and made things happen. Presley did not have the savvy to make things real. That was the Colonel's job, and one that he always took seriously. It was Parker who took care of business.

Parker still kept, at least for a while longer, Joe Bradley on retainer. His job was to be ready to fly whenever and wherever he was instructed. So when Tag contacted Joe to fly *Hound Dog II* back to the Bahamas the next evening, Parker made certain that

Joe was on it. Joe Bradley arrived in Nassau at 6:37 p.m. local the next day.

CHAPTER SIXTEEN

When Tommy, Tag and Aaron Smith arrived at the airport by hotel limousine, they proceeded to the VIP area for private jets. A recent brief summer rainfall had left everything shiny, reflecting the many lights of the busy airport. Multicolored beacons from the terminal, the airplanes taxiing back and forth and the ground crew vehicles—some frantic, others leisurely—all danced together in the fading, evening light.

All customs and immigration procedures were handled in the restricted VIP area. The privileged were immune to the imposing formalities of the normal traveler, and the delay before boarding their private jet was less than five minutes, with neither Tag nor Elvis needing to speak to an authority—only Tommy had that dubious pleasure. Tommy presented all their passports and signed a form, and they were free to leave.

After they finished with the formalities, their black limo followed a security car over to where *Hound Dog II* was parked, and they all go out. Elvis and Tommy boarded the plane immediately, and Tag went to speak with Joe Bradley.

Joe was walking around the plane, doing a last-minute visual check before takeoff. The jet was fueled and ready for the next leg to Antigua.

Tag approached the pilot and said, "Hello, Joe, good to see you. How you doing tonight?"

Joe looked distracted, and he came right to the point. "What really happened, Tag? They say he died of a heart attack or maybe an overdose . . . I just can't believe it." Joe was, understandably, still quite upset by the news of Elvis's death.

"Heart attack, they say. That's all I know, Joe. Ron found E's body in the bathroom. Tommy and I weren't at Graceland that day, remember? We were escorting that record exec here to Nassau."

Joe shook his head. "What a tragedy . . . The funeral was today. I figured you guys would have been there."

"Parker needed us to take care of some business here and in Antigua. And honestly, I don't think I could have gone. It's all just so . . ." Tag let his voice trail off. He wanted to say as little as possible, hoping Joe attributed his reluctance to talk to his being too emotional to discuss it further at this time.

Joe took the hint. "Yes, sir. Well, the plane's ready to fly when you are." He turned and walked back to the jet.

One could argue that flying into a place always gives a traveler the most interesting perspective. Far more dramatic than seeing the destination slowly unfold before you, like an unrolling carpet, as one would when arriving by land.

Seeing Antigua from the air quickly confirmed the beauty of the place, even at night, which was when

Hound Dog II flew over the coast of Antigua and then St. John's on its approach to the V.C. Bird International Airport. The airport in 1977 wasn't all that big, but it could handle the commercial and private jets arriving and departing each day.

After Joe piloted the JetStar to a safe landing, he taxied to the area reserved for private jets. Again Joe paid little attention to the VIP passenger with Tommy and Tag . . . Joe was a pro and knew his place. When his human cargo was clear of the plane, he waved a farewell to the boys and taxied to the fuel area where he would gas up the jet for the return flight. His orders were to head back home that night, and so Joe wasted no time in Antigua. His copilot on this round trip was a fellow named Larry Thompson, also out of Memphis, and he would help Joe get *Hound Dog II* back to the U.S. safely.

*****

Hound Dog II had landed in Antigua at 10:02 p.m.

And again, for the Boss and his entourage, dealing with the customs agent was a mere walk in the park. They showed ID, they stated that the purpose of the visit was a vacation and they were admitted, *no problem, mon.*

The rich are always more than welcome wherever they go, it seems, and an offshore tax haven like Antigua embraced the wealthy with open arms.

After clearing customs, they proceeded to the arrivals area, where a car and driver, supplied by the hotel, was waiting for them. The private car took Elvis, Tommy and Tag directly to the Royal Windcrest Resort and Spa, a short 15-minute drive from the airport.

The Windcrest was an older hotel that had been recently renovated, creating a lovely, old–new resort with all the modern conveniences of the day. It was oceanfront property, with many of the rooms having ocean views. Its pink stucco exterior with white trim was at once friendly and inviting. The limo turned into the paved, semicircular double-entrance driveway and parked in front of the large white double doors that led into the lobby.

The evening was a warm 78 degrees, and the smell of salt water and perfumed tropical flowers filled the air. The sounds of exotic birdlife cracked through the palm trees and tropical bush, creating a pleasant musical theme unique to these tropics. As Elvis stood beside the limo, he stretched and took in a deep breath, enjoying the alluring smells and the salty taste of ocean in his mouth. He felt like he was home. His new home.

Again it was Tommy who led the way into the lobby and to the check-in counter, where a tall young man with a wide smile welcomed them to the hotel.

"Welcome to the Royal Windcrest, gentlemen. Do you have reservations?" the young man said. His voice was firm but friendly, and there was a trace of an accent unfamiliar to Tommy.

"Yes, we do. Two suites under Jefferson. I'm

Thomas Jefferson and I'll be signing for the rooms. Mr. Koury and I will be sharing the two-bedroom suite, and Mr. Smith will have the other suite. Here is my credit card for your files." Tommy handed the young Antiguan his MasterCard for an imprint.

"I have your reservation right here, sir. It says you'll be staying a few days but there's no specific checkout time noted. Is that correct?"

The man's intelligent face regarded Tommy, with a quick glance at the two men with him.

"That's right. We're not sure when our business will be finished here but it shouldn't be more than a week, certainly. That's OK?" Tommy knew it would be.

"Of course, that'll be no problem. Will you need help with your luggage, then?"

"No, we're good with just the keys, please."

The pleasant young man had Tommy sign his name for the file and returned his credit card. That completed, he then handed Tommy the keys to the suites.

"There you go, gentlemen. Have a great stay. My name is Normand Fisher. If you need anything, just ring the front desk and I or one of my associates will be at your service." He smiled brightly at his guests.

"Will do. Good night."

"Good night, gentlemen."

Normand Fisher was the manager of the Royal Windcrest Hotel and Resort. He was a native of Antigua, and like his parents, he had been born and raised there. He was twenty-seven years old when he first set eyes on Aaron Smith, no more than a glance in the lobby of the Windcrest, on the very same day that Elvis Presley's funeral had been held in Memphis, Tennessee.

He spoke perfect English, of course, as that's the official language of Antigua, and he also spoke Antiguan creole, which was a second language on the island. He was a Christian and still went to the Anglican Church most Sundays. His father was British and his mother Antiguan. They met when Normand's father made a career decision to leave England in 1948 to join the medical staff at the University of Health Services Antigua. His mother was a student nurse at the university, and they met there, fell in love and were married. One year after they were married Normand was born. Over the next five years he gained a brother and a sister. Normand and his siblings were brought up in a healthy, upper middle class environment, filled with love and respect for family values, with a strong sense of fair play and honesty in all their affairs, personal or otherwise.

Because his parents insisted he get a good education, and since they had the financial means to make it happen, he attended Antigua State College and received a business administration degree. His smarts, good looks and amicable disposition helped him become executive manager at the Royal Windcrest Hotel and Resort, the largest and finest resort on the island. His promotion to an executive position took less than eight months from the day he started at the hotel as a reception staff member.

Normand also dabbled in local real estate and even freelanced for an island paper called *The Centennial.* It was very common on the island to have more than one source of income, and Normand's strong work ethic served him well.

Antigua is a member of the British Commonwealth, and therefore the English language and English cultural influences are conspicuous. Cricket is the national sport, while football and boat racing are passionately pursued there as well. Antigua Sailing Week is a very exciting and popular spring event that attracts sailing enthusiasts from all over the world during the month of April. Boating and fishing are national pastimes, but like all Caribbean vacation destinations, it was the spectacular weather, beautiful beaches and warm ocean waters that kept people visiting this island jewel and that kept the island's economy thriving. Normand loved the islands and had no intentions of ever leaving.

Normand wasn't married, and he had no children. He was handsome in his way, and his sexual magnetism was mainly because of his easy, confident mannerisms. His young, svelte form had a gracefulness and ease that gave him an air of self-assurance. Tommy noticed Normand's confidence and healthy sense of self-worth when they checked into the hotel that night, and it was comforting to encounter such competence in an unfamiliar country, especially under the sensitive circumstances.

When Elvis and the boys were checking in, Normand had been thinking that these men were a bit different from the usual guests at the Windcrest. For one, they seemed distracted and anxious to get to their rooms as quickly as possible. Perhaps they were just tired from travel and in no mood to carry on any more conversation than absolutely necessary. Most visitors to the hotel were more forthcoming and filled with questions about everything, and all at once. Where's this? And where's that? Where's the restaurant? Is it open? We're starving; can we get room service? How's the food? What's the weather calling for tomorrow?

And on and on.

Other check-ins were already kicking into a more laid-back frame of mind and appeared to be almost drugged by the beauty of the place . . . and sometimes a bit sluggish from the heat and humidity. Not these men. The few words that were said were curt and distant. All business. Mr. Jefferson was the only one of the three who spoke at all, and also, there was little luggage for three men there for a week's stay. Normand guessed that there were no flip-flops, bathing suits and copious amounts of suntan lotions and creams stuffed into the few bags they did have with them.

It was common to see businessmen unaccompanied by family and traveling alone on the islands, obviously. There was plenty of business dealings, requiring visitors with special interests and expertise to come in from around the world, but those types did not usually stay at a place like the Royal Windcrest Resort and Spa. The Fairmont or the Hermitage was more in the corporate style. Less touristy, if that's possible.

Normand gave Aaron Smith an end suite on the top floor. The balcony wrapped around the building and offered unobstructed views of the beach, with the ocean straight ahead and a side view of the beach and downtown from the corner section. Tag and Tommy shared a two-bedroom suite next door. If this hadn't been the slow season for tourism in Antigua, Normand would have been hard-pressed to hold on to those two suites as long as he did without a confirmed check-out date.

But Normand Fisher took care of it. That . . . *and much, much more.*

*****

Elvis was tired, so after the guys escorted him to his suite and dropped off his bags, he said good night and told them he'd see them in the morning. That was fine with them; they also needed some downtime.

His body was feeling the absence of the buffet of prescription drugs that was normally on offer, and he was physically hurting despite his excitement over being safely out of the United States. The enormity of what had happened over the last three days had yet to hit him. Nevertheless, he was exhausted and he wanted to guarantee that he'd get a good night's sleep. His stash had been hidden well enough when he went through customs, not that customs would suspect someone like him, a rich American businessman arriving in a private jet, of being a pill-popping addict; nevertheless, *out of sight . . . out of mind.* He went into his bedroom and procured a couple of Prozac from a black leather bag to dull the senses. The Prozac helped . . . he slept like a baby.

*****

"Good morning, Tag. You guys up yet?" Elvis's famous slur was even more evident first thing in the morning.

Elvis was using the phone on the night table next to his king-size bed. He felt all right, all things considered. He had yet to pop some uppers, but he would do that shortly.

"We're up, Boss, waiting to hear from you. Sleep OK?" Tag was alert. "Tommy and I been up a couple of hours."

"I did and now I'm starving, Tag, so order some room service. I want lots of bacon and some toast with peanut butter. Tell them to burn the bacon. Some fresh coffee, too, and real cream. I don't wanna drink that complimentary stuff here in the room. You guys order something for yourselves, and have it delivered here thirty minutes from now. I'm heading for the shower. See you soon."

Elvis's first look in the mirror that morning made him jump back and then laugh. He was looking at Aaron Smith.

"Good morning, sir," he said to the image reflected

back at him. His now short, reddish brown hair with the side part made him look younger, and he liked that. He smiled. *It'll be OK*, he thought to himself.

He went to his stash and selected two amphetamines. He washed them down with some water from the bathroom faucet before jumping in the shower.

As he was getting dressed, he was feeling excited because he considered it the first day in his new life. He realized he wanted this more than anything he'd ever wanted. And the clarity he was experiencing, surprised him. He had wanted fame and wealth. He had wanted lots of women, and he had wanted Priscilla. He craved drugs and he wanted more . . . more . . . more . . . But now it was this that he wanted more than anything. A new start. Peace.

Elvis was doing the tourist thing that day, so he dressed accordingly. He donned a pair of lightweight, white cotton slacks and a dark blue sport shirt. He would bring a pair of wraparound sunglasses, and he'd buy a hat at the gift shop in the lobby on his way out. He was sure no one would recognize him and he'd be able to come and go as he liked. That kind of anonymity he had never known as an adult, and the idea thrilled him.

He heard a knock at his door—Tommy and Tag.

"Hey, fellas, come on in." They followed him into the suite.

"I'd friggin' love to go for a swim later today," said Tag, going straight to the large windows overlooking the beach. "The humidity here is a killer, isn't it?"

"You get used to it, Tag. It'll be so you won't even notice. It was like this in Hawaii when I was filming there, but after a while you become used to it, you'll see." To tell the truth, Elvis didn't want to be seen in a bathing suit, for a while at least. He was fat and he knew it. But that would change . . .

Tag asked Elvis, "How long do you want Tommy and me to hang out here, Boss? On this island, that is?"

"Let's just see how things go and then we'll talk about that."

They were sitting at a white laminated dining table that was surrounded by six white chairs with rose-colored cushions—a captain's chair at each end and two regular chairs on either side. Elvis sat at one end of the table and the boys sat opposite each other. Overall the suite was much the same as the one in Nassau, featuring a long living room–dining room combination with a kitchenette and a large bedroom en suite at one end. The room was more modern than the one in the Bahamas, but it was very comfortable, with beige carpeting and full floor-to-ceiling windows. The generous balcony sported a table and two floral-print chaise longue chairs. The beach and ocean views were spectacular.

There was a knock at the door and a voice announcing "room service," so Tommy got up. He led a young black man pushing a food service trolley into the suite. The young man started to ask if they wanted him to put the orders out on the table, but Tommy interrupted and said they would do it themselves. He signed the chit and gave the man a five dollar bill as a tip, which he accepted graciously before wishing them a great day and showing himself out. They set out the food and began to eat. Tommy and Tag both had pancakes with fruit, and the three of them ate quietly, each lost in his own private thoughts. No one spoke until the food was gone.

Elvis was sipping his coffee now after having finished a ration of burned bacon and several slices of toast with peanut butter. He started the conversation.

"I wanna have a look around today. Finding a place here will take time, and we'll need to do some research, ask questions and do some sightseeing. I wanna get a feel for the island. Tommy, do you have us a car yet?"

"We got a rental this morning. It's a Ford sedan; it'll do. They drop it off here."

"All right, I want you to call a local real estate agency. Check the phone directory and pick one. Tell them we want advice on where to start looking for homes for sale in the $250,000 range. That should get their attention. Tell them to give you some addresses, and we'll drive around and look at what they suggest, and if we see something we're interested in, we'll call them back and they can arrange a viewing, OK?"

Tommy nodded.

"Good, you get on that now. Use the phone in the next room; I'm going to watch some television. Tag, top me up."

There were only a few channels available, the main

being a broadcast from England. To Elvis's chagrin, his death was still the top story each hour. His funeral had been a major event. The anchorman was saying that thousands of fans had arrived in Memphis after his death was made public, and the numbers kept multiplying. The cameras had filmed people crying, distraught with grief.

There was coverage of the body they believed to be Elvis being returned to Graceland, the hearse slowly making its way up to the mansion where the remains would be on view to the public. The lineup to see the body had stretched for a mile along Elvis Presley Boulevard, with more than seventy-five thousand mourners wanting to pay their last respects.

Elvis stared at the television set in amazement. *Wow, that's crazy*, he thought, sipping his drink. He felt emotionally estranged from the whole situation . . . a silent observer witnessing an event that was only a curiosity, without any personal connection. The station informed its audience that the viewing of Elvis's body continued for several hours before they shut the gate, and many thousands of fans were turned away. They showed pictures of the police and the National Guard, tense and ready for a confrontation. Amazingly there was no trouble from those turned away, disappointed in not seeing the King one last time.

Elvis took a long haul on his drink and gently shook his head.

"Here we go, Boss." It was Tommy returning with papers and notes he had made on the phone with the real estate people. Then he noticed what Elvis was watching and was taken aback.

"Sorry, Boss." He felt uncomfortable and looked away.

"What are you sorry for? I'm not dead. Though if they knew the truth, Tommy, they'd probably lynch me, and then I would be dead." Elvis laughed, and his witticism caused him to cough slightly.

"You might be right, Elvis; they sure are an emotional bunch." Tommy was now fascinated by the coverage on the television. He worked himself over to the sofa, placed the notes on a faux onyx table and then put his feet up.

Tag was standing next to his boss and was also mesmerized by the news, which was now showing footage from the funeral service in Memphis.

"Remember, boys, my name is now Aaron Smith, so when in public, be careful not to call me Elvis or E, all right?"

"Sure, boss," said Tommy.

Tag nodded at Elvis and added, "Got it."

Elvis got to his feet and hit the off switch on the RCA console; they all watched as the image dwindled to black. He grabbed his room key and his sunglasses and headed for the door.

"All right, boys, *let's go shopping*!"

CHAPTER SEVENTEEN

It was a perfect day for mansion shopping. The weather was conveniently gorgeous, and the natural grandeur of it all, for a first full day on the island, was a heady experience for Elvis. A moderate breeze helped keep the heat and humidity from becoming oppressive. The ocean breezes gave the island a comfortable, steady climate without extremes, where back in Memphis during the summer, the heat was stifling and often caused Elvis breathing problems, especially since he became overweight.

But this was a delightful day and Elvis was in a good mood, thinking he might buy himself a convertible as soon as he found a place to live. A place to call home.

Before leaving the Windcrest, they had the concierge draw them a simple map showing them the way from the hotel to the ritzy area located just off a coastal section of St. John's Road. The area was called Senniville. They were told this was where some of the finest homes on the island were located. The kind of area Elvis figured he might find his dream house. His Shangri-la. It would take only about twenty minutes to drive there, they were told. They piled into the rented car and Tag started it up.

"OK, boys and girls, and away we go!" He pulled out of the parking area of the hotel and headed west on Main Road.

Tag drove the four-door blue and white sedan with one hand on the wheel and his other arm out the window, his hand resting on the door. Tommy rode shotgun, a map and the directions to St. John's Road on his lap. He was sporting his new white fedora with a narrow light blue band, perfect for the look he was going for . . . relaxed cool.

Elvis Presley sat contentedly in the back seat, listening to the music on the radio as the car rode comfortably along the streets of downtown. The windows were open and the radio was on a local station that played fifteen-minute segments of prerecorded island music. The sounds emitting from the car radio were intoxicating . . . at times light easy listening, at other times up-tempo tunes with the pulsating sounds of instruments unique to the islands, all the time creating delicious rhythms that teased the body to move. Elvis loved it.

"First stop, gentlemen, is the Coral Real Estate office for some info on where exactly we're going on this fine afternoon and to pick up some listings if we're lucky. They're expecting us, right, Tommy?" asked Elvis.

"Yes they are, E," answered Tommy. Tommy had found the phone number in the telephone book under realtors. There were only a few to choose from that looked promising, and he randomly picked one called Coral Real Estate. He spoke to an agent named Murphy, explained that they were looking for a property in Senniville or that area, and arranged a time to come by for a chat.

"Let's do it."

"OK, turn left here, Tag," instructed Tommy, looking up from the directions he had gotten from the hotel concierge.

The Coral Real Estate office was in a pale blue, single-story cinder block commercial building that contained a florist, a car rental company and Coral's two offices. When Elvis and the boys entered the building, a balding white guy in a white shirt and dark dress pants and brown loafers greeted them openly with a big salesman's smile and a look of hungry anticipation.

"Good day, gentlemen, I've been expecting you. My name is Ralph Murphy and I am at your service. I spoke to a Mr. Jefferson on the phone earlier?" He looked from one to the other waiting for Tommy to identify himself.

"That's me, Mr. Murphy. Call me Tom, please. This is Tag Koury, and this is the man who's looking to buy, Aaron Smith."

"Welcome. I hope your stay so far has been pleasant. Tom, a pleasure. Mr. Koury." He held out his hand to shake Tommy's hand, then Tag's.

"And Mr. Smith, a pleasure to meet you, sir. Can I get you gentlemen a drink? We have nice cold water, a selection of sodas, and if you're in the mood, perhaps some chilled white wine? I admit it's not an expensive vintage wine that you may be used to, but it's not altogether disagreeable," he said, showing lots of teeth.

"Nice to meet you," Elvis said after shaking Murphy's hand. "I'll pass on a drink for now, thanks. I'd like to talk listings with you in a private place, if that's OK with you, sir."

"Of course. Follow me, please."

Murphy led them into a small office that contained several straight-back chairs and a typical office desk. Everyone sat down but Tag, who stood at the door looking in.

"Well, I understand, Mr. Smith, that you're looking for a property on St. John's west shore. Senniville, to be more precise. I pulled a few listings for you to see. There are three properties available for purchase at this time. Homes in Senniville do not come on the market that often, so you're quite lucky in your timing. Three at the same time is almost unheard of."

Murphy all but ignored Tommy and Tag, focusing deliberately on Elvis.

"They are all lovely as I'm sure you'll agree." He handed the three listings that he had Xeroxed to Elvis and sat back in his chair, pleased with himself.

Elvis took in all three in as many seconds, flipping the few pages. A picture of the third listing caught his eye and held his attention.

"This one here. I like this one." He tossed the other two listings on Murphy's desk and looked closer at the one in his hand.

Tommy and Tag both moved next to the Boss to see the picture of the listing he was holding.

"Wow," said Tag. "That's really something, E."

If Murphy noticed Aaron Smith being called E and thought it odd, he kept the thought to himself and said nothing.

"Which do you have there?" asked the agent, quickly reaching for the two that were rejected by Elvis in favor of the one that grabbed his interest immediately. He realized what property Elvis was looking at and said,

"You have excellent taste, Mr. Smith. Villa Selena is one the finest properties on the island of Antigua, if not *the* finest."

"What's the address? I wanna do a drive-by this afternoon." The tone of his voice did not invite discussion, but Murphy still made a play.

"Shall I make a call and arrange a viewing for you?" Murphy was almost beside himself thinking of his commission on such a sale.

Elvis stood as he replied to Murphy. "No, thanks. Like I said, I wanna see the location and get a feel for the area and a casual visual of the property before I bother anyone to view it."

Murphy looked as if he was about to say something—argue to let him make the call, perhaps—but he must have thought better of it, and he resigned himself to having to wait to hear back from the rich American before he could personally pursue the sale further.

"Of course. I'll show you how to get there."

Tag made a left that took them off Main St. and onto the beginning of St. John's Road, which meandered along the coast for about three miles or so before it swung right and inland. The section they were looking for was about a mile ahead of them. There they would find a high-end stretch of large residential properties, amazing villas and mansions only partially visible from the road, but there was just one Elvis wanted to see.

As they drove east and then slightly north on St. John's road, the ocean was to their left all the way. The views were spectacular as the two-lane highway slowly climbed higher into the island, and Elvis and the boys were loving it.

"Beautiful," Tag murmured as he handled the car carefully, respectful that he was driving on a winding two-way street and oncoming traffic would suddenly appear and speed by . . . lots of old cars and trucks as well as the occasional Mercedes or other such personal luxury vehicles, almost certainly from the Senniville area they were looking for.

"We're getting close now." They had just passed a sign announcing Senniville. Tag slowed down.

"Harlowe Lane, it'll be on our left," Tommy said, looking up from his notes. There was really no need to say the road was on the left, as there were only steep rolling hills on the right.

The hills were heavily forested with jabillo trees and trees known locally as gumbo-limbos or, amusingly, as *tourist trees*, because they have red, peeling bark. The land on the left was also hilly, but gently so, and from there the inhabitants of these private estates had a truly beauteous, panoramic view of the Atlantic

Ocean.

Elvis knew what he wanted and he was getting excited. He knew himself well enough to realize that he needed lots of privacy. He knew the main house must be large, with a minimum of four bedrooms and at least as many bathrooms. He wanted a pool, of course. He wanted lots of land and spectacular views. These were his basic requirements, and the property at 354 Harlowe Lane had caught his eye for these reasons. The pictures he had seen at the Coral office had shown a mansion overlooking the ocean. His mansion back in Memphis paled in comparison.

He articulated all this to the guys.

"A place like this is gonna cost a lot of dough. Lots. At least, from what I'm seeing here. Half a million bucks, probably more."

There was no reason to ask if Elvis could afford that much; he could, and easily. But Tommy did venture to say, "Elvis, that's a big dollar commitment in a place you hardly know. Do you wanna consider renting for a while? And if you change your mind, well . . . it's no major deal to pull out."

"Tommy, if I end up not liking the place I buy, I'll torch it and collect the insurance. Don't worry about it." Elvis laughed and turned his attention back to checking out the natural beauty of the area.

"Seriously, guys, I know this island is the place I wanna live. I know it. I feel it. And if I'm wrong about this, we'll fuck off. We're getting pretty good at fucking off." He laughed again and this time the guys joined him.

"There it is." A custom-made mailbox in the shape of a gray stucco house, a miniature likeness of the villa, they guessed, stood at the end of a driveway with a large iron gate. The black, ornate electric gate was closed. The address, 354 Harlowe, was painted on a metal shingle that hung from two chains just below the mailbox.

"I can't see much, E," Tommy remarked, straining to see the villa as he stopped at the end of the driveway.

None of them could see much of the villa. There was just a tease of roof showing through the trees and the tall manicured hedges that fronted the property. The property looked to be well over a few square acres in size.

"Perfect," sighed Elvis. "Complete privacy." Elvis got out of the parked car and stood looking at the entrance of the estate. The boys followed his lead.

"Security cameras," noted Tommy, pointing at two cameras perched high and on either end of the tall iron gate.

After a few minutes Elvis said, "Well, this is as far as we get today, guys, but I'm loving it. We gotta get an appointment ASAP. I got a good feeling for this place, and I don't wanna miss out. Let's go."

Elvis got back in the car, and again Tommy and Tag followed suit. When they were all seated, Tag started the Ford, turned around and headed back toward the highway.

*****

After a couple of hours of sightseeing, Elvis was ready for a nap and they drove back to the hotel. He woke up hungry and wanting to sample some of the local food, so he and the boys headed out and ended up at a restaurant/bar called the Travellers' Rest. They were all having a second beer and sharing a platter of conch fritters. Elvis was not much of a beer drinker, but it seemed the right choice of beverage to go with the deep-fried fritters.

Tag was picking at the label on his beer bottle. He looked up and said to Elvis, "E, the guy at the hotel, the manager, Normand's his name, he said he works part time for Island Realtors. I was chatting with him this afternoon, and he said he'd be happy to help us find a place. He offered to show us around anytime we want. Says he'll get time off work at the hotel, no problem. This guy has a way about him . . . he's smart and I don't think he'll try to fuck us around with touristy bullshit. He seems like a straight shooter. And there's too much at stake here, Boss, to be led around by some dickhead." He looked down at his drink. Did he say too much?

Sometimes the Boss hated to have anyone suggest to him what or what not to do.

But Elvis just looked at Tag and said, "You think so?"

Tag nodded.

Elvis lifted his near-empty St. Pauli Girl and said,

"All right, I'll have a talk with him back at the hotel. Drink up, fellas, it's time to head out. Tag, take care of the bill." He handed Tag some cash. "Easy with the tip, big guy."

They returned to the Royal Windcrest Resort and Hotel.

*****

Normand Fisher was at the front desk when Elvis and his small entourage entered the hotel lobby. Tag waved at Normand as they trooped past the desk.

Normand smiled and waved back. He had just finished his shift and was ready to go home.

As he came around the check-in desk and headed for the door, he heard a man's voice behind him, a strong southern drawl. "Excuse me, sir."

Normand turned to look back and saw it was the gentleman he knew as Mr. Smith, who was staying in the Papaya Suite, and that he was speaking to him.

"Yes, may I help you, Mr. Smith?" Normand replied. He stopped walking and stood in place as Elvis Presley approached him.

"Perhaps," he said. "My associate, Mr. Koury, tells me you dabble in real estate here on the island."

"Why, yes I do," replied Normand.

"I'd like to take a gander at a property up on Harlowe Lane. I understand it's called Villa Selena. A large stucco place, set well back from the road.

Couldn't see too much when we drove by. I hear it's for sale. Do you know the place?"

"Why, yes I do." Normand realized he was beginning to sound like a broken record, so he added, "It's a splendid property, and worth seeing if you're looking for something special."

"Yeah, well, I am. I thought since you know the market and the island as well as anyone, I suspect, perhaps you'd be interested in arranging a tour of the place. If you have the time . . . I realize you're employed here at the resort as well."

Was he interested? The answer to Smith's question, of course, was a resounding *Yes!* But the hotel manager cum real estate agent played it cool.

"Mr. Smith, it would be my pleasure to make the arrangements. My obligations here accommodate my interests in the real estate market and will pose no problem, I assure you. When would you like to view Villa Selena? I'll see what I can do."

"Tomorrow would be great. Anytime tomorrow, but the earlier the better."

"Fine, I'll look into it immediately. I'll go straight to Island's office and start the process. Shall I call you here at the hotel when I know more? I can leave a message if you're out."

"That would be perfect. Thank you, sir. Thank you very much." That southern drawl somehow sounded familiar to Normand.

"All right, Mr. Smith. We'll speak in a while, then."

Normand extended his hand to Aaron Smith, gave

him a firm handshake, turned on his heels and almost ran for the door.

Normand knew the villa quite well. It was owned by an Italian film producer whose company was financially challenged because of bad film choices. Add the fact that he was also in the middle of a divorce . . . he had to sell. "*Vender rápidamente*" had been his directive.

The place was a great find and the timing totally in the buyer's favor. Normally the property would sell in the neighborhood of $1.6 million. Under the circumstances, with the owner trying to unload it as quickly as possible, it might go for as little as a million. Mr. Aaron Smith might have found himself in the right place at the right time. And more important, it might be the right place at the right time for Elvis. *Location, location, location!*

After an hour at the office, Normand called Smith. Elvis answered the phone.

"Mr. Smith, it's Normand Fisher here, and I have some good news for you, sir. We can see Villa Selena in the morning at 10:00, if that works for you."

****

That evening Elvis stayed in his suite and relaxed. He went to bed early, as he was tired from his body's cravings.

Elvis was now in better condition to deal with what needed to be done than he had been when this whole adventure started. But truth be told, it was still a very difficult time for him, drug-wise. Thank goodness he had the drugs he brought with him. His dwindling supply was not enough to make him so wired that even the simplest tasks were impossible to manage. He had pills to get him going in the morning, pills to shut him down at night and painkillers to help him cope with the hurt his abused body was dealing with. The alcohol helped smooth things over as well.

He knew what he was doing had to stop, and he believed he was on the road to getting there. After all, he was taking only a half dozen or so prescription pills a day, down from twice as many less than a week before. And the really dangerous ones he wasn't taking at all. When he got settled, then the detox period would begin earnestly, and under proper supervision. The healing process would take time.

And most important, Elvis was trying. *Where there's a will, there's a way, Elvis*, his mama used to say.

Elvis's mind-set and his determination to succeed drove and inspired him. Young Elvis had been a gifted and consummate professional, focused and tenacious, someone who had a vision and a dream. He made it happen; he became the King of Rock and Roll!

The same gumption that had made him a star would make him a survivor. He had gotten lost along the way; but he was back on track . . . on the path that led to living, not dying.

Long live the King!

CHAPTER EIGHTEEN

Aaron Smith put on some coffee, swallowed a couple of uppers and then had a long, hot shower. While in the shower, he thought of calling the Colonel. So after drying off and dressing, he poured himself a fresh coffee and sat down to place the call.

"Elvis, where the fuck are you now?"

"Antigua, like I said I would be. Have you been taking care of business?"

"Yes, I have, but it's crazy here. You have no idea. I've had your funeral to go to; that was fucking special, knowing you're alive and well and lying on a beach in the Caribbean!"

"Sir, I have some idea. I've been watching things on TV. I can't believe the outpouring of love and the pain people are feeling because of my passing. It's a weird thing, Colonel, watching it all go down. Can't say I like it much, either." Elvis knew Parker was loving it in his own way. "How's my daddy doing?"

"He's in bad shape, Elvis, has been for a while. Let's face it: This situation of you dying don't help things none. No parent wants to outlive their children. He's getting a lot of attention right now that he doesn't want or need, and the same goes for Priscilla and Lisa Marie, but I imagine you knew that would happen, so what's done is done, as they say."

"Colonel, I didn't call you to discuss the consequences of my actions, although I appreciate your concerns for my family." Elvis suddenly felt very tired.

"All right, Elvis . . . You should have all the money you requested by now, or at least by the end of the day. It was wired and there were no problems to jam up the wheels from turning, you hear." This wasn't a question. "There are copies of executed contracts that I'll be sending out over the next few weeks, and I need an address. Not your residence, though, if you even have one . . . Do you?"

"What?"

"Do you have a place yet?"

"No, sir, but soon."

"OK, let me know when you do. No one expects any hanky-panky, but let's be very careful nonetheless. Right, Elvis?"

"Right. I gotta go. Thanks, and I'll get back to you soon. Bye for now." Elvis hung up. He didn't wait for a response. Parker would have tried to keep him talking, and he had work to do.

When Elvis, Tommy and Tag arrived in the lobby together, Normand was waiting and anxious to get the show on the road.

"Morning, everybody. What beautiful weather outside, a perfect day for a viewing. Shall we get started?"

Elvis wanted to use the large Ford, which was

much better suited to the task than Normand's smaller Renault. Once everyone was in the Ford, Tag pulled away from the hotel and headed west.

"I've chosen a couple other properties that seem to fit the profile you're looking for. One is in the same area and the other is farther north. How would you like to proceed?"

"Let's see all the Xerox printouts; I'll have a look while we're driving. Meanwhile, take us to Villa Selena, Tag."

*****

As they pulled up to the property, Elvis admired the handmade stone wall, mostly covered in moss, going off in either direction from the driveway gates. A forest of cultivated trees and sculptured hedges bordered the inside perimeter of the wall, adding to the privacy. A subtle brass plaque embedded in the stone wall stated simply *Villa Selena*. Elvis hadn't noticed that yesterday.

The entrance gate stood open today, inviting Elvis and his party admittance onto the hallowed grounds. The Ford crept respectfully up the white stone driveway, the tires crunching audibly on the gravel.

As they followed the long lane to the main house, it reminded Elvis of what it might feel like to drive up the famous driveway leading to the clubhouse at the Augusta National Golf Club in Atlanta, Georgia. Although E. hadn't started playing golf yet, most everyone from the south was at least familiar with the Masters championship, the club and it's exclusivity.

A fellow agent was waiting at the house. The security systems had needed to be shut off and the house opened and aired.

"Good morning, Nancy. I'd like you to meet Aaron Smith. These are his associates, Tom Jefferson and Tag Koury. Gentlemen, this is my associate, Nancy Turple. She'll be aiding me in showing you the villa today." Nancy shook hands with everyone.

"Welcome to Villa Selena," said Nancy professionally. She was middle aged and white—with short brown hair and a petite stature—and she was wearing a business suit of dark blue with white dress sandals. Tommy thought she was cute and gave Tag a slight nudge and nod in her direction when she turned away.

"Mr. Smith is anxious to see the property, Nancy. I'll start with a tour of the grounds and then we'll be back to view the villa. Will that be fine, Mr. Smith?"

"That's fine with me. Lead the way, Normand."

The property was spread over twelve stunning acres. Most of the estate was made up of manicured lawns and flower beds, radiant with an array of brilliant colors. A variety of bushes and shapely trees such as the silk cotton, the sweetleaf and the tamarind were scattered about with no discernible pattern or grand scheme in mind. It looked natural, and it all worked beautifully.

There were fruit trees: banana, cherry and papaya. There were jabillo and gumbo-limbo trees, which one saw most everywhere. Villa Selena was park-like, and showing the property was a genuine pleasure for Normand. He had been showing luxury properties for nearly three years, but only once before had he shown such an expensive property or one of such beauty as this estate. Normand was thinking it must be a bit like walking about a tourist destination—not unlike Abbey Dore Court Gardens in England—with that feeling of majesty. A Caribbean version.

Normand was just as enthralled by Villa Selena as Elvis appeared to be. Although Elvis said little, his eyes shone with obvious admiration for the splendor around him.

The villa turned out to be a light-gray, two-story, Caribbean-style stucco mansion of 10,000 square feet, with white windows and shutters and an orange-colored half-barrel tile roof. The roofline was broken into sections; some were wide and sprawling, while others were more diverse in terms of shape and size. All of this suggested that the ceilings inside the house were not all the same height and that the rooms were quite varied in style. Elvis was anxious now to go into the house. He was stimulated. *Intrigued.*

"Well, shall we have a gander inside?" Normand smiled at Aaron Smith as he said this. Elvis caught the reference to his southern-American use of slang and seemed to blush a bit.

"Let's do that, Normand. Come on, fellers; be sure to wipe your feet, now." His turn at waggish humor brought a smile to everyone's faces.

Tommy and Tag had been talking quietly to each other during the tour and said nothing to E, but they had lots to say about the property to each other. They were in awe the whole time.

Although Elvis was joking about them wiping their feet at the door, they did nonetheless, almost nervously, like children who had been forewarned and were under surveillance.

The front door and foyer entrance to the villa was as expected: grandiose. Mr. Italian Movie Producer sure had fun with his home away from home. In fact, it was almost garish.

But somehow, it wasn't.

Perhaps it was the muted tones of the island colors, blending the house so skillfully into its native surroundings. The entrance, like most of the house, was opulent but somehow welcoming. Everything worked. Frank Lloyd Wright would have been impressed.

Earth tones encompassing shades of browns—beige, sand, cherry, oak—were mixed with a delicious wash of terra-cotta and rose, along with complementing shades of yellow, burgundy and gold and a variety of pastels. Scrumptious.

The villa had five bedrooms and seven bathrooms. Not counting the bathrooms, there were fourteen rooms in the main house altogether. Big? Yes, but not unmanageable.

When the owner spent extended time there, he employed a staff of five full-time employees. Three maintained the main house and two the property. When the guesthouse was being used, the owner added additional staff to keep it serviced.

The tour went on for almost two hours. There was the guest house to see, plus the regulation tennis court and the beautiful infinity swimming pool, with its large stucco pool house. The guest house was off to the right of the main house, as were the tennis court and pool. The ocean was clearly visible from all areas. The estate's design was brilliantly thought out, created to maximize the natural beauty of the property and feature the million-dollar view.

*****

"Wow! That was really something, Boss, What a place! Can you imagine living there?" Tag was clearly blown away and didn't mind saying so, now that they were finally alone. Elvis and the boys were waiting in the Ford for Normand.

"Not me, I honestly can't," answered Tommy. "I'd get lost trying to find my way around."

"One problem though," Elvis responded.

Tag and Tommy looked at each other, then back at Elvis.

Tag said, "What's that, E?"

"Where do we keep the chickens?"

Everybody laughed hard; they were acting like schoolkids, giddy at finally being let out of detention.

After two hours of concentrating so much, it was likely that an hour from now, the details would be a blur and the facts all a jumble.

Meanwhile, Normand was in the house saying thanks to Nancy and getting her sense of how the tour went.

"What does your gut say about Smith's interest in buying, Normand? Do you feel he's for real?" Nancy asked as she was putting her papers away, giving her fellow agent a sideways glance.

"I think he's a player, Nancy. He was *in the moment* all afternoon. At this point, if he wants more info, that's a good sign, right? On the other hand, he hasn't even mentioned price yet. Maybe that's a sign that he's just kicking our tires."

Nancy now had Normand thinking. Even splitting the commission with her, a sale meant a lot of money coming his way. It would be a sweet, sweet deal.

Nancy said nothing more, but she had to be thinking the same thing.

"Well, I gotta go. They're waiting for me. I'll keep you posted." And he was out the door.

Normand got into the back seat of the Ford with Elvis and asked him, "Which property would you like to see next, Mr. Smith? We can swing by the others and I can set up an appointment for tomorrow, if you'd like."

Elvis was silent. The guys looked at each other. They also wanted an answer. They were positive Elvis wouldn't want something as formidable as Villa

Selena.

Normand turned away from Elvis to stare out the window. Tag started the car and drove slowly away from the estate, pulling to a stop when he reached Harlowe Lane.

"Where we going, Boss?" Tag looked at Elvis through the rear-view mirror and waited.

"Normand." It was Elvis. "How much?"

The agent's heart did a backflip. "How much . . . ?"

"Yeah, Villa Selena. I wanna buy it. How much is the guy asking?"

Normand cleared his throat and swallowed. "Well, in a good market and under normal circumstances, they'd be asking about $1.6 million. But because the seller is having corporate financial difficulties, and with the house and property being an asset to the company, they want to sell. Personally, he's dealing with a divorce, so the bottom line here is this: He's trying for $1.4, but I'd say you might be able to get it for about $1.2, maybe even a bit less. Remember— it comes furnished. It's an amazing score, Mr. Smith. The house just came on the market. It's a special property with a big-ticket price, and it might take a long time to sell, or it may go tomorrow. I believe it won't last long."

Silence.

Tommy and Tag might have stopped breathing; Normand almost did.

"I'll think on it a bit," replied Elvis.

The drive back to the hotel took about twenty minutes. Tag parked the car and everyone jumped out.

"You guys go on ahead," Elvis told the boys. "I wanna talk to Normand."

Finally: "I'll pay the guy $900,000 tomorrow by the end of the day. That's the deal; he can take it or leave it."

"I think you might be better to offer $1.1 mill and see what he says. We don't want to insult the guy; the house and the property are worth close to $2 million. He'll never sell for under a million."

"Make the offer, Normand. I'm going to my room to have a nap." Elvis walked away.

*****

"What are you going to do, then?"

"I don't know."

Tag and Tommy had been discussing the fact that their boss seemed ready to drop a million dollars in a developing country, after being in that country less than forty-eight hours.

Tag said, "I say he's in need of some professional medical help. Perhaps he should be checked into a special hospital. A rehab, I think they're called. I mean, Tommy, think about it! He's allowed his family and the world to believe he's fucking dead! There's a homeless person buried and mourned by millions of people! Why? Because Elvis feels he needs a fucking change in his life. And we're his accomplices! If the police find out this is all a hoax . . . we could be put away—forever."

"Easy, Tag! You'll have a heart attack, and then we'll be burying your sorry ass too. Look . . . we knew what we were doing when we joined on with Elvis, back in Memphis. You can't start freaking out now. Do your job and don't think so goddamn much! If you can't handle it, tell Elvis, but you better be ready for the consequences. By the way, what's wrong with living in a mansion on a Caribbean island, getting paid to mostly enjoy yourself? Maybe you didn't notice, but there's no shortage of women here, either. Yeah, I can handle it, I'll tell you that much."

*****

After Elvis's offer to purchase Villa Selena, Normand got down to business. Although the offer was verbal rather than official and on paper, he convinced the representative for the seller, ConFlicks International, that it was legitimate.

Of course Smith's offer was declined immediately and was countered at $1.2 million. Normand explained that the offer submitted was final. They refused to budge. Normand wasn't surprised.

When Normand called and spoke to Elvis, Elvis told him he could make it a cool million for the estate, with the villa fully furnished, but that was it.

He would transfer the money that day, and the film

producer could remove the villa as an asset. Then he and the company could close their books on the matter and move on. In other words: Take the money and run, boys.

When Normand told them Mr. Smith's counteroffer, they balked. Normand reminded them that if the bank stepped in or divorce lawyers, they could take a bigger hit, so why not take the offer? It was *real*.

They said they would consider it and hung up.

Less than a half hour later, they called back. They'd take the offer.

SOLD!

*****

It had been a long day for Elvis. Seeing Villa Selena and then negotiating the deal had brought on a lot of physical and mental fatigue. With his offer being accepted, he then had to contact the Colonel and get the funds transferred. *Yes, sir*, he thought to himself, *this was quite the day*. It was time to pop a few sleeping pills and crash for the night.

He was about to do just that when the phone in his suite rang. It was Tommy.

"Hey, Boss, how you doing? You need anything? Tag and I are going to the lounge downstairs for a drink."

"I'm fine, enjoy. Tomorrow we're going home."

Tommy couldn't believe his ears.

"We're *what*?"

"We are going home. You'll need to pack up. We're leaving tomorrow."

Elvis had always been compulsive, and Tommy shouldn't have been so flabbergasted. But they were fugitives in a way, and going home to the United States was dangerous. Stupid in fact, under the bizarre circumstances. He could imagine the headlines: ELVIS BACK FROM THE DEAD! Tommy moaned audibly.

"What's the matter, Tommy, you didn't like the villa?"

The villa . . . Villa Selena? Tommy thought. *He bought fucking Villa Selena? He's certifiable!*

"What do you mean, E?"

"I bought Villa Selena today. So we're going to drop by the bank first thing in the morning, sign the final OK for the money transfer to Island Realtors, in trust of course, then drop by Island Realtors, see Normand and sign off on everything and be sure there are no last-minute hiccups to straighten out, and when all *i*'s are dotted and the *t*'s crossed, we go to our new home. And we get fucked up."

When Elvis arrived at the offices of Island Realtors the next day, all was in order and the formalities were all that remained. Within the hour, they were finished all the final business required for Elvis Presley to own the house and the twelve-acre property at 354 Harlowe Lane.

They all stood in the larger of the two offices

occupied by the real estate company. The owner of the company, Mike Onslow, had been invited to join in the celebration, of course; otherwise, there was only Elvis, Normand, Nancy and the boys. They all watched as Normand handed the keys to Villa Selena over to a beaming Elvis Presley, aka Mr. Aaron Smith.

"Congratulations, Mr. Smith. You've done exceptionally well with this purchase. You will not regret it, I'm positive. Now . . . a toast. I hope you like champagne, and that it's not too early for a glass of bubbly," offered Normand.

He had poured each a glass of the chilled champagne, a bottle of Moët & Chandon Impérial, that he'd hurriedly purchased from the Windcrest at cost, and now he held his glass high.

"A great idea. Call me Aaron, Normand. And thank you, thank you very much for your help and for Nancy's help in making this whole experience fast and painless. Painless, that is, if you don't find parting with a million dollars hurtful." Laughter and cheers followed from everyone.

"Normand, Nancy, fellas . . . Cheers!"

"*Salute*," Normand Fisher replied.

CHAPTER NINETEEN

For Elvis, moving into Villa Selena couldn't have been more stress-free thanks to Normand. He had the phone lines reconnected with a new phone number in the name of A. Smith, 354 Harlowe Lane, St. John's, Antigua.

He had all basic services properly registered and activated. There was the company that handled property maintenance: groundskeepers, pool care, and tennis court upkeep. It was the same company that had been doing the work at Villa Selena for a number of years, and Elvis agreed when Normand suggested that he use the same people and to just reactivate the account under his name.

Normand took care of arranging all the details for Elvis so he would be able to move in and be comfortable with the least amount of stress. Elvis could personally fine-tune things after he was settled and more familiar with the villa and the estate property.

So Elvis, Tommy and Tag moved into the villa the day after Elvis bought it. Elvis wanted out of the hotel and could not wait a day longer, even though there was still basic cleaning and airing out of the villa to do, all arranged by Normand. Normand asked Aaron Smith to wait until the end of the day so that the house could be prepared, and then Normand had a small troupe of cleaners start working at 8:00 a.m. to get the villa ready for Elvis's arrival.

Elvis arrived at his new home just after 5:00 p.m. and was welcomed by Nancy, the real estate agent.

"Welcome to your new home, Mr. Smith." Nancy was wearing a flowered sundress, flats and a big smile. She held out a welcome basket.

"Well, hello, Miss Turple, thank you very much," said Elvis, sounding just like Elvis but looking like Aaron Smith. "It's great to be home! Boys, bring our stuff in." He took the basket from Nancy and walked into the house, through the "grand" entrance, toward where he believed the kitchen area was.

"Can I help you with anything? Show you around the house again?" offered Nancy smiling. "I know you've only been here once, and although it was just the day before yesterday, there was so much to see that it's probably all a blurry memory for you today."

"No, that's fine, Nancy. We'll have fun exploring." As he looked around him he added, "This is very exciting, I must admit." Elvis was like a kid, full of wide-eyed wonder. For a guy who had seen and done it all, this was very special for him. A first for Aaron Smith.

"Well, if you're sure, then, I guess I'll leave you to it, but please do not hesitate to call me or Normand Fisher if you need anything."

"Will do, and thanks again, Nancy." Elvis walked her to the front door. Tommy and Tag passed them on their way in toting several pieces of luggage.

"Good bye, Mr. Smith. Enjoy."

Normand decided to drop by the villa that evening,

after everything was more or less in place, but first he called the new number.

The call was picked up after three rings. A lusty southern voice said, "Hello?"

There was loud music in the background. Apparently the guys had found the state-of-the-art sound system and the record collection left behind by Mr. Movie Guy. There was a party going on.

"Normand, here. May I speak with Aaron, please?"

"Is that you, Norm?" It was Elvis. *Norm!*

"Uh . . . yes, Aaron. How are you doing?"

"If I was doing any better, it'd be illegal," Elvis joked as the 50s-style rock music got louder.

The boys were *well on their way*. Normand couldn't help but notice that Elvis's and Tag's deep southern accents got deeper and thicker the more they tippled. He first noticed it at the hotel after Aaron and his friends had a few drinks at the lobby bar and dropped by the front desk for an extra key.

"That's great, Aaron. I was going to drop by, but you sound like you've had enough biz for one day, and it's your time to 'party hearty.'" This was Normand's attempt at laid back.

"Hell, Norm, you get your ass out here." He hung up.

Normand drove his Renault out to 354 Harlowe Lane. As he motored along, he envisioned himself in a new car, a reward for successfully completing a very lucrative real estate deal.

The gate to the villa was open. He wondered if they knew how to close it. As Normand pulled up in front of the mansion, music was pounding away. Some of the front windows were open, and he could hear the partying clearly and voices singing along to some gospel music.

After several attempts to get someone's attention by ringing the front doorbell and knocking on the door to no avail, Normand let himself in and followed the sounds to the "grand salon," where Elvis, Tommy and Tag were in the throes of some righteous gospel singing.

"*What a friend we have in Jesus . . .*" they testified. Tommy and Tag were yelling more than singing. As they belted out the hymn, blissfully unaware of his arrival, Normand noticed that Aaron had a very nice voice and was really into it.

Finally the song finished, and Normand cleared his throat loud enough to be heard above the laughter and back slapping.

"Norm, you ol' hound dog you, get in here and choose your poison. The bar is well stocked, compliments of Cecil B. De Fucking Mille." Elvis was feeling no pain.

Normand drank alcohol rarely and hard liquor not at all. So he accepted a cold St. Pauli Girl offered by Tommy.

"Hey, guys, cheers!" He raised the bottle of beer in mock friendship. Normand didn't really know these guys very well, and besides, drunks made him nervous.

"Great music," he stated loudly in order to be heard as he hoisted his drink in Elvis's direction.

At that moment, a new song began playing.

"*I've just come down from the Isle of Skye, I'm not very big and I'm awful shy . . .* " This was what Normand imagined the Americans called a *shit-kicker*. The boys started dancing in a kind of jig. Round and round, back and forth, singing at the top of their lungs.

"*Donald where's your troosers . . .*"

Normand thought he knew this song. He'd heard it on the radio a number of times. It was a novelty tune by a singer named Stewart, he believed.

They kept dancing and singing until the music slowed right down and finally to a stop. Then it restarted, only slowly this time . . .

But now only Aaron sang, in that slushy, affected southern voice . . . "*I've just come down from the Isle of Skye . . .*"

Now in this part of the song, Stewart impersonates Elvis Presley.

Normand watched as Aaron Smith, with eyes closed shut, sang it perfectly. Better, actually, than the original guy, Stewart or whatever his name was . . . it was as if *the King was right there*.

"*I'm not very big and I'm awful shy.*" Aaron opened his eyes for the last bit, lost in the moment until his eyes locked on Normand's.

As they say, something clicked with "Aaron."

He froze. Then he went straight to the record

player and lifted the stylus, not so gently.

"That's enough of that for now. Let's figure out what's to eat around here." The moment passed. It would be a while before Normand understood the significance of what had just happened.

*****

Elvis and the guys had been living in the villa for three weeks when Normand dropped by late one Saturday morning to say hello and see how things were going. He had not heard from Aaron since they had moved in.

There was a silver Land Rover parked in the carport next to a shiny yellow Mercedes Benz 450SL. A gray Ford station wagon sat patiently near the front entrance. Normand could see the back end of a few other, older cars parked along the far left side of the villa and assumed they belonged to the regular staff or to workers at the villa on business.

He rang the front doorbell and heard a chiming sound resonate somewhere inside the house. A local woman opened the door. She was wearing a pale blue dress and brown running shoes. An apron tied around her slim waist made it clear that she worked there. *She looks pleasant enough*, thought Normand.

"Good morning. Is Aaron Smith in?"

The woman smiled and stepped back, suggesting that he enter the house. At least into the vestibule area. He entered directly.

Behind her Tag appeared with a smile and what looked like a Bloody Mary in his left hand.

"Norm, how's it hanging, man? The Boss was going to call you. Come on in. Let's see if we can find him in this labyrinth."

Tag led him to the kitchen at the rear of the house, and on the way there, Normand caught the scent of bacon wafting in the air.

The kitchen was huge. It had all the latest appliances, as you'd expect in a home like this. There was a marble center island, surrounded by chrome stools with black leather seats. A large circular table that seated a dozen or so people was set for the next meal.

"Good morning, Norm. Just the man I wanted to see." Elvis was seated on one of the stools. He was wearing a dark blue tracksuit and black runners. A white bandana was wrapped across his forehead and knotted at the back.

"Have a seat. Get you a drink, Norm? Tag, Norm wants a drink." He pointed at the bar on the opposite side of the room. *A bar in the kitchen*, thought Normand. *Interesting.*

"Just a coffee, Aaron. Hey, I'll pour it myself, thanks. Let's see, now . . ."

He got up and went to the kitchen counter, where he saw a large chrome espresso machine. He wanted a regular coffee, but before he could pour himself a cup of java, someone stuck the very popular Bloody Mary in his face. He reluctantly took the glass handed to him and stood there, overcome by the thought of drinking alcohol at this hour of the day.

The lady in the white apron who answered the doorbell was named Beatrice, and she was a permanent staff member. She was standing in front of some cupboards, pulling out pots and pans and other cooking utensils.

And right behind her a second woman dressed in similar attire was frying bacon. Her name was Lucinda, and among other duties, she was a cook. The bacon looked somewhat burned. No one but Normand seemed to notice.

"Let's go outside, everybody. It's too nice out to sit in here. Call us, Lucinda darling, when all is ready." Elvis led the way, through the patio doors and onto a sandstone deck that faced the ocean.

There were chairs and tables, covered in royal blue and white striped cloth, and shade umbrellas rising up from the center of each table.

Elvis motioned to Normand to follow him, and he continued walking across the large deck and onto the lawn and away from the others.

Both Elvis and Normand were casually dressed for the day, and a delightful summer breeze was coming in from the ocean. The view was spectacular.

"What a spot, Aaron. It's magical here."

"Yes, Norm, this place is really growing on me. I think I might live here forever." Elvis meant exactly what he was saying—this place had a hold on him, spiritually and physically.

"And who would blame you? It's amazing."

Normand held his tall glass in two hands but refused to drink from it.

Elvis's voice was steady, "Unfortunately, Tag is not as smitten as I am and wants to leave the island next month." He took a swallow from his drink.

It was at that moment that Normand noticed his companion was drinking a diet soda. Normand wanted to trade him.

"Well, island life is not for everyone, Aaron." Normand smiled at him. "He's going back to the United States?"

"Yes, he is, to Dallas. He knows people there. He's a good guy, and he'll do fine. I'll miss him, though. He was with me a lot of years."

"What about Tommy? How's he doing?"

"Oh, Tommy, he loves it here. He's already seeing a gal he met at the local market. He tried to talk Tag into staying, but no dice."

Elvis spit on the lawn near a hedge that ran along one side of the property. It seemed an obscene gesture, spitting on the lawn at Villa Selena. Normand wanted to grab a Kleenex and wipe it up.

"Norm, I been given this a lot of thought, and I want you to work for me starting Monday. This will give you the weekend to pack your personal items for the move here."

"Pardon me?" was all Normand could think to say

"I want you to work for me. I pay very well, and it's a full-time gig."

Normand was thinking, *Am I being bamboozled here? I mean, is he serious?*

He faced Elvis and said in a voice a bit higher than he remembered it being the last time he used it: "Work for you? Doing what?" Normand was wondering if he might have followed those questions with a twitch.

"Do you know what a majordomo is, Norm?"

"No," he confessed. By not knowing, he wondered if he'd knocked himself out of the running. He was hoping he'd ask him something he did know next. To save face.

"That's a fancy word I heard earlier today. Tommy said I could use one. Majordomo, that is. And I said, sorry, Tommy, but who's a major homo?"

Elvis was laughing at his own joke. His laugh was infectious, and he had Normand grinning right back at him. He shook his head and looked at Normand. His southern voice was sounding thick.

"Sorry 'bout that. You might not find that funny." He cleared his throat and continued.

"A majordomo is a pretentious name for a guy who runs the house staff. Administrator. You'd be in charge of keeping the estate in order. You'll see that the house and the property are managed properly and that all things run smoothly. I know you can do it. I did some research . . . I know you're educated, honest and passionate in your affairs, and I think you could do a great job for me, Norm."

Normand thought of Elvis spitting on the grass.

Funny how that still bugs me, thought Normand.

"The entire staff would be under your direction. And once this place is running like a fine-tuned engine, the more time you'll have to sit back and relax. But as I said, it's a full-time job and you'd need to be living here, not going back and forth every day and night to someplace else. I'll supply you with a new car that you can keep if you don't like the job and decide to quit. How's that sound?"

"A new car?" He thought of his old Renault.

"Yes, sir."

"And you can have the Victoria bedroom in the west wing. It has a private bathroom, of course, and a sitting room as well. Views of the ocean. It is sweet, Norm. You wanna see it?"

"I've seen it, Aaron. It is very fine indeed. Well, let me think—"

They looked toward the house as they heard Tommy call out that breakfast was ready. It was 12:15 in the afternoon!

Normand said nothing.

"Look, Norm, don't worry about it. I'll give the job to Tommy—he'd love the challenge. And he's crazy about the villa. Come on, son, let's eat." He started for the house.

Normand didn't move. The untouched drink was still in his hand. He was looking across the manicured lawn, to the distant sea that he loved so much.

"Norm, you all right? Come on, time to chow

down." Elvis had Normand's arm now and was giving him a gentle nudge. Normand nodded and turned to Elvis.

"Will I have to wear a uniform, Aaron? I hate uniforms. I would prefer loose shirts and short pants, with runners. Stylish of course. I'm a bit vain that way."

"Norm, you're a classy guy and you dress real nice. The *major*domo don't need a uniform to get respect." Elvis smiled kindly at Norm.

"Thank you."

"You saying you'll take the gig, Norm?"

Normand looked at Elvis for a brief moment longer and then he too smiled.

"You bet . . . Boss."

CHAPTER TWENTY

Life was just starting over for Elvis. He embraced the island way of life. It inspired him. He appreciated the exotic ingredients that made up Antigua. The sights, the smells, the food, the people and the almost sensual, carefree pace of the island and its people. His taste for living, deadened for so long, was becoming vibrant and alive once again.

Living at Villa Selena was a wonderful experience for Elvis, and Normand was to play a major part in that experience. Normand was also inspired. Now that he was part of Elvis's entourage, he was busy with the daily goings-on in the mansion and property.

His first challenge was to organize the household staff. When Normand took over managing the staff, there were two full-time domestics at the villa, Lucinda and Beatrice. Both cooked and cleaned. Beatrice was the older of the two; she was thin and dark skinned, with lots of silver in her hair. She was in her sixties, but she looked and acted twenty years younger, with her sharp tongue and quick sense of humor. Normand knew of her before they were part of the team at the villa, but he didn't really *know* her. Her husband was a fisherman who went out to sea one morning and didn't come back. That was before Normand was born; he didn't know what happened, and he never brought it up.

Lucinda was in her mid-forties and quiet. She was quite religious and sang in the Anglican church choir in nearby Barnes Hill, where she lived. Her husband was a gardener and worked for a house about a mile farther on, past the villa. Lucinda wanted her husband, John, to work at the villa as well so they could be closer to each other during the week, but her husband liked things just the way they were. The man enjoyed his space, and who could blame him, thought Normand.

Although both Bea and Lucinda were good at their jobs and put in a fair day's work, it was just too much for the two of them, so Normand hired a third person, and that person was named Geraldine.

Geraldine was young, about twenty-five, and a cousin of Lucinda's, and she had worked at an older motel in town called the Ridge Motel. The motel was poorly cared for and the employees overworked and underpaid, so when Normand informed both Bea and Lucinda that he wanted to add a third person to the housekeeping staff, Lucinda suggested her cousin Geraldine.

Geraldine was very attractive in a *whole lotta woman* kinda way. She was big everywhere, but she had something that the local boys liked a lot, and she was busy. Her face was quite pretty, with lovely brown skin, full, sensuous lips and bedroom eyes.

She had three boys from different fathers. One child was five, another three and her youngest was two years old. Normand asked who looked after her kids when she worked, and she replied, smiling,

"They looked afta good by my mama."

Geraldine was not married but had boyfriends. Her life seemed to revolve around men. She was silly in a childish way—always giggling and going on—and poorly educated, but she was said to be honest and a good worker, so he hired her.

Now there were three persons looking after the cleaning and cooking, and that made a big difference in keeping the villa proper.

The company that looked after the property was called Thompson's Landscaping Inc. It was owned by two brothers, and their green three-quarter-ton truck was parked on the property once a week. They arrived at the estate Monday mornings around 7:30 and stopped for a lunch break at noon, usually eating something they made at home and brought with them. They'd eat in the truck with the windows down or sometimes in the shade somewhere on the property, and then it was back to work until about 4:00 in the afternoon.

Elvis had the brothers cut some flowers every Monday and leave them with the "girls" to place around the villa. He enjoyed the look and fragrance of cut flowers in the house, and he had done the same thing when he lived at Graceland. One day Elvis was having some fresh fruit at breakfast when he had a thought.

"Normand, I was thinking it'd be real nice to expand the orchard. Perhaps that open area near the north wall around back would be a good spot. I was thinking I'd like to have some more fruit trees, if they'll grow here on the property. Ask the Thompsons, will ya? See what they think."

"I'll ask them if that's possible, Aaron," replied Normand.

Eventually several apple trees were planted along with mango and avocado. In time, they produced excellent fruit.

The pool and tennis courts were looked after by a young man named James. He also worked one day a week and was quick and did a good job. Geraldine thought he was cute and always found a way to catch his attention, then wave and smile suggestively hoping for a chance to know him better, but James was all work. He ignored her.

"He's a fool, he is," she'd say. Eventually she gave up and gave him a "never no mind." Normand witnessed all this with amusement.

It was an interesting collection of souls who were part of the daily goings-on at beautiful Villa Selena.

*****

The night Tag had announced his intention of returning to the United States, Elvis was in the games room arranging cue balls on the regulation-size billiard table that Mr. Movie Guy had custom made and then left behind. The games room was large and rectangular, with light-colored hardwood floors and area rugs scattered about. There was a marble fireplace—the villa had five fireplaces in total—on one wall. The walls were papered with a British-green felt material, as was the tall ceiling, which was curved like the ceiling of an early 1900s railway Pullman club car, from the golden era of the American art deco period. A row of curtainless windows along one side of the room offered a partial view of the tennis court.

Elvis had a Hugh Hefner look going on, casually dressed in pajamas and leather slippers; a Coke sat on an oak table at one side of the room. The oblong-shaped overhead Tiffany pool light, suspended from the ceiling by brass chains, was turned on, and the surface of the felt table was perfectly lit, while in the rest of the room the lighting was dimmed. The three-hundred-pound slate top was covered in blue felt. The pockets were the classic type, made with open-weaved strips of leather.

"Excuse me, E. Mind if we have a talk, just you and me?"

"Sure, Tag, what's up? Pour yourself a drink from the bar. You want a game?" Elvis pointed his cue stick at the table.

An oak cue rack containing a half dozen cues and two rakes was positioned on one wall alongside a black chalkboard. A circular oak table on the opposite side of the room sat next to a long bar that was fully stocked even though Elvis rarely drank alcohol these days. Pills were still part of his everyday existence, and Dr. Bell helped him with his prescriptions.

Normand had recommended Dr. Edward "Eddy" Bell when Elvis realized he'd need a doctor on the island. Doc was about sixty-five and carried a classic black leather doctor's bag containing all the stuff required to do a routine check-up and tend to minor emergencies. He was old fashioned enough to still make house calls for special patients (especially rich ones), and Eddy was often at the villa.

Eddy tightly controlled the drugs Elvis was taking those days, administering legal prescriptions for Desoxyn, Dilaudid and Xanax, Elvis's uppers and downers. He was also taking various painkillers. If he had quit all the drugs he had been taking when he'd left Memphis, he probably would have died. A sudden stop could have brought on a heart attack, a stroke, an aneurism or some other fatal consequence. *Cold turkey* was not an option for Elvis. He needed to stabilize his body and then slowly decrease the medications until it was safe to stop entirely.

Tag mixed himself a Bacardi and Coke and sat on one of the seven chrome stools along the side of the bar, positioning himself to face Elvis. Elvis was chalking the tip of his cue stick when Tag unloaded the news.

"I'm going back, Boss."

Elvis turned to Tag and said, "Back to Memphis?" Elvis's voice was neutral, showing no emotion one way or the other.

"Not Memphis but Dallas. I got friends there as you know, and I've been telling them I was traveling these last few weeks with a lady friend, not able to deal with your death, Boss, and all the hoopla in Memphis. They said they understood and offered their condolences. They know we go back a long way,

E." This was not easy for Tag.

"Yes, we do, Tag. It's OK. I want you to be happy, and if this life ain't for you, you should leave, absolutely. You can visit us, Tag. Tommy is staying, right?"

"Yeah, Tommy's staying here . . . he loves it here. It was like a duck to water for Tommy." Tag laughed. "And he loves you, man . . . we both do. You know that."

Elvis was thinking of all the years they had been friends, first as neighbors back when he moved to Memphis from Tupelo, then becoming best friends. They were both different from everyone else back then, and their uniqueness brought them together as buddies. Tag—big, intimidating, all dressed in black—and him, with his flamboyant fashion style that upset most everybody he came in contact with back then. Man, did the world change for them both. Regardless, they were friends in the '50s, and they had remained friends for twenty years and counting. Ah, the good ol' days . . . he chuckled to himself and smiled at Tag.

"I love you, man." He went to Tag and embraced him. "I'm gonna miss you."

CHAPTER TWENTY-ONE

Elvis had been living at the villa for a month when he decided to convert a room on the ground floor previously used as a study into a gym. Equipment was ordered, and soon he had a decent home gym that included some weights, a rowing machine, two stationary bicycles (one for Tommy), a treadmill and a few other assorted pieces of equipment to work out with. Inspired, Elvis started to self-train with Tommy.

Normand realized quickly that Elvis's health was an important issue. It was as if he was recuperating from an illness or something.

"Aaron, I know a guy that you should meet." Normand explained that he knew a trainer who could help him with his workout routine and got a thumb's up.

"Sure, bring him by. That's a great idea, Norm."

The trainer's name was Ralph, and he was a white guy from Antigua who owned a place called Ralph's Real Gym. His job was primarily to see that Elvis didn't hurt himself.

"The main thing for you to remember, Aaron, is easy does it. There's no competition and you're not against the clock, so respect that your body needs time."

Ralph worked out a fairly relaxed regimen of warm-ups and calisthenics that would suit Elvis's present condition and goals. These simple routines, along with a diet that was not too difficult to follow, helped Elvis's overall physical condition and were making a noticeable change in Elvis's appearance.

He had nice color and his skin looked healthier. He lost some weight and was even getting a bit of muscle tone in his arms and legs.

"Tommy, see if Eddy will drop by today or tomorrow, will ya," Elvis said one morning after his workout.

"Sure, E, I'll call him now."

Tommy's role at Villa Selena was to be Elvis's right hand guy, driver and companion. Although Tommy's new girlfriend, Carol, was taking up some of his time, he was unwavering when it came to his boss. Elvis always came first.

At times, usually once or twice a week, Elvis would go into the den, close the door and make phone calls. Only Tommy knew who Elvis was speaking to.

Tommy could go in and out, most of the time, when Elvis was making those calls. He always closed the door behind himself after entering or leaving the room.

On this one day, Elvis asked Normand to join him in the den.

"Major."

Elvis was now calling Normand *Major* a lot, although not always. Normand had gotten used to it, but at first he wondered if his boss was making fun of him and his unofficial title, majordomo. But the man loved nicknames . . . a southern thing, Normand came to believe.

"Yes, Boss?"

"How are things running? Everything smooth? It seems so to me, but I like to be sure." He seemed a bit off somehow.

"Oh, yeah, Aaron, the household is basically running without any headaches. The girls are handling their responsibilities just fine. They're very good cooks in a native way, don't you think?"

"I do. I love the way they do fresh fish." The thing about Elvis was he loved most everything if it was prepared the way he liked it. Like his burned bacon.

When it came to meals consisting of meat, mostly hamburgers, ribs or steaks—which Elvis specially ordered from a local butcher—he cooked those himself, on the BBQ.

"The Thompson fellows are handling the maintenance of the grounds competently, and the property looks spectacular. You agree?"

"I do, and you're doing a great job yourself, Major. I salute you. Cheers." He smiled at Normand and offered a toast with the freshly squeezed orange juice Lucinda had made that morning.

The most taxing job at the villa seemed to be the constant cleaning, and that was one thing Normand was adamant about. He didn't want to see dust anywhere, or a dirty window or sill. He wanted the woodwork polished and the floors to shine.

The Major ran a clean ship. Villa Selena deserved no less as far as he was concerned.

Elvis was now squirming a wee bit. He had something to say, and Normand was attentive and curious. It was unlike his boss to be self-conscious and ill at ease.

"I was telling Tommy that I'll be away for four weeks starting Friday. I'm sure I won't be needed around here during that time. You and Tommy can hold down the fort, right, Major?" Elvis smiled at Normand again. "You guys will be OK."

Was this health related, or was it a business trip? thought Normand. It was not his place to pry.

"Sure thing, Boss. We'll be fine."

"I know you will." Elvis stood and made for the door. "I'll see you at dinner, Norm."

"Yes, sir."

*****

Elvis sat in a wing chair in the parlor off his bedroom. It was late on a Thursday night. He was going to rehab first thing in the morning. And staying there. *Alone.*

The decision to seek help had been difficult at first. But he knew he needed support, and there was no other way.

He had to go to them; they would not come to him. No amount of money could change that. The rehab center was on the island of Montserrat, and the facility was called the Kinsale Medical Institute. *I'm being fucking institutionalized!* thought Elvis.

Tommy was the only person, outside of the rehab medical team and Dr. Eddy Bell, who knew a bed was waiting for him. *I'll have to wear a name tag, and a hospital gown, with my ass sticking out! Paper slippers! Lord, have mercy.*

Elvis reached for some pills . . . a couple of "sleepers." He didn't use them very often anymore, and he wondered if this would be the last time he'd be popping downers. *We'll see. One day at a time, Elvis ol' boy, one day at a time.*

The pills kicked in and quickly; he was feeling all warm and fuzzy. Soon he drifted off into a deep, drug-induced sleep . . .

Elvis left Villa Selena early the next day. His luggage that morning was just one black leather suitcase. It contained all he would need for his twenty-eight-day visit. All toiletries would be supplied by the rehab center. His personal items would be scrutinized, and anything inappropriate, such as drugs or booze, would be seized. Elvis was concerned, of course, and nervous, but he knew he was in good hands at the center and no harm would come to him. And when he thought about all the misery the pills had caused him, he was OK with what was to come, although fear of the unknown was making him feel a bit queasy from time to time.

He was groggy as well, and to Normand, Elvis looked apprehensive. Tommy was quiet that morning. He was driving the Land Rover, and Elvis was riding shotgun. It was 6:30 a.m., and just Normand was there to see Elvis off on his "business trip." Elvis wanted to be gone before the rest of the staff showed up for work. He'd booked an early flight out of V.C. Bird International airport, and a car would be waiting in Montserrat to deliver him to the center.

"Have a great trip, Aaron, and a safe return." Normand watched as the Land Rover drove off the estate, going Lord knows where.

*****

During the third week that Elvis was away, an antique jukebox was delivered. It was a classic 1947 Wurlitzer 1015 in excellent condition, with multicolored lights running vertically down the front. It came with a large collection of 45s. The stacked records and the turnstile were visible, and everything worked perfectly. A stunning piece of functional art, fit for a King! Tommy had it put in the games room.

The jukebox was a gift from Tommy. He had found it at a bar in St. John's the week before while there with his girlfriend, Carol, and he had to have it.

"Aaron will really enjoy this, Major. He loves a jukebox. It goes back to his southern American roots . . . it's a cultural thing for some. You wait and see—he'll love it!"

Tommy always had to remember to refer to Elvis as Aaron. Not a simple thing to do, especially when he was talking directly to Elvis with others in the same space, but it was getting a little easier as time went on.

Elvis had told them, "Just remember, it's our secret. It's kinda like a game. It's a high-priority top secret, and we have sworn to protect that secret no matter what." Elvis had a thing about law enforcement officers, military personnel and, well, just about everyone in a uniform. The uniform meant power and respect.

Tommy was very excited at the thought of the Boss coming home.

"It's beautiful, Tommy. Well done!" praised Normand. He felt this gift was more than just a welcome home gift from Tommy to his friend. Somehow, it was much more than that.

While Elvis was away *on business*, things went smoothly at Villa Selena. Normand was proud and relieved at the same time. He had a good team at the villa, and no one wanted to disappoint the Boss. He was the kind of guy you wanted to please, and he was missed by everyone.

One morning, less than a week before Elvis was to return home, Normand was beginning an early morning stroll around the grounds, coffee in hand, when he saw Geraldine walking up the gravel driveway toward the house. She had just been let off at the gate entrance by a male friend.

When Normand saw Geraldine, he automatically waved. He started to turn away but then did a quick double take. Geraldine was wearing her blue work dress with sand-colored clogs. A big brown purse was slung over her right shoulder. Large yellow sunglasses covered half her face, while palm tree earrings swung from each ear. What caused Normand to look twice at Geraldine on this bright, sunny morning was that it looked as if she was carrying some kind of metal cage with her mouth.

When she saw Normand she quickened her step in order to get by him without being confronted. Normand just stared, not saying a thing, slowly turning his head to follow her as she made her way to the rear entrance of the villa, where she disappeared through a door into the mudroom used by the staff.

How odd, thought Normand as he watched Geraldine vanish into the house. But he continued his tour of the property, enjoying the fresh ocean breeze and the delicious fragrance of flowers that followed him everywhere.

A voice broke the quiet of the morning.

"Major?" Now most everybody was calling Normand Major. By now he had more than gotten used to it—he liked it.

Normand looked about for the source of the call. He saw Tommy walking toward him. He was barefoot and had a coffee as well.

"Good morning, Tommy. You're up early."

"Yes, a bit early. What a beautiful morning," exclaimed Tommy. "I might start getting up earlier." He took a deep, exaggerated breath of fresh air.

"The most enjoyable part of my day. Always has

been."

"I can see why." Tommy took a sip of coffee and continued. "By the way, I got a call from Tag last night. He says hi."

"How's he doing?"

"Good. He's working for a security firm in Dallas."

"Security?"

"Yeah, mostly as a handler, he says."

"A handler. So he works with cattle? Horses?"

Tommy laughed, "No, a handler in this case is a person who accompanies and takes care of a celebrity of some sort. A movie star, a sports figure or maybe a singer or a musical group. Last week he was looking after a female pop singer named Pamela who was making a new record in town."

"Pamela?"

"That's it, Pamela. One name, like Cher. Tag says she's an OK person, but he doesn't care for her style of music or anything. But he's not getting paid to like her, is he? But yeah, he's doing well and says he might visit over the winter."

"That would be nice." Normand started walking again and Tommy walked with him.

"You see Geraldine yet this morning?"

"No," answered Tommy. "Why?"

"Nothing."

As they walked together, Normand decided to ask Tommy a few questions about his employer. He didn't want to step out of line and appear nosy, but perhaps with a little prompting, Tommy might offer some insight into the man who was Aaron Smith.

"Do you miss living in the States, Tommy?"

"Sometimes, I guess, but I love it here. I'm thinking I might like to visit back home next spring. Both my parents are alive but quite elderly, and I'd like to spend a bit of time with them."

"Maybe they could visit you here sometime, if they don't mind traveling this far, that is." Normand stooped to pick up a broken branch and then tossed it into the brush.

"No, no, they won't be visiting here." Tommy would never take the chance of E being recognized by his parents. They had met Elvis once when Elvis was in Pittsburgh years before, and it would be hard to fool them.

"They don't care to fly," he lied.

"Flying's not for everybody. Personally I love to fly. I've yet to travel to America, but I flew to London once with my family when I was young. My father has a brother there, and we spent a week with him and his family. I was twelve years old. It was a fun time, and flying was the best part as far as I was concerned," remembered Normand fondly.

Tommy nodded and said, "I wanted to be a pilot once upon a time."

"You could have flown Aaron's jet for him," threw in Normand with a smile. Aaron had told Normand that he'd had his own jet when he'd lived in the

United States.

"Yeah, maybe."

"How's Aaron's trip going, have you heard? I expected a phone call or two while he was away, but not a word."

To this Tommy had to think before he spoke. The purpose of the Boss's trip was personal, and only Elvis would be the one to discuss it with Normand, if at all. Obviously Elvis hadn't confided the true purpose of his trip to the Major.

"He's fine and wishes he was here."

"You spoke with him?"

"Oh, yeah, a few times. He's good."

The fact is, Tommy had heard from Elvis only once while he was away, and that had been a few days ago. At the clinic where he was staying, there were no phone calls or any other form of communication with the "outside world" until the beginning of the last week of his stay. No visitors, either.

Normand couldn't think of a question that wouldn't sound like he was snooping, so he let it go.

"Well, a few more days and he'll have his wish."

By this time they had reached the back of the villa, and instead of continuing on, they stepped onto the patio and entered the kitchen through the double set of patio doors.

The girls were busy preparing food for the day. At least Lucinda and Bea were; Geraldine was sitting at the kitchen table mumbling something about "it ain't easy."

Normand was now staring at Geraldine. *What the hell is that?*

"Geraldine, may I ask you what that is in your mouth? You OK, girl?" asked Normand, no longer able to curtail his curiosity.

Geraldine looked at her boss and managed a grunt and a tight-lipped "I'm OK, Major. I just had my jaw wired shut." She looked like she might cry.

"Why, girl, did you break it or something?" Normand's concern was real. "You need the day off?"

"No, sir, she's fine," interjected Bea. "She had that contraption put in her mouth to stop her from eating so damn much."

"Her jaw is wired so she can't eat anything solid. She's on a liquid diet," added Lucinda.

"She wants to lose weight," said Bea sarcastically.

Tommy said, "You shitting us? Goddamn, that's a bit drastic!" Tommy starting laughing, and Geraldine was now fighting really hard not to burst into tears.

Bea added, "You better not cheat and try eating that fried chicken you like so much, honey. You might could choke to death."

Poor Geraldine. Now her eyes were wide and teary and her chin was quavering uncontrollably, so Normand decided enough was enough.

"OK, everybody, give the girl a break. She's trying to do something positive. It can't be easy. Let her be." He gave Bea a hard stare and then turned away.

"How's breakfast coming along, Lucinda?"

Lucinda said over her shoulder, "It's coming, Major," and went back to frying some hash potatoes to go with the sausages Bea was preparing.

And then old Bea said in a loud, teasing voice, "You want me to puree some pork chops for "Jaws" to have for lunch, Major?"

Tommy started laughing, and Geraldine ran out of the room into the backyard.

"Bea, you get out there and you apologize to Geraldine right now! There'll be no more teasing, you hear me?" Normand's voice was loud and serious. Even Tommy knew better than to say a word, so he went to the espresso machine and started to make himself a café latte without another word or a snicker.

Bea reluctantly put down her spatula and did a brisk walk outside, only to return almost immediately, announcing, "There, it's done. We were only teasing her. That ain't no big deal like you make it." She went back to her cooking.

Normand followed Geraldine outside and found her sitting on a bench by the tennis courts. She had a Kleenex to her nose, and she was crying softly. He approached the bench and said to her, "Mind if I sit with you?"

Geraldine looked up at Normand and shook her head. Normand took that as permission to sit and dropped down next to her.

"Don't listen to them, Geraldine. You know they are just ragging on you. They don't mean to be hurting your feelings." Normand's long legs were stretched out in front of him, crossed at the ankles.

"You hear me?" he said gently when Geraldine didn't reply.

"I hears you, sir. I'm OK, I really am. I'm not mad at them, they just funning with me . . . It's me I'm mad at. I got no good sense when it comes to eating right. I just eat. I eat and I gets big. Too big. Men don't like too big, sir." She blew her nose. Her pretty eyes were red.

"Geraldine, you're an attractive young woman, you know that, and if you want to lose weight, you will. But don't be too hard on yourself. If you want to keep your mouth wired like that for a while, well then, that's your business. Don't let that ol' woman Bea get on your nerves or Lucinda either . . . they like you Geraldine. And it doesn't really matter if you're too skinny or too fat. It's you, the person, that we care for honey. OK?"

Normand had never spoken to anyone like this before or about anything like this before. He wasn't much older than she was. Geraldine was the mother of three, but she was so like a child herself that he felt he had to talk to her. Normand had a big heart and a strong sense of family, and what he had said came naturally for him. Actually, he was starting to wonder if he should have said anything at all . . . Geraldine said she knew the others were just "funning" with her. Maybe he was the one who was overreacting.

"Well, I'm going to have some breakfast. I'm hungry." He stood and for a moment regretted mentioning being hungry.

Geraldine looked up and smiled. "I'm all right . . . I'll be right in. Thank you, Normand."

*****

Twenty-eight days after leaving home, Elvis returned. He sat shotgun again with Tommy at the wheel of the Land Rover as it swung into the yard and crunched to a stop in front of the house. Both doors opened at the same time.

Elvis got out of the car, kneeled down and kissed the ground!

"Hallelujah! I'm home!"

When Normand saw Elvis kiss the ground, he wondered if Aaron might think twice about spitting on the lawn of Villa Selena again!

Elvis was dressed exactly as he had been when he left the villa. It was all smiles and hellos for the staff, who had been standing at the front entrance waiting for him to arrive, as per Normand's instructions.

"I need a drink," he exclaimed in that thick, southern accent. "Airplanes always suck the fluids right out of me, man. Somebody bring me a big ol' mug of cola. And I wouldn't mind a snack. All they had on the plane was cookies. Would lunch be possible, Lucinda?"

Lucinda did a little shuffle and nodded, but otherwise she didn't move, still smiling at Elvis.

Elvis went up to Normand. "Man, how you doing, Major? You had to shoot anybody for acting up since I been gone?"

He gave Normand a quick hug. As he released him, he heard Lucinda say, "Welcome home, Boss. You looking real good, sir." Lucinda was right: He looked very good. Rested. Healthier.

"You look handsome," added Geraldine, batting her long lashes and giggling.

"You watch that kinda talk, girls. I warned you before. I might have to take y'all out back and teach you some learning," Elvis joked.

Geraldine blushed, obviously loving the attention, while Lucinda and Bea laughed out loud. Geraldine no longer had her jaw wired. The girls were enjoying themselves.

Watching Elvis teasing and joking around, Tommy was thinking that Elvis might be trying to find the *old* Elvis. A *younger* Elvis, and not the man he had become over the last several years or so.

It wasn't just about a physically healthier Elvis. It was also an attitude he had about life in happier days . . . it was about getting in touch with his old personality, finding himself. Tommy didn't think E really cared all that much for acting the way *Aaron Smith* was expected to act. He wanted to keep the name Aaron Smith all right, and he wanted to maintain his anonymity—that was the key to his survival—but he wanted to be *Elvis* too. To be true to himself. In spirit. He didn't want to lose the heart and soul of Elvis Aaron Presley. *The Man.*

"It's nice to have you back, Boss. Everyone missed you," Normand said. He and the others at Villa Selena had come to have a strong personal regard for their boss.

"You know what I think I'll do? I think I'll take my time and wait for the girls to make me something light to eat. My mind wants several burgers with a mountain of fries and a couple of beers, Normand." He looked around him, taking in the sights. It was clear that he was thankful and delighted to be home.

"But I was given a new diet by the doctors I've been seeing while away, and I promised to follow their advice. So, I guess I'll have a sandwich." He started walking toward the house.

So that was it, thought Normand. Aaron had been away because of his health.

"How about tuna on brown, with some carrots on the side and a glass of cold milk? Make that a glass of *colored* milk, please, ladies." Elvis pointed at Bea and Lucinda, smiling broadly.

"So, you be wanting some *fine* chocolate milk with that sandwich, sir?" Bea teased.

"Yes, ma'am, I'd like that very much." He winked, and the girls howled in delight. Tommy gave his boss a friendly slap on the back, then went to the Land Rover, collected Elvis's stuff and took it into the house.

Elvis followed the girls into the kitchen, where they made him a healthy lunch.

Elvis looked tired after the food registered with his

brain, and a yawn led to "Great lunch, ladies, thank you, thank you very much. Now if you'll all excuse me . . ."

He went upstairs and had a nap. It had been a long day already.

The next morning, Normand was walking by the den and heard soft guitar sounds emanating from within. He stopped to listen for a few moments, then looked in the room and was surprised to see Elvis, in his bathrobe, gently playing an acoustic guitar. He tapped lightly on the door.

Elvis looked up at him and stopped strumming the instrument.

"Aaron, sorry, I didn't mean to cause you to stop. I heard the music. That sounded very nice. You learned to play while you were away?"

"Thank you very much, Normand." Elvis got up and put the guitar in its case. He had bought the guitar while in rehab. He was allowed to do so after his third week there, and he noticed a few other "clients" had guitars. So he spoke with a counselor, who found him a new Gibson acoustic at a local music store. Elvis was grateful to have a bit of music back in his life. It was therapeutic.

"I wish I could play the guitar. I love the guitar sound. I tried playing the piano when I was younger . . . my mother plays . . . but I guess my talents lie elsewhere," concluded Normand.

"Well, I'm going to the market with Bea. I'll see you later. It was nice hearing you play, Aaron . . . you have a gift."

After Normand left, Elvis closed the door to the den, took the guitar from its case and started quietly playing again while thinking about how to maintain the kind of regimen he was introduced to in Montserrat. Exercise and diet were the two areas he had to concentrate on the most, he realized.

He figured he'd start by walking every morning after breakfast and at the end of the day right after dinner. The coolest times of the day.

Elvis appreciated the fact that he wouldn't be recognized and hassled as he walked along Harlowe Lane. There was a sense of freedom in Antigua that he never had back home. These days Elvis tried hard not to think about Memphis and his estranged family there. That door was closed, for now at least.

Yes, walking at first, and as he grew stronger, he'd try jogging.

And Elvis knew that healthy eating habits would also need to become routine. The nutritionists had given him a list of foods and food groups. There were charts that plainly explained the nutritional value of the various food choices recommended for a healthier, longer and happier lifestyle.

Drinks were another challenge. He wasn't an alcoholic, but one thing could lead to another, they advised, so it was strongly suggested he stay off all drugs, including alcohol, for the time being. *One day at a time.*

All in all, there was a lot to learn and apply. Dr.

Bell would drop by in a few weeks for a brief check-up.

While in rehab, Elvis had to list what activities, sports or hobbies he enjoyed. He gave that a lot of thought. He said he enjoyed shooting pool, doing karate and collecting guns. They suggested he not play with guns for a while. They did suggest swimming as one of the very best exercises he could do. So swimming, walking and then jogging, these would be at the top of his to-do list.

But he also wanted to find some new activities that were healthy *and* fun. While in rehab, Elvis remembered his fishing days as a young man in Tennessee and figured fishing was a natural choice for him. Lots of fresh air when you're fishing, he thought, and some exercise too but not so much as to be a problem. He didn't want to fish off a dock, which was popular in the harbor areas; he wanted to be on the water. So he would need a boat. He'd speak to Normand when he got back and ask him where to start looking.

CHAPTER TWENTY-TWO

E lvis started looking for a fishing craft of some kind a few days later. A combination fishing/ pleasure boat would be ideal, he decided. A boat like that would be perfect for most types of fishing or for cruising, or even for going to an out island for a day on the beach. There would probably be lots of choices in a place like Antigua. Choosing wisely was the challenge when it came to purchasing a quality boat, and as he suspected, Normand had plenty of advice on how to proceed.

The largest boat yard on the island was in St. John's, and Normand thought that would be a good place to start looking. He would also make some calls to people who were connected to what was on the market.

Normand grew up around boats, and he knew a lot about them. For Aaron, he was looking for quality. In real estate it's the *location* that is usually the most important consideration; in boating it's the craftsmanship.

A cheaply made boat would be a liability on the ocean. Even a medium chop could have the boat floundering about like a lightweight fishing bobber, which would be very uncomfortable and even dangerous. Normand had seen cheap boats owned by fair-weather boaters, and it was not a pretty site when the wind came up. He had personally rescued more than a few boats caught in some *weather* and towed them to safety.

Pay more and get more was the way to go in buying a boat that would be trustworthy and safe on the ocean. Two saltwater sport-fishing cruiser companies to be trusted in the boating world were Bertram and Hatteras. There were others worthy of consideration, but their boats were the *crème de la crème* and most often purchased by boaters with demanding standards.

It was a Bertram that was the first high-quality boat Normand heard was for sale. A used Bertram in pristine condition *and* for sale was hard to find, but one had just come on the market, and Normand thought Elvis should see it.

He found Elvis in the games room playing pool with Tommy. Elvis was wearing a red T-shirt with the famous picture of Marilyn Monroe from the movie *The Seven Year Inch*, her white dress blowing up around her as she stands over a subway grating.

Tommy was lining up a shot while Elvis, a glass of water in one hand, the other gripping a pool stick, stood to the side and kidded him about missing.

"Tough shot, Tommy. Glad it's not mine, buddy. Watch that you don't scratch, now."

Tommy ignored his friend, put a smooth stroke on the ball and made the shot to win the game.

"Well done!" congratulated Elvis good-naturedly.

"Thank you, thank you very much," imitated

Tommy. They both laughed.

"You fellas are having fun I see," said Normand as he walked into the room.

"Hey, Major, how's it hanging?" asked Elvis before taking a sip from his drink.

"Fine, thank you, Aaron. I found a boat that might suit your needs very well indeed."

"Indeed!" mimicked Elvis.

"That was quick, Normand," stated Tommy. "Is it local?"

"It is indeed." Normand grinned at both of them. "Here in the bay, at Reiner's Marina. Let me know if and when you wanna discuss it, and I'd be happy to tell you all about it."

"Let's hear about it now. Let's sit." Elvis went to a stool at the bar and sat down. Tommy sat next to him, and Normand walked behind the bar and remained standing. He told them what he knew about the boat he had heard was for sale.

"Well, it'll be expensive, Aaron, but you get what you pay for in a boat, and this Bertram is the real deal," Normand informed Elvis. "It's a fiberglass forty-six-footer with twin inboard Cummins diesel engines. At forty-six feet it's big, but not too big to manage, even by a single person, and it's large enough for a half dozen passengers easily. It's a solid craft, Aaron. If it's offered at fair market value, which I believe it is, then it's worth the money, I can assure you."

Elvis was listening carefully to Normand and had to ask him, "How do you know about all this,

Normand. Have you done a lot of boating?"

"As a matter of fact, I have. I'm Antiguan, comes with the territory," Normand said with a laugh. "Seriously, though, I have spent a lot of time boating and fishing. My dad has a boat, and I have many friends who have boats. I've been around them all my life."

"Really? Can you handle a boat like this one? I mean, I know a bit about smaller fishing boats. My father had a fourteen-footer with a single outboard, but a forty-six-foot cruiser sounds quite big."

"I don't suppose you've captained a boat with a flybridge, then?" Normand smiled, knowing what Elvis's reply would be. He continued: "This Bertram has a flybridge, which is what you want on a boat like this."

Elvis considered this. "I know what a flybridge is, from a fishing charter I was on in the Bahamas once with some friends. The captain let us steer for a while, and that was fun, but that's it. Not much experience at all, really. I found the height of the flybridge and the controls for the twin engines a bit unnerving, but I could get used to it, I guess."

Elvis was being honest. "I didn't want to try docking. Not a chance. I'm sure the captain was relieved," laughed Elvis.

"I'm sure you could get used to it too. I'll help you learn. Aaron, have a look. If it's too much for you we keep looking. But boats this clean are hard to find used. Or you can buy a new boat, of course, but you could save a lot of money if you want this one. Doesn't hurt to see it."

It was a good day to view a boat. Normand, Elvis and Tommy arrived at the dock where the Bertram in question, with the name *Roberta's Way* painted in blue on her transom, was moored. She was white fiberglass with a blue stripe running down either side. She was spotlessly clean and glistening in the early morning sun as she sat in the water motionless, waiting to be taken out and enjoyed. The air was fresh with the smell of the ocean, and the sky held the promise of a fine, sunny day ahead.

"Good morning, gentlemen, and a beautiful one it is," a man called out to Elvis and Co. as they arrived at berth #7 at Reiner's Marina. He jumped out of the back of the Bertram easily and onto the floating dock. Normand went right up to the man and held out his hand.

"Good morning, nice to see you, Alex. How are you?" Alex looked to be in his mid-fifties. He looked fit, with thick salt-and-pepper hair and the complexion of a man who spent time outdoors.

"Hi there, Normand. I'm good, thank you. Yourself?" They shook hands.

"Fine, Alex. Let me introduce you to my friends. This is Tommy Jefferson, and this is the fellow looking to buy a quality fishing boat, Aaron Smith. Guys, this is Alex Court." They all shook hands and then Normand explained Alex's presence at the dock.

"Alex here is an agent for the sale of this Bertram. He knows boats better than anyone I've ever met and is an avid boater himself. You been selling fine boats for about thirty years, isn't that so, Alex?"

"Been a long time, Normand. When I started, though, the boats I had to sell were not all that fine to be honest. But when you're young and starting out in this biz, you take what they give you. But I've been selling the good stuff a long time. I even get to sell yachts these days." He turned to *Roberta's Way* and said. "This Bertram is one fine craft, gentlemen, make no mistake. It's a lovely fishing cruiser, and as you can see, it's in pristine condition."

Elvis and Tommy looked at the boat, and Elvis said, "Nice," momentarily at a loss for words. Tommy nodded in agreement.

"Are you gentlemen boaters?" asked Alex.

"Nothing like this," replied Elvis, intimated by the sheer size of the boat. "Sure is big."

"Well, it's a good size, yes," replied Alex. "But in this style of fishing cruiser, the configuration of the engines and controls and so forth makes it handle, more or less, the same way as the smaller cruisers. The big difference is that you get so much more with this size. For example, the thirty-three-footer is a popular choice, but the difference in the amenities on the forty-six is huge. That extra thirteen feet makes a world of difference. Let me introduce you to this lovely lady."

Alex spent the next hour and a half showing the boat, starting with an outside visual and explanation of the materials and the workmanship that went into building the fishing cruiser.

"The boat is only two years old and has very low mileage. The original owner is a retired local doctor named Jay Nance. You know Jay, Normand. Well, he bought it in Florida new and brought her here. Then he injured his back when a guy rear-ended his car at a stoplight, about eight months ago. Since then he's had problems getting around easily, and consequently, he's used the boat less and less. So he just put her up for sale. You're the first to view her."

Normand remarked, "The cruiser does look new."

They continued to walk along the dock next to the Bertram, admiring her graceful lines.

Alex pointed out, "As you can see, on the bow, there's even a fourteen-foot powered launch to shuttle yourself ship to shore. You simply anchor off shore and use the runner rather than be bothered with mooring the Bertram at a dock. Can be very useful at times, and getting the small boat off and back on is easy with the electric launch that you can see there."

"Cool," Elvis said to Normand. Alex was right. It looked simple and efficient.

After the walkabout, they all boarded the vessel. It was confusing, understandably, with so much to absorb on a fishing cruiser like this, and Elvis tried to keep up. Normand deliberately asked questions he knew the answers to so that it would help Elvis understand more of what he was seeing.

Next came a trip up to the flybridge and the controls for the engines, the steering and all the electronics in the cockpit.

"No worries," said Normand. "It's not as complicated as it appears. It's all rather easy, as a matter of fact.

You just have to know how to do things and then it just requires practice. Like anything else worthwhile. And as I said, I have lots of experience and I can show you the ropes, Aaron. I'll even be your captain or first mate, if you'd like, at least until you and Tommy can handle things on your own."

Yes, there was a lot to take in, but Tommy could tell that his boss was getting into it.

"Let's go down below and take a look in the salon," said Alex.

Elvis quickly appreciated the main salon area, which featured teak cabinetry, beige carpeting, and a table with fold-up wings that could accommodate six comfortably. And there was a three-person sofa and two upholstered arm chairs. A floor-to-ceiling cabinet housed a television and sound system. There were a few lamps on the table . . . all of these ran off the generator. The galley area had plenty of counter space, a refrigerator, a sink and a stove with an oven, and, of course, there was running water. Hot and cold.

But the real kicker for Elvis was the fully functional bathroom, equipped with a toilet and a shower, and the main bedroom with a double bed. There was a night table with a lamp, a mirror along one wall and curtained windows. There was also recessed lighting overhead controlled by a dimmer switch system.

"Lord have mercy, this is real nice!" He looked at Tommy and said, "Man, I could dig this." Tommy just smiled back, nodding.

"There is also sleeping for two in the bow," said Alex. "And the sofa can be used for a bed as well.

They really maximize the space on a boat these days, don't they." It wasn't a question, it was a fact.

"I wouldn't mind sleeping on the deck under a sky full of stars. That would be amazing!" Tommy said to everyone.

"Yeah, I've done it myself many times, Tommy," Normand agreed. "It's very peaceful being anchored away from the lights and sound of a city. The sound of the water lapping against the boat is very relaxing, almost therapeutic . . . at least I've always found it so."

Alex continued: "This cruiser allows you to do what you want, when you want. You know, Bertram has a yacht this same length but with a very different stern and allotment of space, as it's designed for cruising only. It's not set up for fishing like this one is. And not only coastal and offshore fishing, but also deep sea fishing, boys, if you wanna go after the big fish. Very versatile, this particular size and model."

The boys were very impressed.

"You wanna go for a ride, Aaron? I made arrangements to do that if you'd like," asked Alex. When Normand looked to Elvis, he saw excitement in his eyes.

Elvis nodded. "Oh, yes, sir. I'd like that very much!"

By the end of the day, Elvis was the proud owner of one beautiful Bertram cruiser.

CHAPTER TWENTY-THREE

Televised sports events were a big deal for Elvis and his gang. Baseball and football were the two most popular games watched. A new friend of Tommy's who was welcomed to the house was a guy named Lonny. Lonny was a local who loved his football. He followed both pro and college games religiously, and every week during the season he would print out the latest stats, which were available to anyone who wanted an advantage in a friendly wager.

Normand had introduced Elvis and Tommy to cricket, and Elvis found that he enjoyed the game. In early December, the first World Series Cricket competition was staged, and they followed the matches closely.

Whatever the sport, Villa Selena was raucous when the gang gathered to watch a game. Cold beer and pizza were the order of the day. Elvis was just as feverish as the next guy but without the *lubrication* that his buddies liked to indulge in.

Elvis was substance free at this time. No drugs. Offered an alcoholic drink, Elvis would refuse.

This was the new Elvis, and the new Elvis said the famous Serenity Prayer, used by Alcoholics Anonymous and many other support groups worldwide: *God, grant me the serenity to accept the things I cannot change, the courage to change the things I can, and the wisdom to know the difference.* He would repeat it quietly to himself at least once a day. It was a very positive message, and Elvis believed that the world would be a far better place if everyone followed its suggestions. It helped Elvis persevere. *It'll take time; be patient.*

Along with baseball, football and cricket, golf was also watched at the villa. Earlier in the year, Tom Watson won the Masters in Augusta, Georgia. This was the first of the four majors of the year, and many considered it the most prestigious. Elvis knew of this major golfing event because it took place in the Deep South. He knew Georgia quite well from his touring days. But he had only casual interest in the 1977 Masters. His earnest regard for the sport of golf was yet to develop.

The rest of the year went very well for the King of Rock and Roll. His mental and physical health were improving. It's not easy to bounce back after years of abuse. He knew it was going to take at least a year to feel normal. Although he didn't really know what *normal* would feel like.

For a younger man, recovery would be difficult. For a man of Elvis's age, it was even more exasperating. But Elvis was tenacious again in his life, and he believed he could do it.

A big mistake that people make in life is to give up. There was no "give up" in the King of Rock and Roll.

Nineteen seventy-seven was coming to an end, *and*

thank God, thought Elvis. He was reminded of an old black and white television show where a young girl in pigtails says to an elderly neighbor, "All in all, Mr. McGarrity, it's been quite a day!" That's how he felt during that time.

Almost four months had passed since Elvis "died." People worldwide were still dealing with it. Still mourning and refusing to believe.

"Believe it!" he felt like shouting. "I have passed on. Get a fucking life!"

How in the hell did I manage all this? he often wondered to himself. *I'm clean and sober. I live in a spectacular villa in the Caribbean. The Lord works in mysterious ways . . .*

Elvis celebrated New Year's Eve 1977 in Antigua with friends. Villa Selena was a wonderful place, and Elvis was happy there. Life was good at the moment. And getting better.

CHAPTER TWENTY-FOUR

Elvis Presley took up golf a few months after coming out of rehab. He was now comfortable handling *Roberta's Way*, and he, Tommy, Normand and a few friends were having a great time fishing and cruising the waters off Antigua. But Elvis wanted more physical and mental stimulation in his life. One day after a morning swim, he talked to Tommy about this.

They were in their bathing suits and relaxing in a pair of white lounging chairs by the pool. The weather was perfect.

Tommy had played golf in the States, and so when Elvis started speaking about getting a hobby, Tommy suggested he try it.

Elvis had never considered the game. For the King of Rock and Roll, golf was not an option as far as he was concerned, but then again, he wasn't the King anymore, was he?

"A lot of colored people play golf in Pittsburgh, Tommy? I thought it was a game for rich white guys."

"There are lots of great black players, E. Professional PGA players like Charlie Sifford and Lee Elder, not only playing but winning. Golf isn't just for white guys anymore. I like the game myself."

"You any good?"

"Yeah, not bad. My dad was a golfing fan, and he attended PGA events as a spectator when they were playing in the area. He was a big Sifford fan. One summer he started hitting golf balls on a range near where we lived, and we went with him sometimes. It was fun hitting the ball."

"You think I might like it?" Elvis took a long pull on his cream soda.

"Never can tell. But I'll tell ya, E, it's an addictive game. You try it you might get hooked." Tommy laughed good-naturedly. He was acknowledging Elvis's stint in the addiction rehab facility a few months earlier. "If you wanna give it a try, I'll go with you. I'd like to play. It's been a few years."

"There's a course near the marina," Tommy continued. "It runs along the coast and it looks spectacular driving by. It's a semi-private course, I was told, so we could go there and hit some balls."

Elvis was quiet while he thought about it. All he knew about golf was from seeing it on television once in a while. He had been invited to play in celebrity tournaments in the past, but it wasn't his thing. Not the golf or the golf fans. He'd met Arnold Palmer and Jack Nicklaus and other popular golfers backstage at his gigs, though. Everybody wanted to meet Elvis Presley and get their picture taken with him. That was it.

Tommy smiled at Elvis. "If you want exercise that's both physically and mentally challenging, trust me, this game will give you that in spades."

"You can teach me? I don't wanna make a damn

fool of myself."

"I can show you some stuff, E, but if you like it and wanna pursue it, then you'd best be taking lessons from a pro."

"OK. But I won't wear those silly clothes I've seen some of them guys wear, I can tell you that, Tommy. No way. They look like white pimps!"

"They do, don't they, though?" He and Elvis had a good laugh at that remark.

The next day, Tommy and Elvis showed up at the Antigua Golf and Country Club looking to hit some balls.

"This will be a good start, E. You'll see," encouraged Tommy.

Tommy rented two right-handed sets of clubs and a large bucket of balls. They went to the driving range, and Tommy explained a few things to Elvis.

"The idea today, E, is to try to hit the ball. It doesn't matter where it goes, just try to make good contact. Here, I'll show you a simple, proper way to hold the golf club and how to address the ball, and then you're on your own. But first watch me hit some balls, although you don't wanna copy me exactly because I'm not *that* good, but you'll get a sense of what to do. OK?"

"Sure."

At first Elvis was swinging too fast and missing the ball completely and "whiffing," or he would miss the ball and hit only the grass, hard.

"Easy does it, Boss. Take the club back slower, pause at the top, keep your eye on the ball all the time, and now swing down at the ball and follow through. Here, watch me again." Tommy took a nice swing with a five iron, and the ball flew straight with a slight fade about 165 yards. "Not bad," he said of his shot. "That's all the direction you get from me today. Just keep at it. It'll get better."

And it did get better—a lot better. Elvis's sense of rhythm helped him tremendously. Perhaps because he was a singer, where rhyme and timing are so important, the tempo of the swing came to him more easily than most.

"Looking good, E." Tommy was very impressed, and he gave Elvis lots of encouragement.

*****

That evening, all Elvis wanted to talk about was golf. He made plans to go back the next day and hit some more balls.

Elvis and Tommy were having dinner with Normand and discussing the sport.

"You play golf, Norm?"

"Tried a few times. I liked it. I didn't play enough to get good at it, but it was cool," replied Normand over a plate of fried grouper and peas and rice that the girls had prepared for dinner.

"Tommy, maybe I should join the golf club. I think

I could get into the game."

Tommy was glad his boss wanted to go back to the driving range, as he had enjoyed it as well.

"Sounds good to me. Tomorrow we'll hit some more balls on the range, and then we'll go to the putting green and work on your putting."

"I liked hitting the driver the best yesterday."

"Drivers can be your best friend or your nemesis. That club and your putter are the two most important clubs in your bag." Tommy took a drink of his Pauli Girl, loaded up his fork and continued: "Tomorrow you'll need to work with the other clubs more. The irons. And most important, putting. They have a saying in golf that's very true: 'Drive for show and putt for dough.'"

Normand said, "I know enough about golf to know that's true, Aaron. When I played I could get on the green sometimes in a couple of shots, like a par three, and then take six or seven putts to get the ball in the damn hole." He laughed, but it was clear he was serious.

"OK, I guess we'll try putting tomorrow. You wanna come along, Norm?" asked Elvis before taking up a forkful of peas and rice. "The more the merrier."

"I'd like that. We got some water being delivered in the morning, then I'm good to go."

"All right, then, we're three for tomorrow, fellas."

"OK, can't wait." Normand smiled.

Tommy nodded in agreement. "Me either."

*****

"Good morning, ladies," announced a cheerful Elvis the next morning, fresh from a dip in the pool. Elvis and Tommy were now getting up earlier, often going for a swim while the girls were preparing breakfast. Elvis's now-longish brown hair was still damp, and a white towel was wrapped around his shoulders. Lucinda and Geraldine were in the kitchen working. Bea was home sick that morning.

"Good morning, sir," replied Lucinda. "We got some scrambled eggs and bacon and—"

Geraldine interrupted: "And your bacon be burnt like you want it, Boss." She smiled at Elvis.

"Sounds wonderful," Elvis replied amicably. Lucinda gave Geraldine a look and continued explaining what was for breakfast.

"Bacon, *well done*, and some grits just like you like it. And some fresh, homemade biscuits."

"I might wanna go back to bed after eating all that," joked Tommy. He also had a towel with him, but his short hair was dry already. Normand was wearing light brown pants and a blue collared sports shirt. He was ready for the range.

"I had my breakfast a while ago. Take your time, but I'm ready when you are," said Normand.

"Well, let's eat up, Tommy, and get this show on the road. I'm getting anxious to hit some golf balls!"

declared Elvis. An hour later, Elvis and the guys were in the Land Rover heading for the Antigua Golf and Country Club.

They spent the better part of a day there. They hit balls, worked up a sweat, went for a break and some cool refreshments, hit more balls, and then stopped for lunch.

"Food looks good, E," said Tommy after checking out the small lunch menu listing choices for the day. "Think I'll have a burger with fries."

The fact that Tommy called "Aaron" *E* in front of Normand was of no consequence. Elvis and Tommy had discussed it just after moving into Villa Selena and decided that *E* was OK to use. They would tell anyone wanting to know why Tommy called Aaron *E* that it was because the Boss was always right. A regular Mr. Know-it-all, Tommy would explain further, so the guys back in the U.S. had started calling him *E* . . . as in *Einstein* . . . all in good humor.

Normand and the others thought this was hilarious, and they accepted this explanation. Now Tommy could call Elvis *E* and no one would bat an eye.

That day was fun for the three of them. Elvis kept swinging at the ball, taking occasional advice from Tommy and Normand.

"Keep your eye on the ball, E," suggested Tommy.

"Follow through," from Normand.

Normand was impressive. His trim, athletic build and natural body movement over the ball was a pleasure to watch, and Elvis noticed that he hit the ball farther than Tommy and without a lot of effort.

"Looking good, Norm. You know how to play this game," said Tommy as he watched Normand on the range.

"He can hit the ball for sure, Tommy. How far are they going, anyway?"

"Not that far, really. Maybe about 250 yards. I know guys who hit it 300 or more," stated Normand as a matter of fact. "My main problem is keeping the ball in play. My game can be one long roller-coaster ride if I'm not careful, especially if my putting lets me down."

"I hear that," replied Tommy. Tommy hit the ball well, although his swing was unconventional and he held the club with a baseball grip. He managed to be consistent nonetheless with his exaggerated fade.

A few minutes later, Elvis walked back to the bag of rental clubs and put away a persimmon three wood. "I want to take some lessons," said Elvis just after he had been duffing one ball after other. "I wanna know how to hit the damn ball properly. Hell, how about we all take lessons? The three of us. OK?" He looked at the two of them, sweat rolling down his brow.

"Sure, let's do that." Tommy declared. "I think that's a real good idea, E."

"I'm not sure I want to take lessons, Aaron. I can't be hanging out with you guys at this club all day. I've got a villa to run."

"Norm, you can't be a slave to that place, either,"

pointed out Elvis. Elvis knew very well that Normand was a taskmaster and that he ran the villa with a watchful eye. Besides supervising the house staff and the groundskeepers, he also handled the financial aspects. This allowed Elvis to do as he wished, when he wished, knowing everything was in good hands with the Major in charge. Villa Selena could be a busy place, and Normand made sure everything ran smoothly. The Major took his job seriously.

"No, it's OK," insisted Normand. "I can get around the track fine the way I am. You guys take the lessons, and I'll just play with you from time to time."

"All right, then. I'll tell ya what we're going to do. We are joining the club. The three of us. Then Tommy and I can take lessons when we want, and we'll be able to play here when we want. And Normand, when you're able to find the time. And I'll tell ya what, guys, I'm footing the bill, so no bullshit, we're doin' this. Now grab your clubs and follow me."

Normand started to protest, but his boss gave him a look that said *there's no ifs and buts about it*. So he picked up his rental clubs and followed Elvis and Tommy.

And so Elvis joined the country club, along with Tommy and Normand, that very day. Elvis had the guys pick out new clubs, a golf bag each, balls and gloves, even tees . . . everything they needed to play the game. Elvis then had them pick out golf attire from the pro shop, almost needing to force Normand. Everything, head to toe.

"Guys, not one shirt, get three or four. Same with

slacks. Don't be shy, let's do this!"

"Boss, what if you end up hating the game?"

"Then you'll play without me." Elvis gave them a big grin. "Now c'mon, buy up!"

*****

There was no problem joining the golf club, and on the first day as an official member, Elvis met Bob Royce. Bob was an ex-PGA golfer who retired from the European Tour because of a shoulder injury. He was now the head teaching pro at the club.

Bob was a good-natured British gentleman originally from a small town about forty miles north of London. He had spent some time in Antigua on a trial basis at the invitation of the golf club, where he had been offered employment. He and his wife enjoyed the climate, the island and its people so much that he decided to accept the job offer and move there permanently. He had been the head pro for five years when Elvis joined the club. He was thirty-three years old and in good shape.

"Good morning, Mr. Smith, and welcome to the Antigua Golf and Country Club. I'm head pro, Bob Royce." His British voice was friendly, and his hand-shake had just the right amount of pressure.

"Good morning, Bob. Call me Aaron. Nice to meet you. I asked to see you because I want to take some lessons, sir." Elvis in his southern drawl.

"Absolutely. Why don't we go to the range, Aaron, and have a look at your swing."

Under Bob's tutelage, Elvis got good, fast. Elvis was a good listener and even better learner. Bob told him that his natural sense of rhythm probably helped him on the golf course. Elvis's swing was very fluid and more easily controlled than a fast swing, uncoordinated and stiff like so many of Bob's clients.

"You're a natural," encouraged Bob with a smile. "You'll be breaking 90 in no time."

Bob was correct, and within six months or so, Elvis was consistently shooting in the mid to high 80s. Pretty awesome, considering that about 95 percent of all amateurs, if they play honestly and by the PGA rules, can't break a hundred!

Tommy also took lessons from Bob Royce, and he too improved his game. By playing together four or five times a week on average, the guys fine-tuned their game so that after four months of regular lessons, which took place on the range, a few playing lessons and work on the putting greens with "the flat stick," they could enjoy themselves more while scoring respectably. They had fun, the kind of friendly, competitive fun that only golf can offer.

Elvis had only one problem with his new hobby. He found the Antigua Golf and Country Club pretentious. "There's no way I wanna be part of this place, not socially," he said to Tommy.

Elvis had been brought up in a redneck environment. Hicksville, USA. Elvis and his family and their relatives were nothing more than poor hillbillies with chips on their collective uneducated shoulders. Well-to-do cultured folk made him uncomfortable, and he let it be known to his buddies.

Despite the pompousness of the members, according to Elvis, at least, he ended up retaining his membership. He made it clear that he joined the club only to play golf, not to socialize. He patronized the pro shop when need be, and he had a locker to store his golf clubs between rounds, and that was about as much as he used the facilities. Off the course itself, Aaron Smith kept a low profile.

The clothing worn by most of the members made him shake his head in disgust. He said to Tommy, "Man, these people look fucking ridiculous!"

"The guys look like pimps, right, E?" Tommy chuckled. Then he added, "Boss, they got dress codes here, but no one's saying you have to dress like they do."

"You're right." Elvis snorted.

So Elvis wore fashionable lightweight, button-up golf shirts in tasteful colors and designs, with solid-colored slacks. He preferred black slacks. Most members at the club wore golf shoes with the tongue of the shoe *on the outside*, hanging over the toe. *What the hell was that all about?* Elvis thought. He chose to wear more fashionable foot apparel, and he ordered special leather, lace-up golf shoes from Europe.

Elvis had always been fashion conscious; and although his taste in fashion was once loud, gaudy and controversial, he now preferred more subtle yet stylish classic attire.

Tommy, Roy Kempt and Doug Lamb were the regulars in his foursome. Roy was a retired teacher who golfed every day, and Doug was a physiotherapist with his own practice in St. John's.

Elvis managed to get Normand to put business aside and play once or twice a week. Truth be told, Normand looked forward to getting out with Elvis and Tommy and enjoying a round of golf; it was a nice balance between the business of running the villa (which he enjoyed) and hanging out with the guys for some competitive fun and good laughs.

One day while waiting on the first tee for the group in front of them to get out of range, Tommy remarked to the guys that the names of a lot of golf courses were predictable.

"It's always Deer Ridge, or Fox Run, that kind of thing," he said lightly.

Doug offered, "That's true. Not a lot of imagination."

Elvis was standing on the tee, looking down the fairway with a driver in his hand. "You know, fellas, if I owned this golf course I'd call it the Pike's Arse Golf and Country Club. Now that would be different," Elvis joked, and everyone had a real good laugh.

The name stuck.

The Pike.

CHAPTER TWENTY-FIVE

Elvis got hooked on golf, and now golf and fishing were his passions . . . music was nowhere on the horizon. It was the fall of 1978, and Elvis was in a good place mentally and physically, doing so much better than when he'd first arrived in Antigua. Then he had been a man on the brink of death from his addiction to prescription drugs. Tommy was impressed with Elvis's progress and encouraged his boss at every turn while their friendship got stronger and more intimate.

In Tommy, Elvis found a man who was willing to do what was needed to maintain his anonymity and to protect him from the world outside of Villa Selena and the Antigua islands. And conversely, Elvis was there for Tommy, not only monetarily but spiritually as well. It took the men time to adjust to the many changes and challenges of leaving their homeland and starting a whole new life in a world so very different from where they had come from. Even though they both embraced the move from the States and came to love the islands and the lifestyle, there were still times when they both needed each other for reassurance . . . to believe they had done the right thing.

It was clear to Elvis that his salvation required a complete geographical change as part of the cure for his illness and his escape from his vices. And Tommy knew and appreciated this. But most of the time, both men were content and all was more than all right in the secret, idyllic world of Elvis Presley. It was a blessed life of new friends, new ways and sunny days. *Fish are jumpin' and the cotton is high* . . .

They took the Bertram out a few times a week, usually to fish and occasionally to just cruise around the out islands, sometimes stopping to go for a swim in the warm waters of the southern Atlantic. Sometimes the guys would release the skiff from its ties on the front of the Bertram, using the electric winch to lower it into the water so that they and a few friends could spend the day enjoying the peace and tranquility of one of the island's beaches, far from the hustle and bustle of St. John's.

Although golf took up a good deal of time, Elvis mostly loved to fish, as did Tommy and Normand. Elvis even had a club record at the Antigua Angling Club, which was run by the Royal Antigua Yacht Club in St. John's. On the day Elvis's name went into the record book, as Aaron Smith, of course, he had been on the Bertram, but with neither Tommy nor Normand.

His witness that memorable day was a record holder herself; Elvis had taken *Roberta's Way* on a fishing run to the out islands of St. Angelic with his friend Patricia Everett. It was just the two of them on board the Bertram on the morning they set out. The islands were a couple hours out of St. John's, and the cruiser left home dock just after 6:00 a.m., an unexpected adventure awaiting them on the unpredictable Atlantic Ocean.

*****

Meanwhile, as Elvis was getting his life together and finally enjoying his new freedom, back in the United States, Colonel Parker was in the middle of a self-inflicted shitstorm.

During that first year after Elvis's "death," Parker was having a grand ol' time selling Elvis Presley as if his star act was actually still alive. He made more money in the first year of Elvis's posthumous career than any other single year that he was alive. It would be a few more years before it all came crashing down on Parker, but the legal interventions regarding Elvis's estate and the Colonel's blatant "conflicts of interest" as Presley's manager were well under way. Parker's insatiable greed for money would eventually destroy him. Elvis on the other hand was content with the fortune he had amassed during the "old days" as the undisputed King of Rock and Roll.

When Elvis moved to Antigua, his money followed him. A great sum of American money, more than Elvis would ever spend, was safely out of the United States and out of Parker's greedy clutches. And the money kept coming. This was timely for Elvis because three years after his "death," the courts would squash his ex-manager financially and spiritually, and consequently no further funds would flow through the Colonel and his team of lawyers and accountants to the island of Antigua. But of course, Aaron Smith was a very wealthy man, and personally he didn't really care that the source of money had finally dried up. He was actually relieved that at least that part of the charade was over. There was no longer an active connection between him and America.

Yes, Elvis had all he needed financially and more. His priorities now were golfing, fishing and living a healthy, stress-free lifestyle with his friends. And as it turned out, his last *record* was not made in a recording studio; it was made on the waters off the islands of St. Angelic.

*****

It was on the golf course that Elvis met Trish. Trish was sexy and "salty" at the same time. Salty as in she loved being on the ocean, and fishing was a passion. She was a member of the Royal Antigua Angling Club, where she had registered no fewer than thirteen all-time club fishing records, two of which were *world* records.

When fishing, she usually wore men's shirts, often with the arms cut off at the shoulders. She had a deep, dark tan, the color of polished sandalwood, and she had dirty blonde hair that was often windblown and casually askew. Her *sea legs* were shapely. Everyone knew that Trish cleaned up real good. And if all that wasn't special enough, she had blue eyes to die for, or so Elvis thought.

She was also an excellent golfer. She carried a seven handicap comfortably. A natural athlete.

A few years younger than Elvis, she was a unique person, a fascinating lady, born and raised in Antigua.

Her mother's side of the family was the major liquor distributor on the island. Her father was a retired dentist.

Elvis fell for her during a round of golf. He and his friend Doug had been looking for a game, but the course had an outside tournament that day and was quite busy. The only option that morning was to join Trish Everett and a golfing friend of hers named Linda Sareault or go home. The men were reluctant, but the starter, Rolly, told them both ladies were very good golfers and fun to play with. So they said all right, and the four of them had a great round of golf together.

After nine holes of play, they stopped at the snack bar and each had a hotdog and soda. Elvis sat next to Trish, while Doug went off to speak with another golfer on the tenth tee. Linda had gone off to the washroom.

"You're a very good golfer, ma'am. I wish I had your consistency. I believe you shot a thirty-seven on the front," said Elvis.

"Thank you, Aaron. Too bad about going out of bounds on the five-par fourth." She laughed. "I tried to hit it too damn hard. That hole demands patience. I know that." She smiled at him. "But easier said than done, right?"

"Yeah, it's an unforgiving game." A cliché he had heard many times since taking up the sport.

"That's why we love it. There's no such thing as a perfect game." Her blue eyes remained on Elvis, and he felt a tingling all over. He looked away quickly, hoping he wasn't blushing.

Elvis was very attracted to her, something he'd realized as he watched her swing the golf club on the very first hole. Her shapely body and the smooth, unhurried timing of her fluid swing was . . . sexy. She was wearing a pale-green cotton golf shirt and a white pleated skirt. A green and white visor protected her eyes from the morning sun.

"You've been playing a long time?" Elvis didn't know what else to talk about. He realized he was nervous, and this was a new feeling for him. Since he'd stopped using, he was reverting back to the shy Elvis of old, when he was just a country bumpkin from Tennessee and tongue-tied around pretty women.

"Yes, my dad's a member here. He brought me with him and had me take lessons when I turned eleven. I really enjoyed the game, and I stuck with it."

"I started not that long ago. I'm sure you can tell." He wished he were a better golfer. Elvis had improved greatly since he'd joined the club but was not yet the consistent player he would turn out to be.

"You have a nice swing, Aaron. You're doing well for being at it only a short time. Don't give up on it. Just take a break if it starts to get overwhelming. You'll enjoy the game more, I believe," she offered warmly. There was no hint of the ego that Elvis noticed from some of the better golfers when they gave him advice on how to play.

"How do you like the island life? Your American accent is hard to miss. Have you lived here long? Rolly mentioned you were a member here."

Elvis was happy that she cared to know how he felt. Or perhaps it was just polite conversation. He hoped it was the former.

"I love it here, Trish. It feels like my home now."

"You don't miss living in the U.S.?"

"No, not really. There are a few things I miss, but not enough to ever move back." He was starting to feel a bit uneasy with the direction of the conversation. He often thought about his daughter, Lisa Marie, and his dad, and it was still a very emotional subject that he hadn't completely come to terms with.

"Are you from here?" He wanted to talk about her.

"Yes, born and raised. No plans of ever leaving either, which I guess is obvious. A person my age would have left long ago if they wanted to live somewhere else. No, I would miss the lifestyle here. It's laid back on the island and I like that. I love to fish and there's no better fishing anywhere as far as I'm concerned. But I'm biased, I suppose."

"Do you have any brothers or sisters?"

"No. I wish I did. Growing up a single child is not nearly as much fun, I don't think. My dad was wanting a son but it never happened . . . which explains why I'm such a tomboy." She laughed at this. Elvis liked her throaty laugh a lot.

"A tomboy?"

"Yeah. Dad took me fishing and had me baiting my own hooks longer back than I can truthfully remember. I was swimming by the time I was four. I can remember diving with him, my arms around his shoulders, holding my breath while he dove for conch in the shallows off the out islands. And of course he introduced me to golf. Speaking of which, I believe we're up, Aaron."

Linda and Doug were on the tee, and Doug was waving for them to get their asses in gear and join them before they lost their spot.

For the rest of the round, Elvis's thoughts were more on Trish than on golf. Everyone had a nice time, and then it was over—all too soon, as far as Elvis was concerned.

After the game, they all walked to the parking lot. They decided not to go to the clubhouse lounge for a drink afterward because of the tournament. It would be too busy and too noisy.

When Elvis said goodbye to Trish, he asked if she would like to play another round sometime.

"That would be nice, Aaron. Sure. You can get my home number from the members directory. Call me and we'll do it again."

Patricia Everett was all Elvis could think about for the rest of the day . . . and then some.

They had played golf together on a Monday, and on Wednesday he called to invite her to go fishing on his boat. He suggested a day trip to the out islands. She readily accepted the invitation, and it was arranged for that Friday morning. She wanted to know what she should bring along, but he told her he had everything they would need and not to worry.

"Just bring yourself and we're good to go," he said.

"I'll bring a couple of my own rods and some gear that I'll want to use . . . no offense," she said sweetly over the phone.

"None taken, Trish. I'd be surprised if you didn't want to use your own gear." *This lady can fish*, thought Elvis. It was going to be a great day, even if they caught nothing at all. Fish was not the real catch he was hoping for anyway, he realized.

Friday morning at 6:00 a.m. they met at the dock where *Roberta's Way* was berthed. Elvis was waiting on the boat when Trish arrived, and he waved as she approached. She had two rods clasped in one hand along with a tote bag and a medium-sized tackle box in the other.

"Good morning, Trish. Let me help you with those things."

"Here, I'll just come on board with this. I can manage." Trish was no stranger to taking care of herself. She crossed over the short gangplank onto the boat. Elvis held her arm as she stepped on board while relieving her of the red tackle box. He noticed it had some weight to it.

"This is a very nice Bertram, Mr. Smith. I'm quite looking forward to this, you know." She gave him a big grin. Her short hair was mostly covered by a red cap frayed along the edges, with the word *Mercury* embroidered across the front in silver.

"You and I both, so let's get outta here, shall we?"

"Aye aye, Captain."

She sat next to Elvis in the flybridge holding a lit

cigarette between her first and second fingers. A large plastic glass filled with ice and Coke sat in the cup holder on her side of the console.

The trip to St. Angelic went smoothly, and the time passed comfortably for both of them. They enjoyed the weather and talked about fishing all the way there.

As they approached the string of five small out islands collectively called the St. Angelic Islands, Elvis slowed the Bertram to a crawl and they surveyed the sights. They were alone.

"My, it's lovely here . . . so peaceful. Not a soul around but us this morning. We've got all the fish to ourselves."

"Yes, we do, Trish," agreed Elvis.

"You wanna cast or what do you have in mind?"

"What say we troll for a while? We'll try for anything that's out there. We got that fresh squid. Let's bait a few lines and see who's hungry this fine morning."

"Sounds good, Captain."

Trish scampered down the ladder and went to the bait box, where there was a collection of fresh bait. She took out the clear bag of squid that Tommy had purchased the day before and put on ice overnight. He had driven Elvis to the dock that morning to help prepare the boat for the run and then taken off, leaving Elvis to it.

Trish selected two squid and then chose two of the four rods that were ready and in position. She baited two hooks (she refused Elvis's offer to help) and

placed a rod on either side of the boat, using the out-
riggers so she was free to move about or to sit while
they waited for a strike. She let out the right amount
of line on each rod and adjusted the tension on the
reels. Then she wiped her hands on her jeans and
shouted up to Elvis, who now had the boat barely
moving across the calm waters, "All set, Aaron. Let's
fish!"

"You go it!" Elvis increased the speed on the twin
diesels until he reached the perfect trolling speed and
then sat back in his captain's chair, waiting to hear
Trish call out from below, "*Fish on!*"

As the morning went on, they caught a nice variety
of fish. Neither of them wanted to go out to the deep
water where the "big boys" were. If, for example, they
got a large marlin on, it would be much more than
the two of them wanted to deal with, so they stayed
closer to the islands, trolling back and forth and
catching all the fish they wanted. Elvis manned the
bridge most of the time, but Trish took over the controls while Elvis went below and had a turn fishing . .
. they were a good team. Together they caught several nice king mackerel, which are great eating so they
kept those. They landed two good-sized pompanos
and a few bonitos and some other fish. A few fish got
away, and they released others for various reasons. By
noon they had plenty of fish and were getting hungry
themselves.

Lunch was sandwiches the girls at the villa had
made at Elvis's request. They ate down in the galley with the air conditioner on. The weather was still

nice, and the boat sat perfectly still in the water about three hundred yards off shore of the largest of the St. Angelic Islands.

"This has been nice, Aaron. Thank you for inviting me." Trish was eating a ham and cheese sandwich and drinking a cola from a tall plastic tumbler.

"Yes, it has. I was thinking we try for some snappers and some jacks after lunch and maybe get us a nice grouper. I love grouper."

"Absolutely, Aaron. I'd like that."

After they ate and cleaned up, they brought up the anchor and slowly guided *Roberta's Way* to an area of water in the lee of one of the smaller islands, where they felt it would be a good spot to fish. Elvis re-anchored the cruiser, and they baited up and started casting from the boat.

The fishing was excellent, and they soon had a respectable number of yellow jacks and snappers and a few other assorted fish. Trish had caught the only grouper, but it was a small one, so she released it.

They felt the change in the weather about ninety minutes after their first cast following their lunch together. It started with a north breeze. Not a strong one, but it was noticeable, and between the tide and the breeze picking up, the bow was pointed due north, as if looking for trouble.

Trish noticed first.

"We'll need to keep an eye out, Aaron. There might be something up north that could turn into something unpleasant. It doesn't look like anything to worry about now, but you never know."

Elvis saw it too and agreed with Trish. They would have to monitor the weather.

Fifty minutes later, Elvis got a strike. It was a barracuda. Fish on! It was at this very moment that the wind picked up and the temperature dropped several degrees. The sky in the north was now dark, and storm clouds were forming and appeared to be coming their way.

At first Elvis was excited at the weight of the fish on his line, but then he realized it was a barracuda and said to Trish, "It's a damn 'cuda! Pass me the knife. I'm gonna cut the line."

"You're sure you wanna cut your line?"

"He'll break it anyway, Trish."

Trish came over to his side of the boat to have a look. She caught sight of the fish that had swallowed Elvis's bait. It was about twenty feet from the boat, arrogantly doing a lazy swim, not yet trying to fight.

"What size line you using, Aaron?"

"Six pound, I think. Why?" He looked at her.

"That's a lot of fish for a six-pound line. But if you can land that fish with that line, you might have a new record on your hands. That guy looks to be about forty pounds, maybe."

"Really?"

"I have several records with the angling club, and to me this looks like it could be a record. If you can get it in the boat, so we can measure and weigh the damn thing, we'll know. What were you trying to catch with that light a line?"

"I saw a school of small jacks."

The 'cuda decided he'd had enough of whatever was in his mouth and tried to shake it free, but the line was still there as the bait and hook were deep in its long, torpedo-like body. It ran, jumped and stopped again, then swam slowly, aimlessly, and then it would feel the line and bolt again. This kept up for a while.

Elvis was now *playing* the fish, letting him run and then, when the fish came about, carefully reeling in some of the slack line. Setting the drag on the reel was the key . . . that and patience. If he tried to force the fish to the boat, the line would snap. It would probably break anyway, either from the sheer force of the fish running and jumping or because of the long, sharp, ugly row of teeth in its large mouth.

The clouds were now rolling in over the St. Angelic Islands, and the sky overhead was an ominous gray-purple. The barometric pressure was dropping quickly. The air was starting to smell of the impending weather conditions. Rain was on the way.

"Uh oh. I see a waterspout off to the left, Aaron. We might need to get out of here real soon," warned Trish.

Elvis was now intent on getting this large barracuda into the boat. He heard Trish but didn't answer.

"OK, play him easy, then. We have some time yet."

Trish grew up on the ocean and was not easily scared but was always respectful. Her dad had taught her well.

The barracuda was near the boat.

"I'll get the gaff, Aaron. Bring him in slowly." It was then that the fish took off like a freight train, straight away. The six-pound filament line was leaving the spool fast, making the reel sing out a high-pitched *whizzing* sound. If the 'cuda went too far, the line would run out and simply break at the reel, and Elvis knew this.

But the fish went down and around to the left and then swam back toward the boat in a wide arch. It slowed down and Elvis reeled in some line.

Meanwhile the wind had died down a bit, but the atmosphere was getting heavier and the humidity was thick. The purple-gray sky overhead cast an eerie glow.

"Aaron, there are now two spouts and they're big."

Elvis looked up and around him. He saw the water-spouts. *Water devils.* They looked like tornadoes, and they both went from the surface of the water up and into the sullen cumulus clouds, now low and menacing.

"Shit. I'm gonna try once more to get this thing in the boat." With that Elvis started turning the reel handle while tightening the drag a bit. He held the rod in his left hand and was turning the handle and setting the drag with his right.

"Come on, come on, you're tired old boy, come in

close."

Trish was standing next to Elvis, trying not to get in the way but ready to gaff the fish so they could toss it in the boat and get out of there.

But the fish got his wind back and took off again. Not as fast or as far this time. It was getting tired.

"Aaron, we gotta go. Like, now."

"Let me try again. He's getting tired."

"Aaron, there's a third spout and it's really close!"

Elvis started reeling, trying not to go too fast, but he understood that now they were in danger.

"That's it, Aaron, you have to bring him in right now or cut the line. Time's up."

"OK."

Elvis tightened the drag considerably and started reeling. Trish came in close, glancing at the three water devils and then back to where Elvis's line disappeared into the water, ready to strike with the gaff if the barracuda came near. The ocean reflected the dark color of the sky, and it was getting harder to see the fish clearly in the inky water.

"Here we go." Elvis started reeling in earnest now, and the six-pound test line was taut and ready to snap . . . but it didn't. Elvis kept the line coming in, smooth and steady.

"He's almost here, Aaron."

The fish now swam toward the boat, confused and tired. Then the long silver and black form, its large jagged teeth clearly visible and the fishing line disappearing into the dark cavern of its cruel mouth, was alongside the boat. The ten-foot gaff struck with surprising force, down and then back, embedding one of the two six-inch steel barbed hooks into the creature's flesh as Trish pulled back hard to set the barb.

Elvis quickly put down the rod and grabbed the long gaff with both hands, and together they brought the barracuda up high over the side of the boat, slamming it hard to the deck, where it flopped once and lay still.

"We did it!" Trish gave Elvis a big hug. "Now let's get the hell out of here."

"I heard that." He also felt *that* . . . the hug. It felt real good.

Elvis shot up the ladder to the flybridge. Trish followed him after quickly placing all rods flat on the floor of the boat. There would be time to clean and stow everything later. The barracuda was left were it lay slowly suffocating. Trish remembered the 'cuda and hesitated halfway up the chrome ladder. She looked back at the dying fish and paused for a moment, then went back down the ladder and made her way to her own tackle box.

"What are you doing, Trish?" She had been beside him one second and gone the next.

"I'm gonna weigh this fish and take a picture of it."

"What . . . now?"

"Yes. This bruiser doesn't have to die like this . . . needlessly." With that she pulled a hand scale out of the tackle box, carefully placed the scale's hook in the barracuda's mouth and lifted it off the floor with two hands.

"Thirty-eight pounds, seven ounces. Excellent, Aaron!" she shouted. The anchor was up and the engines caught instantly. Elvis moved the throttles forward, and the twin diesels started to propel the boat steadily through the choppy waves.

With the boat heading in the direction of home, Elvis took a glance over his shoulder and saw Trish measuring and recording the length of the fish. Then she grabbed a camera from her tote bag and took a picture before finally taking a pair of wire cutters from her tackle box. She cut the fishing line at the 'cuda's jawline and then lifted their scaly, weakened prize by the tail, carefully lifting it over the side of the boat and letting go.

"Good luck," she said as the barracuda disappeared into the dark water.

They headed home.

*****

Roberta's Way carried Elvis and Trish to safety, and within two hours of leaving the troubled area off the islands of St. Angelic, she was moored back at her spot at Reiner's Marina in St. John's. All the way back to port they talked about their first fishing day. They were enjoying the time together.

After the boat was tied up, they removed all the fish from the boat and placed their gear on a wood and metal trolley that was left at the dock for members to transport items back to their vehicles. The fish they would take to an area that had large wooden tables used for gutting and dressing the day's catch. But before the fish were prepared for transporting home, they cleaned up the boat.

"What a blast!" exclaimed Elvis as he ran a water hose over the hull of the Bertram. He was talking about the fishing and the bad weather, but he was also referring to being embraced by Trish. He wanted a lot more of that.

Trish was mopping up the deck. *She's quite the woman*, thought Elvis as he watched her work on the boat. He thought about how she had gaffed that nasty barracuda, and then after she had recorded the size, length and weight, she had tried to save its life.

He pictured her, fearless of the storm but respect-ful, helping him through his first intense foul-weather experience at sea. They acted as a team that day, and that really impressed Elvis.

Together they washed and scrubbed the cruiser until it was shiny and clean again.

*****

"You're very good at this, Trish." Elvis was in awe of Trish's technique at gutting, scaling and dressing the fish they had caught. In her right hand she held a sharp fillet knife that she had fine sharpened on a honing stone at the cleaning station. She held the fish with her left hand. First she removed the gills and the guts and swept them off the large table into a garbage bag fastened next to the cutting table. Then she scaled the fish, tossing the mixture of scales and salt in the garbage. Next she filleted them expertly, careful not to waste any meat by cutting too deep or too thin.

"Thank you. Now watch and learn, sir," she said with a smile. Her hands were a mess of blood and guts, but she didn't care one bit. "Why don't you grab a knife from that drawer and one of the fish, and watch and do as I do?" she suggested.

"No, thanks. Next time. I'll just watch for now, if you don't mind." Elvis was tired and lazy now.

"No problem." And she went at it while Elvis watched her work.

Elvis was thinking that he knew little about Trish. No personal stuff. They had chatted on the trip to St. Angelic, but mostly about fishing. They talked golf a bit and about Antigua in general, and the time passed quickly. There was no personal information shared. That was just dandy with Elvis as he was always careful with strangers and new acquaintances, for obvious reasons, but now he was intrigued and wanted to know more about the person he'd spent the day with.

He wanted to ask if her parents were still living, but that could lead to trouble, so he asked her if she worked.

"It seems funny that after our golf game, and after our time together today, that I don't know what you do . . . you know, if you work?" He assumed she must work somewhere.

"Do you work, Aaron?" she answered his query with one of her own.

"Uh, no. I'm retired."

"Me too," she replied as she ripped the kidneys from a red snapper. She placed the snapper with the rest of the clean catch and picked up another and gutted it.

"Really? That's nice, Trish. Good for you." He was delighted to hear she wasn't tied down with a job and a boss, five days a week. She had *means* . . . that was excellent news.

"You sound surprised." She gave him a quick look of amusement. "It's OK, Aaron, I'm joking with you. Of course you would think I worked. I'm not sixty-five or anything. I hope I don't look it." She laughed at Elvis. "You're blushing, Aaron."

Elvis *was* blushing.

"It's OK, Aaron. I know exactly what you mean, and I'm flattered that you care enough to ask." She smiled.

"I like you, Trish, and I'm interesting in getting to know you better." There. He had said it. There was a time when one could say *he ain't nothin' but a hound dog* . . . but that was another lifetime ago. Now he was bashful and unsure, like the teenager he had been back in Tennessee.

"And I like you too. There, all finished. Let me clean up and we'll be good to go." Trish headed for one of the nearby changing stalls reserved for members of Reiner's Marina and their friends.

Elvis went to the cooler and started loading in the fish. "I'll make two piles: one for you to take home with you, Trish, and one for me. OK?" he called out.

She called back, "No, thanks, you take them all, Aaron. We have a freezer full of fish at home."

We? Who's we? thought Elvis, his stomach suddenly feeling queasy.

"OK," Elvis answered, but not as loud this time.

She added, "Dad brings home so much fish that we can't eat it all. We end up giving a lot away."

Elvis's stomach felt fine all of a sudden. "You live with your parents?"

Trish came out of the stall, wearing clean clothes and looking great. *She sure cleans up good.*

She went up to Elvis and said quietly, "No, just my dad. My mother died when I was young."

Elvis instantly thought of his own dead mother.

"Oh, I'm so sorry to hear your mom died young, Trish. That must have been tough."

"Yes, it was, Aaron." She shrugged and then picked up her tote bag. "Shall we go, then?"

"Yeah, let's go. It's been a long day."

Elvis grabbed the cooler of fish and another bag with his stuff, and they walked to the parking lot where Trish had left her Ford Bronco.

*****

Trish insisted on driving the Bronco, although Elvis had offered to drive.

"I have a good general idea where we're going, Aaron, but I'll rely on you not to let me get us lost in the back hills of St. John's."

Elvis was surprised. He would have guessed that Trish knew every square inch of the island.

"Where I live is not exactly in the boondocks," he replied lightly. He was anxious to get to the villa. He was excited for Normand and Tommy to meet Trish and for Trish to see Villa Selena.

"I know, I was just kidding. I know the area well, and your house is amazing. I've never been on the property, though." She turned her face toward him and smiled. "My dad was there once when he was still practicing."

"Really? What was he doing there?"

"He got a call from a friend of his who was visiting the house one night. The host, a movie producer or something, had a bad toothache, and Dad's friend asked him to come out to see what he could do to help the guy. It was at night, I remember."

"Your dad's a dentist?"

"Not anymore. He retired young."

"I thought he was a fisherman for some reason." Elvis laughed. "The way you described his passion for fishing and all."

Trish decided to fill Aaron in on a few more details of her life.

"Dad has fished all his life. It's his real joy. His parents wanted him to become a white-collar professional, and so Dad decided to become a dentist and then regretted it. He often said he was an outdoorsman and wished he had become a fisherman or had started a boat charter company or something instead of spending so much of his life in an office. After he was established professionally, my dad would leave work at noon on Fridays to go fishing, and then after a while, he didn't work on Fridays at all. He's retired now and fishes mostly, and he manages to play golf a few times a week these days as well. And he's very happy."

Elvis nodded in Trish's direction as the blue Bronco approached a lazy bend in the road. The ocean lay off to the right, hazy now and stretching out as far as the eye could see. The sun would start its decent soon.

"We're close now, Trish, just after the next bend, second driveway on the right. The one with the large gates, but they'll be open. I called ahead from the marina and they're expecting us.

Trish paid her first visit to the villa that day, where she met Normand and the rest of the staff and felt welcomed by all. In a way, she never really left the villa until many years later, when there was no longer a reason for her to come by.

CHAPTER TWENTY-SIX

Almost two years after Aaron moved to Antigua, Normand heard that Vernon Presley, father of Elvis Presley and the last member of Elvis's immediate family, had died. Normand heard the special news update on Island Radio-Antigua just after he got out of bed that morning. He always listened to the radio in the morning as he prepared for the day, enjoying a local station that played a variety of music in different styles, interspersed with news items on the hour and half hour. That morning there was a special announcement that was repeated several times, starting with the 7:00 a.m. news update. At that time he had no idea that Aaron Smith was Vernon Presley's son, Elvis.

Elvis was told of his father's death by Colonel Parker, who called him from the United States on Elvis's private line at the villa. Elvis sat quietly at his Louis XII–style desk as Parker explained the details of his father's passing. When Parker had finished saying all he had to say, Elvis thanked him solemnly before hanging up the receiver.

Elvis was stunned and remained seated, digesting the news without showing any outward emotion, his thoughts deep and troubled.

He and his father had been close most of Elvis's life, and his leaving the States, with his father and his daughter believing he was dead, caused him pain like no other. So many times over the last twenty-two months he had considered calling his father and telling him the truth, perhaps even convincing his father to leave Tennessee and join him at the villa. But he never did. He believed his father would spill the beans, and the public would soon discover that he was still alive and where he was living, and that was a chance he was not willing to take.

No, the secret had to remain a secret. There was no other way. His father and his daughter must never know. These circumstances were, without question, the hardest part of his existence, and he believed there was nothing he could do about it. He prayed to God for guidance, and despite all the guilt and remorse and soul searching, he remained convinced that his ultimate decision to stay "deceased" was the correct one.

Now learning that his father had died not knowing the truth, and feeling the pain of not being there at his father's side at the end, had set off a whole new wave of emotions. And he was carried away to places he had never explored emotionally. Most people who knew the *old* Elvis would think it strange that he didn't break down like he had when his mother passed away during his military service days years before, but there were no tears . . . he was just very sad and numb. The tears would come later.

The thought of drinking alcohol to ease the pain he was feeling was dismissed as quickly as he considered it. He had come too far in his sobriety to "fall off the wagon," knowing he would end up in a far worse place than he was now. He understood his addiction enough to realize and admit that one drink would lead to another. *One drink was too many and 100 not enough.*

Besides, he knew that getting drunk would not bring his father back, and so he wisely abstained.

Elvis didn't go down for breakfast that morning. Instead, he sat at his desk and recalled memories from days long past. He was brought out of his thoughts by a gentle tapping on his bedroom door. It was Tommy. He had heard from Normand that Vernon had died—Normand had casually mentioned the news, not realizing it's great significance. Tommy wanted to check to see if his boss knew, and if so, if he was all right. At first he had waited for Elvis to join him for breakfast, but as time passed, he felt that looking in on him was the right thing to do.

"Who is it?" Elvis said without looking up.

"It's me, Boss. You OK?"

There was no answer.

"E, there's something you should know. It's important." Elvis realized it was Tommy and that Tommy *knew* about his father's death, but he didn't want any company.

"It's OK, Tommy. I got a call from the Colonel." His voice was thick, so he cleared his throat before continuing, wishing he had some water. "I'll be fine. I'll be out later. And thanks."

Tommy crept away from the door, knowing a reply

wasn't needed. It was best to just let Elvis be.

CHAPTER TWENTY-SEVEN

As majordomo at Villa Selena, Normand had become indispensable to Elvis. There was precious little that went on in the house that he did not know about. Nothing that escaped his tireless attention. His efficiency and pleasant manner were appreciated by everyone under his supervision. Normand's duties eventually expanded to managing most of Elvis's personal affairs as well. Everything was directed Normand's way, from scheduling a doctor's appointment to a tee-off time at the Pike.

Elvis was grateful to Normand and acknowledged his worth with encouragement and generosity. And so because of the nature of some of the business Normand helped Elvis with, the two men spent a lot of time together. Their relationship grew more personal, and consequently, they became good friends.

Tommy and Normand also became close over the years, ganging up on their boss whenever possible . . . all in good fun. On the golf course it was often Tommy and the Major teamed against Elvis and his partner on that particular day. It gave them great pleasure to relieve their boss of a few dollars and to earn bragging rights in a two-dollar skins game.

As the years passed, Elvis, Tommy and Normand shared many good times together. They had a camaraderie that was real, based on mutual respect.

As happens in life, there were a few bad times along the way as well. Once Elvis had severe chest pains, and an ambulance took him to the hospital in St. John's, where Tommy and Normand spent several hours in emergency worried that their boss and dear friend might be dying of a heart attack. They were finally relieved to hear that it was a gastric problem. Although it was painful and scary, a generous dose of an anti-acid medication calmed the irritation and Elvis was released. He went home feeling embarrassed and apologetic.

"Must have been those damn cabbage rolls Bea made last night, boys!"

The boys just smiled at each other, happy to be out of the hospital, with their friend healthy and full of good-natured "piss and vinegar."

In 1995 Normand's father died unexpectedly. He had been hit by a delivery truck in the center of downtown St. John's and killed instantly. Elvis and Tommy both attended the funeral and were pallbearers along with Normand, his brother and two family friends. After the funeral, Elvis and Tommy returned to the villa while Normand went with his immediate family to his mother's house, where she would now be living alone. The house had been his parents' home for more than forty years. Normand's family was a close, caring family, and they were devastated by the loss of the head of the household. Normand offered to move in with his mother, but she kindly refused, insisting that he remain where he'd lived and worked for so many years. And so Normand returned to the villa.

His home.

Life for Elvis was nearly perfect in his "retirement." With his health good and his friends close, he felt blessed and grateful. He still sometimes thought about his daughter, Lisa Marie. He'd long ago accepted the fact that he would never see or speak with her again. But he knew the estate was taking care of her financial needs, and her mother was there for her emotionally. As the decades passed, that somehow made it possible for him to carry on. Tommy never brought up the past, and for that his boss was thankful.

*****

Less than a year after turning pro, Tiger Woods was already famous. He had been touted as golf's latest savior. And the world was watching—with great expectations.

A child protégé, Woods had a spectacular foundation in golf. His talent was carefully honed by his father and various golf coaches all his young life, and by the time he stood on the tee for his PGA debut—in August of 1996 at the Greater Milwaukee Open—he appeared ready to take the world by storm.

And that he did. Although Tiger didn't win that first event, he went on to win twice that year, registering the first win of his career at the Las Vegas International in October. He was named Rookie of the Year for 1996. And in April of 1997, he teed off at his first

Masters tournament in Augusta, Georgia.

Elvis watched from Villa Selena, as curious as the next guy in the room, if not more so. Elvis had now been playing golf for almost twenty years, and he was excited to watch the coverage of any major golf tournament, especially the Masters. He was mesmerized by this young, charismatic black man who many expected to inherit the title of golf's new king. *Times they were a-changin'*. Palmer and Nicklaus, move over!

*****

Normand's relationship with Aaron grew more intimate as the years rolled along. It evolved, was redefined and was strengthened over time. All through those years, Elvis remained Aaron Smith to all at Villa Selena but Tommy. Normand would not find out the truth until 1997, the year Tiger Woods won his first Masters in Augusta.

The 61st Masters championship took place from April 10 to 13, and Tiger Woods was set to play in his first major tournament. Tommy and his girlfriend, Shawna, were already sitting comfortably in front of the television, working on a couple of cold St. Pauli Girls. Even Normand had joined in and was enjoying a mango monkey, a mixture of peach water, cranberry juice and banana with an ounce of white rum and crushed ice mixed in a blender until smooth. He was comfortably perched on a high-back wicker chair facing the screen. Bob Royce was there with his wife, Alicia.

"What's your poison, Trish?" Elvis stood at the bar. The broadcast was just starting.

"Bacardi and Coke, if you have it, please. Need some help, Aaron?"

"Sure, honey, you can get some fresh ice for me."

Elvis prepared Trish's drink. He was still not drinking alcohol so his own "choice of poison" was a cold Coke straight from the bottle.

"Let the games begin!" shouted Bob. Elvis and Trish sat down next to Bob and Alicia at a long mahogany table, upon which Lucinda had set out a variety of snacks. Geraldine no longer worked at the villa; she was now married with four children and happy, as far as Normand knew. Bea had retired a dozen years earlier and was well into her eighties. In the last few years of her employment, she mainly sat in the kitchen and bossed around the young'uns.

"Hey, Bobby, where's the smart money?" asked Elvis although there was really no need to. His southern drawl always present.

"I'm thinking Tiger Woods," replied Bob.

There was a buzz about Woods, no doubt.

"Yes, I'm thinking Tiger too," Normand chimed in.

Tiger started off shooting a lackluster round of 40 on the front and 30 on the back, for a two-under-par 70—three strokes off the pace.

"Well, it's only the first round; lots of golf left." Tommy was a Tiger fan all the way.

Everybody would be happy to see Tiger win. To

witness sports history being made that weekend would be a wonderful thing. The excitement was contagious.

"I like Freddy Couples," said Alicia. "He's cute."

Yeah, everybody loved laid-back Freddy "Boom Boom" Couples. He was a terrific golfer with a smooth but very powerful swing. Always a contender, Fred was also in the mix at the end of day one.

"Wouldn't it be cool to see Nicklaus win one more time?" This from Trish, who often favored the underdogs in this world. Although it was hard to think of the Golden Bear as an underdog. His win in 1986 is still considered one of the most popular wins ever.

Elvis took a pull from his Coke bottle and then stated the obvious, "I wanna see the colored feller win this shooting contest. He'd be the first man of color to win this thing." Elvis's roots were still embedded in the Deep South, where blacks were still referred to as colored folk by some. He was just a redneck deep down and meant no offence. He was a big fan of Tiger Woods and hoped to see the young man make history on Sunday afternoon.

Of course, that was the big story that year. Would Woods be the first African American to win the Masters?

"I'd keep an eye on Tolles. He could be the sleeper here," offered Bob.

"Tiger," countered Alicia. Needless to say, she and millions of others wanted Tiger to win.

On day two, the weather was perfect and so was

Tiger's golf. At the end of round two, he was leading the tournament and Colin Montgomerie by three.

To say that this was incredibly exciting is to obviously underplay the significance of the moment. Were they witnessing history in the making? Most believed so.

At the end of Saturday, day three, Tiger finished nine strokes ahead of the field. They may as well have started engraving his name on the trophy.

On Sunday, April 13, Eldrick "Tiger" Woods claimed the 1997 Masters championship with an unbelievable 270, 18 under par!

Elvis was lost for words. As everyone with him that day jumped up and down, high-fiving in celebration of a remarkable feat, Elvis sat quiet and still, bereft of speech.

As a southerner, Elvis regarded Tiger's win as especially significant. All the memories of the prejudice he had seen firsthand toward blacks during his travels on the road flooded back to him. Christ, he hated that bigotry. It still stuck in his craw all this time later. Here was a black kid showing all the rich, pompous whites that he, Tiger Woods, was the Master over all others in the field, donning the coveted green jacket and kissing the trophy.

When the celebrating was done and his friends had gone home, Elvis sat in the den and reflected on what happened that day.

How was Tiger really feeling about all this? How would this young, single, good-looking champion handle all the pressure and the trappings that went with winning the most prestigious tournament in golf? Elvis had found himself in a similar situation when he took the world of rock and roll and shook it by the tail, declaring, "I'm the new king. I'm the future of rock and roll." He had become the most famous face in the civilized world almost overnight. He had it all. The youth, the fame, the money, and millions of woman at his fingertips. He experienced the trappings that sudden success brings, and finally he was a victim of it all. And it nearly killed him.

What was Tiger thinking about all this fame and fortune?

Elvis decided he'd ask Tiger himself.

CHAPTER TWENTY-EIGHT

Colonel Parker was very busy after fake Elvis died in the crapper at Graceland, with legal hassles in particular. Most of the beefs concerned Elvis Presley's estate as Parker tried to control the many millions that continued to roll in. He not only tried to get more of that fortune for himself but also worked hard to keep what he already had. As Elvis's manager, he took a management fee, of course. But in most people's opinion, his 50 percent share of the whole enchilada was too much and yet typical of Parker.

Colonel Parker's whole life had been centered around the quest for the almighty dollar. From Holland originally, he was never in the military, as he suggested, and certainly never a real colonel; he was in fact an unsophisticated character of dubious integrity . . . a con artist and rapscallion! Certainly smart enough to take a relatively innocent upstart like Elvis Presley and not only polish and promote him but also exploit him to the point of conflict of interest.

From the time of Elvis's "death" in 1977 until Parker's death in 1997, the discreet phone calls between the two of them had been amazingly few and always brief. Parker was able to set up a system whereby Elvis's share of revenue from past and more recent enterprises was simply directed to Aaron Smith's offshore accounts. With legal and accounting firms in compliance, things ran smoothly, so there was no reason for Elvis and Parker to be talking much. This arrangement suited them both fine.

Back in 1977, Elvis had the Colonel appoint a "second" to replace him and to handle the basic business of transferring funds, in case something happened to him. Protocol would continue to be carried out regardless. The replacement's name was Ralph Patrick. The day after Woods won his first Masters tournament, Elvis called Patrick.

"Ralph Patrick's office. How may I assist you?"

"Aaron Smith here. I'd like to speak with Ralph."

"Yes, sir, let me check if he's available. One moment please," Patrick's receptionist said. The line went quiet.

It took only a few seconds for Ralph to come on the line. "Aaron, how are things in Antigua?"

"Fine, sir."

Aaron Smith's good ol' boy courtesy didn't fool the lawyer. Smith was a no-bullshit client.

"It was a real shame losing the Colonel like that," Patrick said, although he didn't mean a word of it. Parker's passing meant a sizable increase in Patrick's income after he'd taken control of Aaron Smith's affairs. "Heart attack; sudden, really. I hear his wife found him. Still, he was up there. Eighty-seven, wasn't he?"

Elvis wanted to interrupt but waited until Ralph Patrick had finished.

Parker's wife had indeed found her husband, not dead but unconscious after having a stroke. He died the next day.

"Yes, sir. A shame." Elvis didn't want to correct him on the details; he wanted to get down to the matter at hand.

"Ralph, I need you to help me with something."

"How can I be of service, Aaron?"

"Do you know who Tiger Woods is?" He waited.

Laughing, Ralph Patrick replied, "Yes, of course I've heard of him, Aaron. You a golfer? Although you don't have to be a golfer to know who Tiger Woods is, right? Why do you ask?"

"I wanna meet him."

"You wanna meet him? Well, there are probably millions who would like to meet Tiger, especially now after winning the Masters yesterday. Everybody wants to meet Tiger Woods! He's so hot right now, Aaron, the president might have trouble getting a game with him!"

Patrick chuckled at his own joke until he realized Aaron Smith wasn't laughing with him. He cleared his throat and continued.

"If you wanna meet him, maybe we can try to get you in a Wednesday celebrity practice round with him, as a playing partner. Sometimes the pro may join you and your group for a hole or two, and then move on to the next lucky players who dished out, oh, say . . . $20,000 apiece for bragging rights. You want I try that?"

"No, I'm thinking he might come here to spend a day or two with me." Elvis waited for a reply with a smile on his face. The guy had no idea what was coming.

"What?"

"Listen, contact his management team and make them an offer to fly Tiger to Antigua for eighteen holes of golf. First class, all expenses paid. Accommodations will be taken care of, along with all food and drink, of course. He can stay at the main house at Villa Selena, or the guest house, or if he prefers, he can stay at a hotel of his choosing. Being a handsome young man, he may wanna bring a lady with him. No problem. He will be required to play eighteen holes only, and tell them that our group would just be the two of us and a caddie. The caddie works for me and is knowledgeable and discreet. The course is the Antigua Golf and Country Club, where many local natives are members; therefore the color of his skin will not make him stand out, especially if he's golfing in shorts and wearing relaxed golfing attire and so on. He'll never be recognized."

Elvis continued, "No one would ever expect to see Tiger Woods on their golf course. His anonymity is guaranteed. Tell them he will be met at the airport and driven straight to my estate or a hotel, whatever's his preference. There will be no press whatsoever. I even promise that not one picture will be taken. It will be like it never happened. No one but Tiger, me and the caddie will ever know that he was even here."

Elvis paused for effect. "Questions?"

"You're serious, aren't you? I mean, you've given this some thought, Aaron. But why would you want to do all this—the planning, the costs, everything. Do you really think he'll say yes?"

"Can't hurt to ask, can it?"

"No, I guess not. Anything else?" He sounded incredulous still.

"Yes. Tell his agents I'll pay a fee of $1,000,000."

The fact that Tiger was intelligent worked in Elvis's favor. The last thing a terrorist negotiator needs is a *stupido* on the other end of the phone line. You have to know when the price is right.

It's a fact that Tiger was, and still is, constantly besieged by the press and the paparazzi, so this opportunity offered a discreet getaway with a friend: an all-expense-paid escape to an exotic Caribbean island, and guaranteed anonymity to boot. The plan must have some appeal to it. Just getting a break from his superstar life must put some serious enticement value in Elvis's favor.

Furthermore, it was well known that Tiger took some time off after every major, which worked out perfectly. Add another check mark to the plus column for Elvis.

Speaking of checks, throw in a check for one million dollars, and you just might have yourself a ball game!

Elvis spoke to Ralph Patrick on Monday; the call back from Tiger's people came on Wednesday.

Tiger Woods was going to tee it up with Elvis Presley!

CHAPTER TWENTY-NINE

Earl Woods, Tiger's father, had been having health problems since the mid-'80s. Woods senior had undergone quadruple bypass surgery years before, and he suffered a minor heart attack in October of 1996.

This experience led to surgery and a long road to recovery. There were complications that caused a lot of pain—physical for father and emotional for son. So when Tiger was closing the deal in Augusta, his father was present but feeling poorly, and his well-being had been in question. It was through sheer willpower and his desire to be there when his son won the championship that Earl Woods was able to postpone further surgeries until the event was over.

All these were contributing factors that influenced Tiger's decision to accept Elvis's invitation to Antigua.

Tiger could use a break after winning the Masters and before his father's upcoming surgery and his next scheduled tournament, the Byron Nelson Classic in May.

Because of the time frame involved in Earl's scheduled heart operation, Tiger could go to Antigua the following week, get some rest, and be back several days before his father went under the knife again. His father also needed some quiet time, a time to build up his strength. The timing of all this perfectly coincided with Elvis' invitation to Antigua. Otherwise, it probably would never have happened. Elvis got lucky.

So Tiger informed International Management Group, the firm that represented him at the time, of his travel schedule so they could make arrangements with Mr. Aaron Smith. He would arrive in Antigua on Sunday, April 20, accompanied by his companion, Teresa Long.

Tiger would accept Aaron Smith's offer to stay on the Villa Selena estate, choosing the guest house. He felt the guest house would offer him the most amount of privacy.

Both parties agreed to the final arrangements, and a contract was drawn up and signed. A check for a million dollars was made out to International Management Group, in trust to Tiger Woods.

CHAPTER THIRTY

On the evening of April 19, just after dinner, Normand was in the kitchen when Tommy approached him and said the Boss wanted to speak with him in private.

"Sure, Tommy, where is he?"

"He's in the library." Tommy turned and Normand followed.

The library was a bit ostentatious in an old English kind of way, with the polished oak paneling and the marble fireplace. One whole wall was filled with books that no one at the villa had ever read. The room, for all its old-school splendor, was seldom used at all. Normand would occasionally go to the library to relax, knowing he'd have all the privacy he desired in this magnificent yet neglected room. The door was open and they walked in, Tommy first.

The fireplace was burning. It was seldom used except during the Christmas holidays. Not that it was cold here in December, of course, but the ambience helped create the Yuletide vibe. The Boss was seated in a comfortable, brown leather arm chair dressed in gray silk pajamas under a burgundy smoking jacket. The lights were dimmed to half, and additional light came from the fireplace.

"Come on in, Norm. Here you go." He handed Normand a snifter of Gaston de Lagrange cognac. Normand still didn't drink much but he took it instinctually. He was more than a little curious by now and wondering . . . did Aaron think he needed fortification?

"Sit here, please," Elvis added. He pointed at a comfy chair across from him, and Normand sat down. Tommy took a seat off to the side. At this point, Normand was wondering why Tommy said Elvis wanted to see him in private and then sat down instead of leaving the room. He also noticed that his boss hadn't offered Tommy a drink.

"What's up, Boss?" Normand managed.

It was quiet for what felt like a long time. No one spoke. Then Normand heard Aaron Smith say, "I'm not who you think I am, Norm."

Normand looked at him, smiled, and said, "What?"

"Norm, I want you to listen and not interrupt me, OK? As a matter of fact, don't answer that, just listen to what I have to say. Tommy knows what I'm going to tell you; he knows it's the truth. Tommy has been with me through this whole thing. As fantastic and as unbelievable as this is going to sound, it's the God's truth. I swear to you. I care for you like the brother I never had, Norm. I have known you for twenty years, and I've come to trust you like I trust Tommy, completely. But you, well, you don't know me, Normand. Not the real me."

Normand shifted in his chair, not understanding where this was going.

"Until tonight," Elvis added. "It's time you know the truth."

Normand sat back and tried to relax. He had yet to try the cognac, but he had a feeling he might any time now.

"My name is Elvis Aaron Presley, and I'm from Memphis, Tennessee. You mighta heard of me." A smile teased Elvis's lips despite the seriousness of the conversation.

Normand just stared at him.

"Excuse me, Boss, but what are you talking about?" He looked from Elvis to Tommy and back to Elvis. "Is this a joke?"

"No joke, my friend. Just sit back, relax and have a drink while I explain everything to you."

Then he started to tell Normand how he was Elvis Presley. *The* Elvis. How he had gotten tired of performing and how he was unhappy. And how, when he was looking for a way out, it came to him by happenstance and divine intervention. He told of how an Elvis look-alike impersonator had dropped dead in Graceland Mansion, some twenty years earlier, and how this had given him his way out.

He explained how he used the incident to fake his own death. And that dead *fake* Elvis was buried in Memphis and that people believed it was the real Elvis, and that the real Elvis, he himself, became Aaron Smith. He explained that he chose the name Aaron because that was his real middle name, of course, and Smith was his mother's maiden name.

He said that Tommy knew the truth and so did Tag. (Good ol' Tag, who still dropped by once a year for a few weeks, partied with Elvis and Tommy, and then disappeared back to the States again.)

He patiently explained how Colonel Parker, recently deceased, had helped keep the hoax alive for all those years, and how the Colonel handled the finances that allowed Smith to live a luxurious lifestyle. He lightly expounded on how the Colonel set up a financial management team in the U.S. to handle all the monetary demands and requests of one Aaron Smith, without knowing Mr. Smith's true identity . . . and would continue to do so. He explained how and why he chose Antigua as his new home.

Normand remembered their arrival at the hotel all those years before. He remembered how Tag and Tommy took care of the business of checking in, while Smith was trying his best to be inconspicuous. How they carried Mr. Smith's expensive luggage to his suite, refusing help from the hotel porters. How they all seemed a bit anxious. They had showed none of the normal behaviors of tourists or visiting businessmen.

He remembered Smith having his own private suite, not unusual of course, but Tag and Tommy had acted like body guards and insisted on an adjoining suite.

And of course, Smith had bought a million-dollar estate within two days of arriving in St. John's. Fast and discreet. Very unusual, even for a millionaire eccentric.

Elvis explained how the prescription drugs almost did him in before he arrived in Antigua and how he needed to get some help as soon as he was settled in at Villa Selena. He admitted that he went to rehab in Montserrat to stop doing drugs and to stop drinking.

My God! Could it really be Elvis? thought Normand. He was starting to believe that his boss and friend might be telling him the truth.

He took a small sip from his snifter of cognac. He needed a bit of intestinal fortitude to loosen his tongue, which was now thick, his mouth dry.

"When you disappeared from here for four weeks, way back, just after you got settled in . . . that was to go to the rehab, wasn't it?"

This was the first time Normand had spoken since "Elvis" had started telling him this remarkable story. He then took a second sip of cognac.

"That's right, Norm." His voice was deep, rich and from the south. His blue eyes were shining. It was as if Normand had never really seen him before. Even his hair, which he'd been growing long and combed up and back lately, could easily belong to a sixty-two-year-old Elvis.

"After that hiatus, I never saw you take a drink of booze again. Your whole lifestyle changed . . . you were a different man after that." When Normand said "you were a different man," the hair on the back of his neck stood on end. He felt light-headed . . . everything became surrealistic—the room, them, him.

There was a silence that was all encompassing, a

little like being under water.

"Norm?" It was Tommy. "Everything you just heard is true. I'd like you to meet your boss, Elvis Presley." He laughed, a kind of laugh that told Normand it was all real. The whole account was truth.

Normand suddenly knew, as well as he knew his own name, that his boss was indeed Elvis Presley, the King of Rock and Roll!

Normand started to chuckle. He could not stop himself if he wanted to. All he could think of saying at that moment was: "Ladies and gentlemen . . . Elvis is in the building!" He started laughing.

They all laughed. Elvis went up to Normand, took him in his embrace and said, "It's great to finally, *really* meet you, Normand."

****

This new revelation was a joyous one for Normand! For a few hours they talked openly and honestly. He asked many questions and listened respectfully to Elvis's replies. He had the feeling that this could be his last opportunity to talk openly about the subject of Elvis Presley, aka Aaron Smith, and that after this evening, the door to the past would be pretty much closed. Normand could understand and appreciate that.

Elvis had spent the past twenty years redefining himself. Two decades of keeping himself protected from the millions who would never accept or understand that he'd done what he had to do to survive. Elvis made a leap of faith when he decided to share the truth with Normand that day. Normand believed that trust was the ultimate show of respect anyone could ever bestow on him. He thanked Elvis and swore to keep the secret just that, a secret. *Their* secret.

Normand didn't want to leave the library that evening, but he eventually sensed that Elvis was feeling tired. It took energy to rehash the past the way he had. So Normand decided it was time to take his leave. He set down his glass, which was empty for the second time, and was about to speak when Elvis, who must have anticipated his intention, said:

"Norm, have a seat. There's another thing I wanna tell you."

"Sure, Aaron. I mean Elvis." Normand sat down. Calling his boss *Elvis* was definitely going to feel odd for a while. Of course, he would still have to call him either Aaron or Boss in public.

Elvis cleared his throat and said:

"Tiger Woods will be visiting us tomorrow. He'll be with us for two days, and he'll be staying in the guest house. I need this to stay between just the three of us. And I need your help with a few last-minute details."

Without batting an eye Normand replied, "OK."

Well, wasn't that interesting. Tiger Woods. At this point Normand wouldn't have been surprised if Elvis told him that James Dean and Marilyn Monroe were also still alive and dropping by for dinner.

It was that kind of day!

CHAPTER THIRTY-ONE

For the record, Normand had never caddied before in his life. He played golf, of course, because Aaron Smith had taken up the game and insisted that he join him and Tommy on the links, but now he was going to caddy for Tiger Woods and Elvis Presley. Remarkable!

Normand was assured that all he needed to do was carry the bags, keep an eye on the balls when they were hit, hold the flag on the green when they were putting, and rake a sand trap or two.

Normand thought to himself, *I can do that. No problem!*

He was also instructed to personally handle all Tiger's wants and needs during his stay at the villa. This included, but was not limited to (as they say in legal jargon), taking meal and drink orders, or any other requests, and delivering items to the guest house discreetly.

Hopefully he would get to rest between the carrying of golf clubs and the "catering." But it was only for two days, and the thrill level made it all agreeable to Normand.

And Elvis made it clear that Woods's anonymity was *priority*.

Actually, the fact that Tiger wanted his anonymity

protected as much as Elvis wanted *his* to be protected helped matters immensely. Elvis believed that Tiger would absolutely make every effort to remain incognito during his stay in Antigua. He certainly hoped so. Elvis did not want attention drawn to Tiger, which would bring unwanted attention to himself. Lord, imagine the headlines: Elvis and Tiger teeing it up in Antigua!

Elvis had Tommy make arrangements for a tee time at "the Pike's Arse" for 8:00 the next morning, which was a Monday.

The course was rarely very busy on Mondays, and Elvis picked 8:00 a.m. because Rolly, the starter, said there would be no one in front of them to slow them down and no one behind them breathing down their necks. In actual fact, Rolly had accepted a hundred dollar bill from Elvis to *guarantee* that the tee times were staggered before and after they teed off.

Of course Rolly had no idea who Mr. Smith's guest was. Or who Mr. Smith *really* was for that matter!

Late the next afternoon, Tommy took the Cadillac and drove off to get Tiger at the airport. Normand watched him drive away and then he set off for the guest house, where Tiger and his friend would be staying.

There was perfect weather in the forecast for the next few days. *All should be great for the golf game tomorrow*, thought Normand as he made the short walk to the guest house. He just had some last-minute checks before Woods arrived. As majordomo, Normand felt the extra responsibility that came with having such a special guest at the villa, and he wanted to be quite sure all was ready for the most recent Masters champion when he arrived.

*****

When Tommy returned from the airport with Tiger, he parked in front of the guest house and helped Tiger bring in his golf clubs and his two pieces of luggage. Tommy noticed the golf bag was plain black, with no writing on it other than Nike stitched in silver on one side. Tiger explained to Tommy on the drive from the airport that his friend was unable to join him because of a re-shoot "emergency" that had come up. Tommy assumed that Miss Long was a model or actress or something. He wasn't about to start questioning the man. Tiger said she had to be in L.A. in the morning and was flying directly there from Florida, where Tiger lived.

After Tommy took care of getting Tiger settled in the guest house, he returned to the main house to find his boss and inform him of Tiger's arrival. He explained that Tiger's girlfriend had not been able to travel with him. When Elvis heard this, he had Tommy call Tiger at the guest house to invite him for dinner. He was anxious to meet the young superstar in person. He was relieved that Tiger was alone and not having to think about entertaining a girlfriend or, even worse, having a girlfriend tagging along on the golf course.

Tiger accepted the offer, and Elvis sent Tommy

to collect him. Elvis had thought about going to the guest house himself to meet his guest personally, but he was feeling a little nervous and decided to have Tommy bring Tiger over to the main house instead.

Elvis wasn't nervous about meeting Tiger the celebrity—he was more concerned about being recognized. It had been twenty years since Elvis had left the U.S. and he'd never had his anonymity jeopardized. His attempts at a disguise by simply dying, cutting and combing his hair differently and wearing clear glass lenses in dark frames had worked perfectly. But the main reason he was never recognized as Elvis Presley was because the world believed Elvis Presley was dead. If anyone had ever looked at him twice, thinking he looked familiar, Elvis was not aware of it.

Still, here was Tiger Woods, an American, spending time under the same roof, albeit less than forty-eight hours, ready to exchange pleasantries, share meals and even play a round of golf together. It was not without some concern to Elvis, and he could not help but wonder if he was taking too much of a chance in his eagerness to meet and get to know this extraordinary black athlete who was changing the sporting world as he once had in the music world. Nevertheless, here he was and here was Tiger, and so far he had no regrets.

Tommy brought Tiger in through the front door of the villa and on through to the kitchen, where Elvis and Normand were waiting for them. Normand had wanted to be at the front door when Tommy arrived with their guest, but Elvis had preferred the more informal approach.

Elvis stepped forward as they entered the room. "Welcome to Villa Selena. How was your flight in?"

After introductions by Tommy, they were all now seated at the kitchen table, at Elvis's direction.

The domestic help had already left for the day, so only Tommy and Normand were present for this remarkable first meeting between Elvis and Tiger. Elvis had given the staff the next two days off to ensure Tiger's privacy.

To Elvis's initial question, Tiger's reply was open and friendly, "The flight was great, Mr. Smith. "Aside from a few bumps on approach, it was all good."

"That's excellent, Tiger. I prefer you call me Aaron, if you don't mind. I'd appreciate that."

"Sure, Aaron." Tiger took a sip from a cold bottle of Budweiser offered by Normand. Elvis made certain that this particular American beer was always on hand, although Pauli Girl was the most popular beer on the island and a favorite at the villa.

"That's settled, then. So, congratulations on winning the Masters. That was really something, son. And it was great that your daddy was right there with you, and your mama, of course."

Normand wondered what Tiger thought of a grown man calling his parents Daddy and Mama.

"It was. You sound like you're from the south, Aaron. Is that right, sir? I mean, I know you're American. I was told that."

"I'm originally from Tennessee. Don't you worry none, I'm no redneck hillbilly." Tiger could hear Elvis's low chuckle.

Tiger replied with humor in his voice, "Good to hear it. I felt some of that vibe last week in Georgia. Not from everyone, mind you, but from too many nonetheless."

"I can appreciate that. How's your daddy doing? He got some surgery coming up soon, right?" His concern was genuine.

"He does. I'll be with him for that, soon as I get back. He's a tough guy and he'll be fine, but it's still hard to deal with at times. He's not a young man anymore."

The conversation went on for nearly an hour, with the discussions being light in substance, and often it was Tiger asking questions about what it was like as an American to be living in Antigua. Did Aaron and Tommy miss the States? How was the fishing? Did they miss the changing of the seasons here in the Caribbean, as the temperature never really changed much from the summer to the winter months? Even in Florida and Tennessee, there was quite a noticeable change in weather patterns through the year.

It was starting to get dark, and the setting sun was gloriously reflected on the waters of the Atlantic when Normand set to heating up the food Lucinda had left for them. They feasted on honey-baked chicken with peas and rice, topped off by macaroon pie for dessert.

Whey they'd finished their meal, Elvis asked if Tiger would like to join him in the den for an after-dinner drink. Tiger stated that he was tired and preferred to go back to the guest house and get some rest since they had an early day coming up.

"It's been a long day, so if you'll excuse me, Aaron, I'll see you tomorrow. If you don't mind that is?" He was polite but a bit hesitant, not sure if his fee of a million dollars meant he had to be social all the time.

Elvis was disappointed but didn't show it.

"Of course. Well, have a good rest, then, son. Feel free to use the phone in the guest house; the calls are on me. Tommy will meet you at 6:30 tomorrow morning and bring you over for breakfast, OK?"

Tiger nodded. "Nice meeting you, Aaron, Normand. See you in the morning, Tommy. I'll be up and ready. Thanks again, Aaron, and good night."

"You bet." Elvis watched as Tommy led Tiger from the kitchen and back through the villa and to the guest house.

*****

In the morning, Tommy was waiting to pick up Tiger at the guest house. He had eaten breakfast already and was keen to get going. He was still in the kitchen when Normand arrived a few minutes past 6:20 a.m.

"This is one glorious day we got going, Major."

"Sure is. This will be quite the day, Tommy." Normand took a sip of his tea and sat back in his chair. "I'd better start preparing some breakfast for the Boss and Tiger. The golfers will need some sustenance this morning." *So will I*, thought Normand. The idea of carrying golf clubs for Elvis Presley and Tiger Woods was daunting, and he was feeling a bit overwhelmed.

"Yes, they will, Major. Well, I'm gonna head out now. I'll be back in no time." Tommy left the kitchen, leaving Normand to his thoughts.

Normand was still psyched. *Elvis is in the house!* Not only that but soon Tiger Woods would arrive and they'd all be sitting around having breakfast, talking golf and whatever . . . *What a remarkable thing it is*, he mused. Shaking his head, he got up from his chair and started preparing some bacon, cooked real crisp, just the way his boss liked it.

Meanwhile, Elvis was up and getting dressed after an invigorating early morning swim in the pool. He arrived in the kitchen wearing a pale green short-sleeved shirt and black cotton golf slacks.

"Morning, Boss, care for some coffee?" Normand left the eggs he was scrambling and started toward the kitchen counter, but Elvis said, "I'll get it." He added, "How you feeling, Norm? You feeling strong this morning?" This was a direct reference to Normand's ability to handle the caddying duties expected of him on the course later that morning. Of course Normand was very fit and would handle the physical challenges of being a caddie with ease. The mental challenge, well, that was a different thing.

"I feel good, and you, Boss?"

Elvis answered, "Right as rain, Major, but a little nervous. I'm hoping it doesn't show too much." He laughed lightly as he poured some coffee for himself. A container of fresh cream was sitting nearby in a bowl of ice. The ice was just starting to melt a little.

"Boss, you have every right to be a little anxious. You're going head to head with the current Masters champion. Damn, isn't that something."

"Thanks, that helped calm me down, Norm." The sarcasm was duly noted.

"Try not to worry. You're gonna be just fine." It was then that Normand heard Tommy's voice as Tommy and Tiger made their way into the villa.

"Oh, here they come now, Aaron." Normand had automatically called his boss Aaron, the first time since he'd found out he was really Elvis . . . What a strange thing it really was. It would take some time to get used to. If ever.

Tommy walked into the kitchen with Tiger, and Elvis turned to face them, coffee in hand, waiting to greet his esteemed guest.

"Good morning, Tiger. Sleep well?"

"I did, Aaron, thank you," replied Tiger, looking not quite as awake as he pretended to be. It made Elvis smile.

"Coffee?" offered Elvis, pointing to the coffee maker. "Normand's got some food all set for us. I hope you like bacon and eggs."

This was Elvis's version of southern hospitality, and Normand could tell Elvis was a tad nervous. He wasn't sure if Tiger noticed, though.

"Some coffee would be nice. I don't usually drink coffee before I play in a tournament. It makes me a bit speedy when I need to be alert but also relaxed. But this is pleasure not business, right?" He flashed a big smile.

"That it is, young man," answered Elvis, smiling back.

Normand had been buttering some toast, but he put down the butter knife, wiped his hands and poured Tiger a cup of coffee, which he accepted with thanks. He indicated that he didn't want sugar, but he poured himself a bit of fresh cream and stirred the mixture gently.

Elvis watched Tiger as he took his first cautious sip of the hot java.

Tiger Woods was being a total gentleman at the villa, in a situation where he could, if he so desired, be a complete prick and distant to his host. Tiger was already a golf icon, in just the second season of his professional career. Here he was, a Masters champion, hired by a rich southern white man to tee it up for a check, albeit a million dollar check. He had basically been hired to play with Aaron Smith—for Aaron's sole amusement, really.

But Elvis noticed this young black athlete showed no animosity at all. In fact, by calling the game they would be playing that morning "a pleasure," he had everyone feeling at ease and, oddly, somehow welcomed on their own turf.

Very classy.

Elvis said, "Let's dig in. I'm having some bacon with my scrambled eggs. I like my bacon on the burned side, don't I, Major? I don't eat as much of it as I used to, not good for the ticker they say. Doesn't stop me from having some, though." Elvis took some tongs, pinched a bunch of bacon from the skillet, and placed it on his plate. He added two pieces of toast and sat down at the center counter. Normand placed a glass of mango juice in front of Elvis, his favorite juice these days.

"We're gonna help ourselves this morning, son, so don't be shy. I gave the kitchen staff the day off." Elvis nodded amicably to Tiger.

"Well, I'm gonna have some of that fruit. I imagine it's real fresh."

"Sure is. Straight from our own orchard! And Normand, make sure you eat a good breakfast. Caddying takes energy, and you'll be needing lots of that this morning." Elvis gave his friend a wink.

Normand nodded and filled a plate for himself before sitting down at the table. Conversation was limited, as eating breakfast was their main concern at the moment, and they were soon finished and ready to begin the adventure that lay in store for them that lovely spring morning.

It was Tommy who announced, "Time to head out, Boss? The van's loaded and ready to roll." Tommy got the nod from Elvis. They all headed out the front door and made their way to the van and piled in, with Elvis up front next to Tommy, and Tiger and

Normand comfortably seated in the back.

"All comfy, then, are we?" All replied that they were and without further ado, Tommy put the van in gear and they were off to the Pike.

CHAPTER THIRTY-TWO

I t was a great day for golf. The sky was wonderfully blue, with a few wispy clouds of white slowly passing overhead, no threat to their golf outing and therefore pretty much ignored.

Being a Monday it was a typically quiet day at the club, and the course was all theirs aside from a few members who had already teed off and were of no concern to Elvis and his formidable guest.

Elvis suggested to Tiger that they change into their golf shoes at the van. They were less likely to be recognized if they stayed clear of the locker room, Elvis pointed out. This suited Tiger just fine. Tommy helped unload the clubs from the van, and after wishing them all a great day, he climbed back into the van and drove off with a parting wave. Elvis headed to the starters station with Tiger and Normand in tow, Normand carrying the two golf bags despite Tiger's offer to help. They had decided to skip the driving range and go straight to the first tee, where they would stretch a bit and take a few practice swings and then get on with it.

Elvis walked up to the starter, who had been watching them approach, a professional smile of welcome on his round face. "Morning, Rolly, we good to go off?" asked Elvis.

"Yes, sir, Mr. Smith. You and your guest can tee off whenever you're both ready, and have a great round. It's a perfect day for a golf game."

At this point Normand was thinking that he'd watched many hours of professional golf on television over the years. He'd watched Jack, Arnie, Tom and even Tiger Woods, plus a slew of other golf greats who amazed mere mortals with their prowess with a golf club. He'd been in awe of their dexterity and imagination as they went about their business of winning tournaments. But to stand next to a great player such as Tiger, one of the greatest golfers the world had ever seen, and witness him taking a ferocious swipe with the driver, usually resulting in almost dart-like accuracy, was well . . . mind blowing! And that's what Normand and Elvis saw from Tiger Woods time and time again that morning.

The first hole was a 352-yard par four. A slight dog-leg left, the first half of the hole was slightly downhill and the second half sharply uphill. Woods and gullies on both sides of the narrow fairway spelled potential trouble. Elvis went first and hit a very nice 200-yard drive slightly left of center, leaving 152 yards uphill to the green.

Tiger unleashed a drive that landed 47 yards in front of the green. His chip lipped out, and he had a kick-in birdie. Elvis's second shot rolled just off the back. He chipped to within five feet of the hole but two-putted and made a bogey.

That's kinda how it went.

The conversation during the round was focused on

the game at hand. Many clichés were uttered as they played: nice shot, great putt, you were robbed.

Normand raked seven or eight sand traps after errant shots found the beach. Once for Tiger, and the rest for Elvis. He got used to carrying the bags and tired only a little, on the last two holes. But he wouldn't relinquish either bag for anything. It was a phenomenal experience he would replay in his memory forever.

On the back nine the course got harder, mainly because it is tighter back there, with many more trees. The thirteenth for example is not a long hole at 363 yards. But the tee shot comes out of a long tree-lined chute almost halfway to the green, then it sharply doglegs left and downhill to the green, which was quite large with an extremely steep back-to-front middle. The green is shaped somewhat like a bronco rider's saddle. It's really easy to three-putt there.

The green is surrounded by nasty, tight-knit trees and bushes. If the ball goes long left, you're looking realistically at double bogey at best.

The tee shot is key, as Tiger found out. A safe shot need only be hit about 200 yards straight out, center or right of center, which leaves a short iron in to the green.

He hit a powerful drive with his one wood. A mid-iron was plenty for such a short downhill hole, but he took out "the big dog."

"This will be more fun," he said smiling. When he smiled at his decision he looked like a kid, like any youngster out to have fun, throwing caution and good sense to the wind, just going for the bragging rights.

The fairway sloped right to left, and so when Tiger's powerful tee shot hooked slightly on him, it hit the fairway hard and flew even farther left and long. The ball ended in the middle of the twelfth fairway and almost pin high, a long way from his target. A shot at the green from there seemed impossible.

At least impossible for us mortals. It seemed that Tiger had more fun deciding what to hit and where to hit it on this second shot than he had on any of his other easier approach shots thus far. The shot was about 185 yards uphill and almost entirely blind, over trees that stood high on the hill he was facing. How in the wide world of sports do you get the ball up so high and have it drop fast and not only find the green but also hold the green? Impossible. Most would have thought so, but they'd be wrong.

When Tiger hit the shot, he just started walking. He wasn't going to run up that hill, but he heard Elvis, who had stayed on the proper fairway to watch where the ball went. "You're on! You're on the green!"

Elvis was yelling. He was so blown away. Elvis and Normand could not believe what they had just seen. Tiger was all smiles. You could tell at that moment when he saw his ball on the green, a mere eight feet from the cup, how much he loved the game. He made the putt and a birdie! High-fives all around.

Sportsmanship is the backbone of the PGA. The organization and the players advocate proper etiquette at all times. Cheating is relatively unheard of. Players will call attention to themselves and suffer a self-imposed infraction rather than try to sneak one by. Players such as Palmer, Byron Nelson and others, all the way back to the great Bobby Jones, a southerner who founded the Masters back in 1934, all stressed the importance of gentlemanly fair play.

Throwing tantrums and golf clubs and swearing and so forth are discouraged, to say the least. Fines are imposed on those who ignore warnings from the governing Professional Golfers Association.

The point here is that Tiger was a great example of how to conduct oneself on the golf course. He was attentive, he was courteous, and he had an encouraging attitude toward the nervous, completely out-of-his-league amateur he had been playing with that day.

They finished the round in three hours and ten minutes. They all shook hands, and the "thank yous" were genuine. *A good walk spoiled* did not describe this game.

Elvis finished with a five over par 78, and Tiger played to a nine under par 63, a new course record, albeit a score that was never officially recorded.

"That was a lot of fun, guys," Tiger said, meaning it.

"Thank you, Tiger, it was a great honor." Elvis was feeling very pleased. He had gotten his money's worth. But that was not all he had paid for . . . not by a long shot. It was conversation Elvis really wanted.

Then Elvis said, "Let's head back to the ranch,

guys. Tommy should be on his way to pick us up."

The conversation on the drive back was mainly Elvis making plans with Tiger for a private get-together, just the two of them.

Normand heard Elvis say he wanted to talk about how Tiger was feeling about the success and the adulation that was happening in his life. And how he personally felt about the win in Augusta.

"A few hours of your time, Champ. Just me and you over drinks after dinner, OK?"

"Sure, Aaron," replied Tiger, ever the gentleman. And as to whether the million had any influence over his compliance to a private conversation? Sure, probably.

Normand could have used a nap after walking and carrying the two golf bags for eighteen holes. Besides the physical fatigue, there was the mental exhaustion as well; he now had a newfound respect for the professional caddie and his expertise in being an integral part of the success of a winning professional golfer. Although he didn't need to advise or counsel "his guys" on club selection or how many yards it was to the center of the green, he nevertheless felt mentally drained trying to be helpful while keeping out of the way at the same time. He had successfully come to terms with the numbing realization that he was caddying for Elvis Presley and Tiger Woods and was able to keep his head in the moment.

And now he was knackered. But first he had to see about lunch.

*****

Normand retired to his room after lunch for his much-needed nap. Elvis had given Tiger a leisurely tour of the villa and the grounds, enjoying his chance to play host. And then Tiger had returned to the guest house and Elvis to his bedroom for some downtime.

It was early evening when Normand headed back to the kitchen. He found Tommy seated alone, sipping at some hot java. Columbian brown.

Tommy gave the Major a welcome smile. "So, a great time was had by all, I take it. I haven't had a chance to speak to E yet. Was he impressed with *Tigger*?" Tommy pronounced Tiger's name like the pouncing character in Winnie the Pooh books.

"You should ask him, but I believe so. The whole round was a blast." Normand couldn't conceal his enthusiasm, so why try? Although he didn't want Tommy to feel bad about not being part of the group that morning, he told Tommy that it had been exciting and challenging, while being careful not to sound like he was bragging. When Elvis said in front of both of them that only he and Tiger would be golfing and that Normand would be caddying, Tommy hadn't seemed upset or disappointed. Elvis had made his decision and that was that. Normand figured Elvis probably explained his reasoning privately to Tommy.

Normand assumed Elvis wanted the intimacy of not being distracted by even one other player, not even a close friend like Tommy. Anyway, it was forgivable that a guy who forked out a million bucks might be a tad selfish with the merchandise.

"I'm sure it was, Major. I'm happy for Elvis; he wanted this thing to work." Normand could detect no jealousy in Tommy's reply. "What's for dinner? I could eat the arse end out of a big ol' Mississippi possum!"

"Lucinda made us stewed lamb, with some sweetened plantains and steamed okra. Looks real good. Just gotta warm it up in the oven. When does Elvis want to eat?"

"He said about 7:00. I'm gonna bring Tiger over here at six-ish, in about twenty minutes or so. We'll indulge in one or two before we chow down I suppose."

"Probably. I'll start heating things up in a bit."

There would be just the four of them having dinner, of course. So far, there had been no snags in the plan. No flies in the ointment. Nobody suspected that the great Tiger Woods was on the island, let along there at the villa. As Elvis had predicted, Tiger didn't stand out from any of the other players at the club that day.

Unless someone had seen Tiger hit a shot or two, there would be no reason for anyone to be curious. But to see that swing of his, and the result of that swing, well, you can be very sure that eyebrows would have been raised and a question or two put forward.

But it all went as smooth as the underbelly of a

yellowtail damselfish. No worries.

Elvis entered the kitchen looking good in loose, cream-colored cotton slacks and a Bogosse Bana short-sleeved shirt in lavender. Brown Top-Siders; no socks.

"What's on the menu, boys?" he asked. Normand told him.

He seemed satisfied. He then went to the temperature-controlled wine storage room, returning with a bottle of 1981 Cote de Nuits, and carefully opened it. He brought the cork to his nose and breathed in slowly, enjoying the aroma. He then chose a beautiful crystal decanter and slowly poured the French wine into it. He wanted the wine to breathe before serving it at dinner.

When Elvis was finished with the wine, he went to the refrigerator, produced a chilled bottle of Galvanina still water, poured a glass and came and sat down next to Tommy and Normand.

"Well, here's to a momentous day, fellas." He held up the glass of water. "Rock 'n' roll!"

Normand looked amused. "Rock 'n' roll" from the King of Rock and Roll.

"Back atcha, Boss." From Tommy.

"Rock on!" From a still slightly astounded Normand Fisher. He'd had a lot to absorb in the past twenty-four hours.

When Tiger arrived at the villa, Tommy ushered him through to the kitchen, where Elvis and Normand were sitting.

Elvis offered him a drink straight off, and Tiger chose a bottle of Budweiser. With drinks in hand they all went to the games room, where a soccer match between Italy and England was being shown on the large projection television.

Tiger, on entering the capacious room, made a bee-line for the custom pool table.

"Wow, what a great table! I think this is the most beautiful pool table I've ever seen. I'd love to play a few games before I go." He stood at the table smiling. "Any takers?"

This Normand would love to see. Tiger, a fantastic athlete whose expertise relies absolutely on deft eye–hand coordination, must be formidable at shooting pool.

"After dinner, how's that sound?" suggested Elvis. "I'm too hungry to concentrate on a pool game right now."

Normand took this as a clear message to go back to the kitchen—*vitement*—and check on all things delectable and prepared for consumption.

Dinner was very good. After the meal of lamb and veggies, they sampled some of Rosie's homemade key lime pie (Elvis's favorite) for dessert. Everyone had wine with dinner and when the meal was a finished deal, the four of them retired to the games room.

The conversation was enjoyable and at times raunchy. Elvis and Tommy could get quite crude at times to be honest, and Tiger was a bit reluctant to join in at first, but soon he was as colorful as the next guy and seemed very at ease.

They all had an after-dinner drink. Normand sipped his glass of chilled white wine, a Madeira dessert wine from Portugal. Tommy stuck with beer, and Elvis and Tiger sipped some Gaston de Lagrange, which they warmed slightly by turning the glasses gently in the palm of one hand, back and forth like a cabasa player might.

There were three televisions in the paneled games room. Each TV was tuned to a different channel and the volumes were all turned down except for the one being watched. A local network was showing golf highlights, and of course it was all about Tiger winning the Masters. Tommy had cranked the volume.

Everyone turned their attention toward that set and watched excitedly. Tiger observed quietly and with a sly smile, not unlike the cat that swallowed the canary. And why the hell not!

Elvis and Tommy were whooping it up every time they showed Tiger making a great shot or draining a putt. Groaning when they showed Tiger missing a shot. The situation made Normand feel a bit like an impostor or a nonmember of a very exclusive gentlemen's club.

A private gentleman's club where (*Hello!*) Tiger Woods and Elvis Presley were members!

Nonetheless, Normand also got caught up in the revelry and enjoyed the film coverage, which ranged from golf course play to Tiger hugging his parents, his father in particular, as he walked off the eighteenth green victorious. They all quieted down as they watched the emotional scene unfolding before them once more, and that would continue to be reshown again and again, as if caught up in a repetitive time warp—what is now referred to as a classic *Groundhog Day* moment.

No one commented as the sports reporter talked over the images that had been burned into their collective memories. When Earl Woods's imminent heart surgery was mentioned, the mood shifted from unchecked commotion to concern. Millions were seeing the same footage as they were, but they were in the presence of Tiger Woods as they sat and watched the televised images of his venerable father. It added to the gravity of the situation.

Tiger's mood of despondency was apparent to everyone.

As the telecast shifted direction and focused on the seniors tour standings, Elvis stood up and, with a touch on Tiger's shoulder as he passed, said, "Let's take our drinks outside, Tiger."

Elvis started toward the sliding glass doors that led to the pool area. Tiger stood and followed Elvis, happy to move outside and get some fresh air.

CHAPTER THIRTY-THREE

Before I get back to my uncle's account of what occurred in Antigua between Elvis and Tiger Woods that night, I want to reemphasize the true purpose of relating this extraordinary adventure.

Back in 1997 when Elvis explained to my uncle that he was not Aaron Smith but really Elvis Presley, my uncle swore an allegiance of upmost secrecy. As you now know, only Tommy and my uncle and one or perhaps two intimate conspirators back in America knew the truth of what actually happened to Elvis after August 16, 1977. When I convinced my uncle Normand to let me share the story of his amazing life and times with Elvis, he allowed me to read selected parts of his personal diary.

In his diary, he wrote eloquently of his feelings and his reasons for deciding to finally talk about Elvis. It will be clear after reading this excerpt—taken directly from his diary—why he changed his mind and that he really understood the circumstances and repercussions of a tell-all account of the truth.

Here is one of the last chapters from his diary, which I will share with you now:

So why would I, all these years later, decide to "spill the beans," as they say in America? What happened that I would renege on a personal promise to someone who entrust-

ed me with a most profound and personal secret, someone who became my most cherished friend?

Elvis certainly was an enigma. Even with us few privileged confidants, he was forthcoming but there was always that point at which he "closed the door" and posted a clear message: "No trespassing!" And that meant everyone.

As far as I know, his secret has remained undisclosed until this telling, so here is why I believe this story can be told now.

First, no one will believe it.

No matter how much I might try to persuade people that it wasn't Elvis who died of a heart attack, in a bathroom, back in Memphis thirty-five years earlier, no one would believe it. The only possible way might be for the Presley estate to exhume the body buried at Forest Hill Cemetery in Memphis and do a DNA test, do the same with the body of my friend buried in Antigua, and try for a match from the samples of Lisa Marie's Presley's DNA, or take it even further and dig up his father, Vernon, and his mother, Gladys, and have a field day with the DNA testing. Then have them get back to the public with the results. Wouldn't that put a wrench in things? The moral consequences of such a discovery would be traumatizing to say the very least. The financial ramifications staggering.

And that is why this is not going to happen, at least not in my lifetime. So, the real truth is in these pages. And the truth is in what I shared with my nephew, Craig, who plans to share it with the public someday. Those who want to believe will, and those who don't won't. (And let's face it, the Presley estate couldn't handle the truth.)

My dear friend, Elvis Aaron Presley, passed away in

his bed here at Villa Selena on March 7, 2012. He was seventy-seven. That's the truth.

After being hospitalized for complications due to a heart condition (his early years of drug addiction and obesity may have contributed), he was released and sent home to recuperate with us, his friends, but he succumbed in his sleep several days later.

I was the only one with him at the time.

Tommy had been killed in 2004, when a private amphibian plane crashed off a small out island some one hundred miles southwest of Antigua. There was no foul play and pilot error was blamed. The pilot, a local friend of Tommy's, also perished; their bodies were buried here on the island. Elvis took care of the arrangements and costs. Elvis, myself and Tommy's longtime sweetheart, Shawna, along with the staff at Villa Selena (where Tommy had continued to live) and some local friends, attended the funeral.

We didn't hear from Tag when Tommy died; we hadn't in a few years, not since he called and told us that Ron Fielding, a friend of Elvis's, had succumbed to cancer. Since then, nothing.

Elvis was the only one of us who knew how to reach Tag, so we could not tell him of Elvis's passing.

Elvis was depressed for some time after Tommy's death. Tommy had been his best friend, and his death may have been a contributing factor to his own declining health.

This account, in part, documents the coming together of two remarkable men, Elvis and Tiger. Both heroes to many millions. From two different, yet certainly connected, paths of life. Both stirred the imaginations of the planet's popu-

lace, and both breathed a fresh breath of change that stimu-lated people the world over. Elvis holding a guitar and Tiger a golf club, they rocked the world. Furthermore, they both self-destructed. At least temporarily . . .

For Elvis all those years ago it was overindulgence. Same for Tiger in more recent times. Elvis was addicted to drugs. Tiger is addicted to sex. (He has admitted it.) Sex is like a drug say some, and so is money and power, of course. And they had it all. But if you spiral out of control during life's journey and abuse your blessings . . . it can kill. Kill the spirit. Kill relationships. Kill the body and the mind. Every-thing can be given and taken away. Addition and subtrac-tion. Both of these superstars learned that the hard way.

It must be remembered that these men were human at the time their common sense deserted them for a while. To err is human, to forgive, well . . . divine. If you can forgive the use of one more cliché for the moment, there was one I heard from Tommy when we all started playing golf together years ago: Every golf shot makes someone happy.

What I'm trying to express here is . . . have compassion for our fellow man.

When Tiger's marital troubles were being splattered all over the media, and the world was aghast at his indiscre-tions, I could not help, sitting here in Antigua, but think of Elvis and HIS well-publicized indiscretions, which occurred before he moved to the island. Same stuff in a different decade.

In Elvis's case, he found a spectacular escape from his own personal prison that included the downside of fame and fortune. He did not handle the pressure well.

The list of famous persons who did not handle success

favorably is a long one. Unfortunately, many went from the gossip columns to the obits far too fast, much too soon.

Let's face it, Elvis the Pelvis behaved poorly; he let his ego blind him to what was really going on and what was really important until he turned into a self-centered, pill-popping, delusional mess. Sad.

Luckily he came out of it alive. A different person. He was "reborn," and that's the Elvis I got to know, love and respect as a person and a friend.

Now Tiger . . . he's not that much different. There is addiction . . . check! Enormous ego . . . check! Self-destructive behavior (family- and career-wise, at least) . . . check! Fall from grace? Absolutely.

Tiger has caused a negative reaction that rivals Elvis's, any day. That rivals John Lennon's being misunderstood when he said that "the Beatles were more popular than Jesus," which resulted in a witch hunt and the burning of Beatles recordings. Those frivolous headlines and idiotic accusations did not escape our little island of Antigua, either.

My point is, the damage done to Tiger's public image was colossal. One can only imagine how his father would have reacted to all this. Earl himself had reportedly been a womanizer.

As far as I know, his mother offers little or no comment on this subject. About either of them.

As I stated earlier, honesty and integrity are not only part and parcel to the game of golf but crucial, and that was obliterated by Tiger's unfaithfulness to his wife and children. And his lying and public denial of what was really going on at home.

And not unfaithful once, but many times . . .

He and his father had established the Tiger Woods Foundation, which helps kids become better educated and offers them more opportunities to overcome adversity. Kids believed in Tiger and his sense of fairness and honesty. Their parents believed in Tiger. Tiger Woods was a role model for millions.

After his fall from grace, Tiger was dropped like a hot potato by major corporations that didn't want that kind of association.

And perhaps the most severe damage was done to himself. It's now hard or even impossible to imagine people ultimately perceiving Tiger as "the best golfer of all time," regardless of the number of wins he may eventually record. Once a sure bet, it is unlikely that he will ever be hailed as the all-time best professional golfer the game has ever known. As they say in America, "the smart money" is on Jack Nicklaus; he not only shattered golf records that have yet to be broken but he was and is a gentleman as well, and a role model you can believe in. The real deal. Guys such as Couples, Gary Player, Ernie Els, Nick Price, and the King, of course, the iconic Arnold Palmer . . . are on a stellar list of great gentlemen golfers for the newcomers to aspire to.

Anyway, I'm not writing this to convince anyone of anything, not even that Elvis lived to the age of 77.

I'm only telling the truth about Elvis's life after he left America because it has to be told. If I do not share my experience with Elvis, as my nephew said to me, then it would be a great injustice to this great man. Elvis had redeemed himself. After so many years of drug abuse and de-

bauchery, he'd gotten clean and lived a good life. His fans deserve to know the truth. His daughter deserves to know the truth. That's all there is to it.

*****

Elvis and Tiger took their drinks outside and sat down to relax. A warm, salty breeze swept over the property, and the smell of eucalyptus was pleasant and soothing.

Now that they were alone, Elvis asked Tiger, "How you doing, son?"

"I'm all right. But it's hard to think that it's possible my father might not survive this next operation. This will be his third heart surgery in about as many years, and it does not get easier. Frankly, Mom and I are worried sick."

Elvis was thinking that Tiger was much too young to lose his father.

"Your daddy's a tough cookie, right?" Elvis knew of Earl Woods's military history. "He's a fighter and that goes a long way in these things. He put in a lot of years seeing that you got to where you are today. I'm thinking he'll be hanging around to witness a lot more . . . you'll see."

Tiger looked down at his drink and smiled. "Yeah, he's a tough guy, all right. Thanks, Aaron."

"When you get home tomorrow, you going to see him right off, or you heading back to Florida first?"

Elvis didn't really care where Tiger was going from here; he was just "chewing the fat" to help Woods feel at ease. There was much he did want to know, but it wasn't about Tiger's travel plans.

"I'll go by my house to collect some things and then visit Mom. I've got the Byron Nelson Classic coming up as well, so there's a lot on my plate at the moment."

"I do appreciate you coming here for a visit. I really enjoyed the day. Thank you, son, thank you very much." Elvis raised his glass to Woods and then took a drink.

It was the first real "drink" Elvis had had in a long, long time. A bit of fortitude was called for.

Elvis must have been wishing he could tell Tiger the truth, but he of course couldn't. Not now, not ever.

He wanted a meaningful conversation with this young champion and not the shallow, superficial gabfest he heard on telecasts when Tiger was interviewed. He felt a deep need to relate to Tiger. Relating as equals. Unfortunately, withholding the truth from Tiger made that a moot point. Elvis was paranoid of being "found out."

A few drinks would help him relax.

"I had a great time, Aaron. It was nice to get away, if only for two days. I've had time to think without the pressures at home. You wouldn't believe how the media people can get on your ass! I can't leave the fucking house without someone sticking a microphone and a camera in my face. It sucks!"

Elvis smiled to himself. *Oh, I can believe it*, he mused.

"How do you handle all that attention?" This is where Elvis had been going all along. He'd been through it himself long ago. This was a kind of soft-shock therapy session for Elvis. Who else would be a better choice for him to talk with? Tiger was one of the most famous people in the world.

"My father started me very young . . . everything was about being a golf professional. And once he saw that I had an aptitude and love for the game, he became obsessed with me becoming the best in the world. I was just a kid, and I got used to having people tell me how amazing I was. A protégé. Aaron, I was on *The Mike Douglas Show* when I was two years old hitting golf balls in front of what, a million people? A whiz kid at two! My dad was, in a way, the sports equivalent of a Hollywood Mom who drags her kids to every audition in town. It can get very sur-realistic, and it makes a lot of normal kid stuff impos-sible. But like I say, I loved golf, even at that age. I knew golf was my destiny. Does that sound weird?"

"No, it doesn't. I knew when I was a kid what I wanted to be. I had a hard time fitting in. My hair was different, I dressed different, I talked different, and I rubbed a lot of the other kids the wrong way. But all the time I knew what I was going to be when I was older. It's like that for some of us."

"Whatever you did, you did well," Tiger said as he looked around at the property. "This is one beautiful place you have here."

"Thank you very much, Tiger. Yeah, I was successful . . . a lot of folks said I was the best. They still do." He drank deep.

"What did you do, Aaron?"

"I was in the entertainment business until I retired about twenty years ago."

"Management?" asked Tiger. Tiger understood management and how profitable that could be—managing the right talent, that is. Just a percentage of a guy like Tiger himself could make a man very rich indeed.

"No, I had me a manager. I was "the fighter," you might say." *I could have been a contender.*

Elvis thought of Marlon Brando for the first time in a long time. The two of them had a history. The alcohol was allowing Elvis's thoughts to drift.

"What did you do, then?" Tiger asked. He was genuinely interested. Elvis would have to change the topic or be very careful. Tiger waited for Elvis to finish his swallow of drink before he got a measured reply.

"I was a singer, and a darn good one, they say. But I gave that up and moved here. I don't miss it."

Elvis took another sip of his cognac, then remembered he wasn't used to drinking alcohol anymore. He'd have to slow down a bit before he fucked up and said something he'd deeply regret.

"You sing, Tiger? You folks are supposed to be

naturals at singing." At this, Elvis laughed a friendly sort of giggle. There was no nasty, underlying preju- dice aimed at Tiger, and therefore Tiger did not feel offended.

Tiger laughed right along. "I suck Aaron. You do not wanna hear me try to sing, trust me, sir. What did you sing? What kinda music?"

Elvis couldn't help himself.

"Rock and roll mostly, at least at first. Then I got more into Gospel. I always loved spirituals. I'm from the south and colored music really got to me. Know what I mean? My mama loved church music. She said it brought her closer to God. She's with Him now." Elvis felt his throat tighten at her memory. Was the drink making him maudlin?

Elvis realized he'd better ask Tiger a question. That was the whole point, he reminded himself.

"You like that style of music? Colored music. Choir singing and such?"

"I'm not sure it's called "colored music" anymore, but I guess back then it might have been. Black or African-American music would be politically correct these days, Aaron." Elvis noticed Tiger tense up just a little.

"No, I understand, man. Colored music, race mu- sic—yeah, that's what white people called it all right. "The devil's music" it was called when black artists introduced rock and roll to the white kids. Guys like Little Richard and Chuck Berry. Music's got all kinds of names now, and it's not identified by a person's skin pigmentation, either. Jazz, RnB, the blues, funk, all this music played and sung by blacks and whites . . . it don't matter no more what it is. It just has to be good, and that's the way it should be. You agree with me on this, Tiger?"

Elvis drained the last of his drink, and then he leaned forward to better hear Woods's reply.

"Yeah, things are a whole lot different these days. Still lots of room for improvement, though," Tiger replied quietly before finishing off his drink. "Looks like we could both use a refill, Aaron. You ready?"

Elvis was so they returned to the games room. The room was empty now, the guys having drifted off somewhere, and Elvis and Tiger were alone. They poured two more cognacs and went back outside.

Once they were comfortably seated again, Tiger said in a weary voice, "You know . . . I got a lot of hate mail in the beginning and now after winning the Masters I expect to get even more. Some white people aren't willing to see me, a man of color, even playing at Augusta let alone beating all those white guys at their own game. Calling me a nigger! You believe that shit, man? Bigots sending me and my parents hate mail. I need to have security walk the course with me during tournaments. To protect my ass again racists. Fuck!"

Tiger took a slow drink of cognac after first letting out a sigh. "Sorry," he added, but Elvis knew he wasn't.

Elvis's life had been threatened many times in the past. Not from bigots, but from resentful contemporaries, jealous husbands and begrudging boyfriends, and other assorted nutcases. How could he tell that to Tiger? Elvis was feeling frustrated, big time!

Elvis took a long drink and then asked, "You carry a gun sometimes?"

"Nuh uh, no way. I'm not into violence Aaron. I could never shoot somebody."

"Self-defense is sometimes necessary, son. How about judo? I tried that. Worked my way up to a black belt too. I was pretty good." *Careful, Elvis.*

"You ever carry a gun, Aaron?" asked Tiger seriously.

"Hell, yes. Back in Tennessee we all carried guns. I even had a permit to carry a concealed weapon. Got a permit from the DEA themselves to carry. I made arrests for the police in Memphis a few times. I was a badass, son!"

Elvis sensed that he had just crossed a line and quickly added, "But that was another world ago, Tiger. That ain't me no more."

He raised his snifter of Gaston de Lagrange in acknowledgement of another time. Ancient history. He took a sip.

"You got a girlfriend, Tiger?" Elvis decided to move on to a lighter subject.

"Not really. I date."

I bet you do, thought Elvis. "They must be throwing themselves at your feet, young fella. You're rich and famous and good looking. A winning combination. I know. I've been there."

Tiger looked over at the man beside him. He could see that Aaron was handsome, no question about that. And rich. When he was a younger man, women probably threw themselves at him.

Tiger added, "It's hard to tell how they really feel about you. Do they like you? Or are they just star fuckers?" He smiled a sideways smile at Elvis, who was staring at him with a grin on his face.

"Well put. I know what you mean, son. Cheers!" He raised his glass. They drank.

"Does it really matter at your age, though? Why not just bask in the glory. Catch and release. Lots of time to get serious later."

"I guess." Tiger blushed a bit. Elvis noticed.

"Well, I suggest you sow your oats while still young, son. Don't rush life . . . enjoy the ride. And ride every one of them beauties that you can along the way!" Elvis started laughing.

"I'll try to remember that, sir. Cheers." They gleefully toasted each other again.

"Come with me, Tiger. We'll refresh our drinks and then I wanna show you some things." Elvis led the way into the games room, where they topped up their swill again and then headed off to the den. Elvis was feeling great as he closed the door behind them . . .

CHAPTER THIRTY-FOUR

When Elvis died, it left a void that could not be filled. A nothingness that suffocated my uncle with anguish for a long time. But the distinct, almost tactile memories of Elvis, Tommy and the time they all spent together at Villa Selena slowly gave way to a more peaceful sense of reverence.

Uncle moved out of Villa Selena and never returned. The new owners purchased the estate from an American company called Hound Holdings Inc.

The same company, Hound Holdings, personally guaranteed my uncle an annuity of $200,000 a year for life, with a cost of living index automatically built into the agreement. *You ain't nothin' but a hound dog!*

Thank you, Elvis. Thank you very much.

My uncle Normand had been an empathetic observer of Tiger Woods's personal goings-on, and he was glued to the television whenever Tiger was in contention on the golf course. Which was most of the time.

He'd been around to see a *gentleman of color* become the president of the United States of America! So was Elvis, and he had wept with delight. That was a wonderful, exciting day.

My uncle remembers how enraged Elvis was as he watched in disbelief at O.J. Simpson's acquittal after

being accused of blatantly slaughtering two innocent, affluent white people. "The man's guilty as sin!"
shouted Elvis furiously. He never got over that.

Both those occurrences were extreme signs that
anything is possible in this day and age.

Yes, my uncle had seen extraordinary occurrences
in his time, as had Elvis. But nothing compared to
what he experienced at Villa Selena. He was with
Elvis Presley almost every single day for close to
thirty-five years.

As majordomo and a best friend of the King of
Rock and Roll, his existence had been enriched
beyond words. Life with Elvis Aaron Presley was precious to Uncle Normand. He felt that his life had
been truly blessed.

When Elvis didn't show up in the morning to bid
farewell to Tiger after their night of drinking and
their hours of private conversation behind closed
doors, Uncle saw personally to Tiger's send-off.

Tommy was waiting in the van, ready to drive Tiger
to the airport.

My uncle explained to Tiger that his boss wasn't
feeling great that morning, and that he was sorry Aaron couldn't be there to say goodbye personally. Tiger
understood.

"Have a safe flight home, Mr. Woods. Good luck
to you and your family. I hope your father gets better
soon, and perhaps you'll visit us again one day. Mr.
Smith would love to—"

Tiger stopped him. He put a hand on my uncle's

shoulder and said quietly, "I know."

My uncle started to speak again but stopped when he saw the look in Tiger's eyes. Slowly Tiger turned to look toward the villa and then back.

"It's all right, Normand. I know . . ."

Epilogue

Later that evening, on the same day that Tiger Woods flew home, Elvis walked into the kitchen looking tired. Uncle made him coffee and some toast. Elvis was slow moving and obviously hurting from the night before, which had extended into the wee hours of the morning.

My uncle was curious about what Elvis and Tiger had talked about, and he wondered just how much Elvis had had to drink, but he let him be. It would be cruel and unwarranted harassment to pester him for details. Besides it wasn't his business.

Elvis looked at him shyly and said in a weak voice, "I feel like shit on a stick."

"Yes, I can see that you do. More coffee, Elvis?" Normand said quietly.

"No, I'm off to my room. Tomorrow I'll be fine . . . I hope. How could you allow me drink so fucking much? My God, I feel awful! Elvis started to leave the kitchen but then stopped and turned back to Uncle Normand, suddenly aware that he'd forgotten to inquire about his esteemed guest's departure.

"Norm, did Tiger get away all right this morning?"

"Yes. He said to tell you he had a wonderful stay, and to thank you for your kindness and generosity."

"Anything else?"

"Not really."

"Oh."

Both men were silent, preoccupied with their own thoughts about the night before. My uncle spoke first.

"Boss, did you tell Tiger, uh, you know?" He couldn't help himself.

Elvis knew exactly what he meant.

"I don't know, Norm. I don't remember. He say anything . . . ?"

"No."

Elvis turned to leave.

"Good night, Norm."

My uncle watched Elvis limp off to bed. They never discussed what happened or what was said that last night Tiger spent at the villa.

Ever.

I asked my uncle why he never told Elvis that day that Tiger knew who he really was. That Tiger knew he was not Aaron Smith, a retired American, but in fact, Elvis Presley. *The* Elvis Presley.

It was possible that Elvis told the truth to his house guest when the two shared drinks and conversation, one on one, behind closed doors that night and well into the morning. After all, alcohol had not passed between Elvis's lips in years, and who knows how the sudden drinking affected his reason and his candidness.

Or, Tiger might have guessed the truth somehow.

Either way, Tiger knew.

But my uncle didn't say anything because he didn't want Elvis to spend the rest of his days wondering if Tiger would tell the world that he, the King of Rock and Roll, was alive and well and living in Antigua.

My uncle did what he believed was best for his boss and friend to protect him from carrying around that burden of uncertainty for the rest of his life. In every respect my uncle was a good, compassionate man, and the decision he made that night made sense to me.

Elvis is gone now and so is my dear uncle Normand—may they both rest in peace. Their adventure on earth together has ended and their secret was never disclosed.

Until now.

THE END

www.ingramcontent.com/pod-product-compliance
Lightning Source LLC
Chambersburg PA
CBHW071847020726
47502CB00003B/634